DEFYING THE ODDS

John Noble Thrillers
Book Two

David Mackenzie

SAPERE
BOOKS

DEFYING
THE ODDS

Published by Sapere Books.

24 Trafalgar Road, Ilkley, LS29 8HH

saperebooks.com

ISBN: 978-0-85495-713-2

CHAPTER ONE

RAF Catterick, North Yorkshire, June 1940

Flying Officer John Noble was in the lounge of the officers' mess at RAF Catterick, chatting with two of his fellow squadron pilots, Greg Somerville and Richard Cowles. They had completed their duties for the day and were now relaxing in the warmth of the early evening sunshine flooding in through the open French doors. It was four weeks since John's squadron had been involved in Operation Dynamo, the evacuation of the British Expeditionary Force from France, and the pilots were, as usual, discussing what might happen next in the war.

'The boss made it clear,' Greg said, referring to the recent briefing the squadron members had received from their Commanding Officer. 'The view at the top is that the RAF will be the Luftwaffe's prime focus. Jerry will want to ensure that we have limited capability to intervene when their invasion force crosses the Channel.'

'Yes,' John replied, 'and as well as attacking us in the air, I think they will go for our operating infrastructure, particularly our aerodromes, and the radar stations of Chain Home.'

'I agree. Chain Home is going to be vital to our ability to respond, no doubt about that, so if they knock that system out, we'll be in trouble,' Greg said. 'We're a much smaller force than the Luftwaffe, and we will need to be able to be precise in positioning ourselves to ensure we can respond to all the aircraft sent over by Jerry. They will try to mount a war of attrition against us, I expect, looking to wear us down using their superior aircraft numbers. They'll send a lot of aircraft over in each wave and maintain continuous waves throughout the day. We will need to be able to allocate our lesser resources accurately and effectively to stop the buggers if that's what happens.'

John nodded his approval of Greg's view. Quite apart from Greg's skills as a pilot, John had always thought him to be a careful thinker. What he said was usually well-considered and logical.

'We are fairly well placed here in Four-one-five Squadron in terms of aircraft availability and pilot experience,' Richard added, 'and we are certainly better off than some down in Eleven Group. I have heard there are squadrons there with up to a third of their pilots having less than twenty hours in a Spit.'

'And probably very little time, if any, on war ops, and we know where that leads. We had some *new chums* ourselves when we started over Dunkirk, and it didn't go well for a number of them,' John said, using the standard squadron description for inexperienced pilots. 'But some learnt quickly, or maybe they were lucky, but either way we are now better placed, both experience-wise and capability-wise, with Dunkirk behind us.'

As he said that, John thought about what he had seen during Operation Dynamo. Despite the losses they had suffered at the time, he had admired the dogged determination of every one of the squadron's pilots, whether experienced or not. As the evacuation had progressed, some of the new chums had developed their aerial warfare skills well. In fact, as a consequence of the pilots being exposed to the short but intense period of aerial warfare over Dunkirk, John agreed the squadron was now much better placed to fly and fight in the impending Battle of Britain. That was what Prime Minister

Churchill had named it after the fall of France. John accepted that the expected battle would be a fight for Britain's survival. Failure would encourage the Germans to cross the Channel.

'I think Four-one-five Squadron is as ready now as it ever will be for the Luftwaffe,' John continued, 'but we are going to be really pushed, no doubt about that. The odds are stacked against us. However, I'm confident the chaps will cope, and we will be able to successfully resist Jerry.'

'I hope you are right, John,' Greg said. 'I suppose we will probably be sent back to Hornchurch when the balloon goes up. The Battle of Britain will be fought over southeast England, not up here in Yorkshire.'

John nodded his agreement, sighing as he looked around the room at all the young men who would soon have to fly well, and be absolutely steadfast against a large and powerful Luftwaffe.

John had joined the RAF halfway through 1938. He had been accepted for pilot-training after responding to a notice published in New Zealand inviting young men to apply for flying roles with the service. Now, two years later, he was a capable and experienced Spitfire pilot. Prior to joining the RAF, he had been working on his family's farm in Otago, a province in New Zealand's South Island. He had travelled to the United Kingdom to obtain his flying qualifications, training at RAF Stations Desford and Hullavington. On earning his Wings, John had been posted to 415 Squadron at RAF Catterick, arriving there at the beginning of May 1939. The squadron had just started operating the Spitfire at that time, and he had soon completed his type rating, consolidation flying, and advanced training in that aircraft. Over the months that followed, his aviation skills had rapidly developed as his experience grew. Those who knew John appreciated that he was one of the squadron's more capable pilots.

As he had become more established in 415 Squadron, John had recognised that there was an issue with the squadron's leadership. He understood it had been a matter of importance to the squadron pilots for some time, but nothing had been done. The problem was that their Commanding Officer, Wing Commander Christopher Bland, had shown he was unable to provide quality leadership in the air during war operations. He was simply not up to the task.

John had experienced some unsatisfactory episodes of Bland's leadership himself, when engaging with the Luftwaffe at Dunkirk. In the end, the concern felt by all who flew with Bland had become too much, and a group of the squadron's pilots had recently asked John and Greg Somerville to approach Bland's second-in-command, Squadron Leader David Sidey. They were to ask Sidey if he could help resolve Bland's leadership failures.

Sidey had given John and Greg a good hearing. While he was himself aware of the CO's failings, he made it clear that achieving a change of leadership in the squadron would not be easy. Quite apart from Bland likely resisting any suggestion that he not lead in war operations, Sidey doubted that anyone at Fighter Command would be interested in intervening, to remove Bland from his post. During the meeting John had hinted that perhaps Sidey's friendship with the station's medical officer, Brian Berryman, might be useful. Could Berryman be persuaded to consider whether Bland should be grounded for medical reasons, had been his not-so-subtle message?

It was now two weeks since John and Greg had met with Sidey, and there was still no sign of anything happening with the CO. Whether Sidey would pick up on what John had suggested and follow it up, and, more importantly, how Berryman would respond if he did, were matters that exercised John's mind. One thing was clear, though, as far as John and the other pilots were concerned: if Bland led the squadron into battle against the Luftwaffe, the outcome could be disastrous. Pilots may well be lost, as a consequence of their in-flight leader making poor decisions in the air. *God, I hope Dave can do something*, John had thought as he and Greg had left their meeting with Sidey.

There were other concerns squadron members had about Bland as well, beyond poor leadership and operational capabilities. They related to his personality. John was aware their CO was considered a thoroughly unpleasant person, well known for his rudeness and elitism. Those matters were usually shown by Bland ignoring anyone he considered not to be from the "right" background, while fawning over those he considered socially important.

Richard Cowles was a member of the British aristocracy, the son of a lord, and he occasionally had to tolerate some good-natured banter from his fellow squadron pilots as a result. But his family connections also meant that Richard was a target for Bland. Richard had told John he had been embarrassed on a number of occasions by his Commanding Officer's obsequious behaviour. Conversely, since John had joined the squadron, he had noted that Bland had shown him nothing but hostility. He did not know why, but he suspected it reflected the views held about Bland by the members of the squadron. Because John had joined the RAF from New Zealand, where he had worked on his father's sheep farm, he did not fit the CO's preferred type. John had felt that on several occasions. Apart from being treated by Bland in a rude and dismissive way, there had also been several unjustified verbal attacks on John since he had joined the squadron. On one occasion, Bland had gone as far as trying to suggest John had some responsibility for a fatal training accident.

While his prime concern was Bland's ability as an operational leader, John also intensely disliked his character, and he had never forgiven Bland's attempt to claim he had been at fault in that accident. One of John's close friends had been killed, and being wrongly blamed had compounded the stress and upset he had felt at the time. Although he was keen for Sidey to get on and do something about the squadron's leadership problems, John had accepted it was not a pressing matter. Nevertheless, he did want the issue to be resolved before Germany increased its activity over Britain and 415 Squadron became regularly engaged in battle.

At the beginning of the second week of July, the squadron pilots were called to a special briefing to be given by the CO. The calling of the meeting indicated to John that the question of Bland's leadership may now be about to become even more important. *If we are about to be told that the Luftwaffe is beginning its campaign against us, we need to get the Bland situation resolved*, John thought. *We cannot meet Jerry with him in charge in the air.*

'We have been ordered to reposition the squadron to Hornchurch,' Bland announced to the assembled pilots. 'The Luftwaffe has been stepping up its attacks in recent days. Ports on the south coast are being bombed, as is shipping in the Channel, some of it quite close to our coastline. We are going down there to boost Eleven Group, departing from here at o-nine-hundred hours tomorrow.'

There was a buzz of conversation as the pilots commented to one another regarding this development. They all knew it was the beginning of what was likely to be some very demanding flying and fighting.

'Squadron Leaders Smallbone and Sidey will act as leaders of the squadron on war operations from Hornchurch. They will share that role, alternating as required between operations. I regret to have to tell you that I won't be travelling with you to Hornchurch. It seems I need to have some follow-up tests after my previous medical grounding. I am not able to fly until those tests are completed and evaluated. Hopefully I will be able to join you soon. I'm told it's a matter of days, rather than weeks, before my situation is sorted out.'

John stole a quick look at Greg, who smiled back knowingly. John then glanced towards Sidey, who was standing with the CO at the front of the room. He was looking straight ahead, impassive. *He's not going to catch anyone's eye*, John thought. *Thanks, Dave.*

The squadron's transit from Catterick to Hornchurch the next day was without incident. The weather was good and none of the aircraft had a serviceability issue. After they arrived, John was pleased to see he had been allocated the same room that he had used while based there for the evacuation from Dunkirk. Richard Cowles had the adjacent room on one side, and Charlie Ross, another of the squadron's pilots, the other side.

'Dave Sidey and Tony Smallbone want us to meet to discuss our operating plans,' Charlie said, as he poked his head through John's door.

'Roger that,' John responded. 'Do you know when and where?'

'Main briefing room at sixteen hundred,' Charlie replied.

'Welcome to Hornchurch, gentlemen,' Tony Smallbone said, once all the squadron's pilots had arrived for the briefing. 'You are familiar with the airfield here, following Dynamo, so I don't need to take you through local aerodrome detail and procedures. As well as this station, RAF Manston will be available to us. We are going to use that as our forward base when required. It won't be used tomorrow, as all our ops are planned to begin and end here.'

John understood the proposal to use Manston. It was closer to the coast than Hornchurch, and they would be better placed to more quickly intercept inbound German aircraft from that forward base. But, he realised, it also meant the squadron would have an increased exposure on the ground there. Being relatively close to the Channel, and thus more accessible from the aerodromes in northern France where the Luftwaffe had recently taken up residence, it could easily become a preferred close target for the Germans.

'At present, Jerry appears to be concentrating on our coastal shipping and the southern ports. Dover has taken a particular hammering in recent days,' Smallbone continued. 'Vessels in the Channel are inevitably relatively close to the new Luftwaffe bases in France, so protecting them in a timely way is proving difficult. Warnings about approaching enemy aircraft, usually through Chain Home, are available, of course, but other squadrons have found the warnings aren't being received in time. On occasions they have been unable to reach the required area and intercept enemy aircraft before they attack.

'Coming off a forward base such as Manston will provide us with the ability to intercept enemy aircraft sooner, but I accept it's not the complete answer. Consequently, our strategy, at least initially, will be to run regular shipping protection patrols using less than a full squadron muster on those operations.

That will give us a better ability to ensure continuous cover over the closer waters of the Channel; Command does not want us going anywhere near the French coast at this stage. Those aircraft we hold on the ground will take their turn on patrol when the preceding patrol is back to refuel. We plan to operate using six aircraft only on each of these patrols, but we will of course respond with a full muster where circumstances dictate. We will fly our patrols in an echelon formation. The default positioning will be thirty-yard lateral spacing, with the drop back being your nose level with the preceding aircraft's tail. On any engagement with the enemy, the flight of six will go to pairs, with aircraft one, three, and five taking the lead for each pair. Any questions?'

There were none. They all knew the inadequacies of Vic formations, and with a six-aircraft flight, a finger-four formation was not going to work. Pairs, consisting of a lead aircraft and wingman, had been the positioning successfully adopted for some of the engagements they had experienced over Dunkirk, so what was being suggested suited the pilots.

'Take-off time tomorrow is to be confirmed, but it's likely to be early, so the first flight up, A Flight, will need to be ready by o-five-hundred hours,' Smallbone continued. 'The remainder of the squadron, B Flight, should be ready to go two hours later. That's based on the interval we expect to have between our patrols. Then the flights will alternate during the remainder of the day, to provide virtually continuous coastal coverage. We are currently planning three missions per day for both A Flight and B Flight, so you are going to be busy,' said Smallbone with a grin.

'You will understand that whatever we set up now may get changed at short notice. Flexibility is going to be key. The enemy's intentions are unknown, so we may have to change tactics if something develops, but in the meantime it's these scheduled patrols. That should ensure we are not too far from any engagement we are called to while patrolling. Please note too, gentlemen, the French coast is only about twenty-odd miles from England at its closest point. That's around five minutes' flying time, even less if you are already some distance out over the Channel. Don't get so focused on chasing Jerry that you end up over enemy territory. It wouldn't be too hard to make an error like that in the heat of pursuit, especially if there is a cloud layer beneath you and you don't see the French coastline coming up. That is all, thank you. Until tomorrow.'

The next morning, John was in the first patrol of six aircraft, to be led by Smallbone. Sidey would take the second patrol up after they returned.

'In the air today you'll be part of Red Section, one through six,' Smallbone had said as they were preparing for the day's operations. 'Barton will be red two, Cowles red three, Noble red four, Ross red five, and Bentley red six.'

John was happy with the pilots designated to fly the patrol. Flying Officer Roger Barton was the squadron's aerobatics ace — a valuable chap to have along, particularly if they met any enemy aircraft and became caught up in some dogfighting. The aristocratic Richard Cowles was a reliable and capable pilot, and John was always happy to fly with Charlie Ross, despite colliding with him in mid-air many months ago, during a training exercise. John accepted it had just been one of those no-fault accidents that could happen sometimes when a series of chances and circumstances align, and allow an event to occur. He did recognise, however, that they would all have to watch out for Tim Bentley, flying today as red six. He was relatively new to the squadron. His logbook showed only eighteen hours in a Spitfire, and he had never been involved in any aerial warfare, other than a brief exposure to some basics during his advanced training. Today's patrol would be his first war operation.

John had spoken to him briefly in the mess at dinner the previous evening. Tim had told John he had recently got married, and was very proud of the fact that he was about to become a father. John understood the mathematics involved, but he was not judgemental. He recognised that Tim had a lot going on in his personal life, but it was about to get much busier as the Luftwaffe launched its expected air offensive against Britain. Flying into battle against experienced German pilots was no place for a *new chum*, let alone one who was shortly to become a father for the first time.

John tried to put his concerns to one side as he tuned back in to what Smallbone was saying.

'Control has no targets for us at present, but they want us to patrol east of Dover, at twenty thousand feet, as soon as we are ready. They have designated us Jonty Patrol. So mount up, gentlemen, start your engines, and await my call,' Smallbone instructed the pilots.

Five minutes later, all the pilots were sitting in their cockpits, Merlin engines rumbling. Soon they would take their Spitfires up into the early morning sky. John could see the sun slowly coming up, causing the clouds to glow bright red above the distant eastern horizon.

"Red sky in the morning, shepherd's warning," he said aloud in his cockpit. He tried to recall the meteorological reasons for a sky full of cloud reflecting red in the early morning. Something to do with high water content and low atmospheric pressure, which meant poor weather to follow. But there had been no mention of bad weather in the briefing.

'Red Section, we are cleared for take-off,' Smallbone called over the radio.

They took off, three aircraft at a time. After becoming airborne, the pilots formed up into a six-ship echelon-right formation, off Smallbone's Spitfire, and climbed towards the English Channel. They maintained a standard thirty-yard lateral spacing from the track of the aircraft ahead and to the left, holding a position against that aircraft by trying to keep their nose level with its tail. Level at twenty thousand feet as they crossed the coast at Ramsgate, the sky was clear. No enemy aircraft had been reported. When the patrol was about ten miles out into the Channel, Smallbone called for a turn onto a southerly heading.

'Red Section, this is red one. Turn right to one eight zero. Open your positions laterally when established on heading. Fifty yards, please. Maintain angels twenty.'

The patrolling Spitfires turned and established themselves on the heading he had set, widening their spacing to fifty yards between aircraft, as instructed. After flying south for a few minutes, John could see a smudge on the horizon. It was the French coast. The cape southwest of Calais, Cap Gris-Nez, he recalled.

'Red Section, left turn to zero four zero,' Smallbone instructed.

The six Spitfires now turned towards the northeast. They were paralleling the French coast, about ten miles out.

'Jonty patrol, confirm current position,' a sector controller called on the radio.

'Jonty is approximately eighteen west of Dover, at angels twenty,' Smallbone replied.

'Roger, identified, please proceed directly towards Dover. We have three merchants being attacked by dive-bombers, six miles off the port.'

'Wilco, Jonty patrol is on the way. Red Section, follow me, and down to twelve thousand.'

John watched as Smallbone's Spitfire rolled left and began descending. One after the other, each of the aircraft comprising Red Section followed, rolling into their left turns and accelerating to maintain their echelon right formation.

'Eyes peeled, please, chaps. Dive bombers reported. It will be Stukas we are looking for. They will be starting their runs from around eleven or twelve thousand feet, I expect,' Smallbone called.

John was familiar with the Junkers Ju 87 dive bomber of the Luftwaffe, or at least with its reputation. Usually just referred to as a Stuka, it had caused havoc while supporting German ground forces invading various countries in Europe. A Stuka had a banshee-like wail that increased in volume as it dived down to drop its bombs. The noise came from a siren installed under its nose, designed to scare and destabilise those being attacked. That had worked well, he understood from some of the tales he had heard about Germany's *Blitzkrieg*, but he also knew that while Stukas were considered to be one of the most frightening aircraft you could encounter if you were a target on the ground, that was not so in the air. The Stuka was proving no match for the superior fighters of the Royal Air Force, the Spitfire and the Hurricane, and the Germans were very quickly becoming aware of that, according to Fighter Command. John had not encountered Stukas before, but he had read the intelligence reports distributed to the fighter squadrons expected to meet the Ju 87 at some point, so he had some idea of what to expect regarding the in-air capability of a Stuka.

The six Spitfires were flying at high speed as they reduced their altitude to the height at which they expected to find the Luftwaffe dive bombers preparing for their attack runs.

Richard saw them first. 'Red one, this is red three. I see them. Five miles at one o'clock. Fifteen Stukas. They are two to three thousand feet below our current level.'

The Spitfires were passing through thirteen thousand feet at that time.

'I have them, thank you,' Smallbone replied.

'Stop descent at twelve thousand. We will abandon echelon right and attack in close pairs, but aim to maintain at least fifty yards from an adjacent pair. Watch for any fighter cover. I don't see any at present.'

As Red Section approached, John could see that some of the Stukas appeared to have completed their dive-bombing run against the vessels below. *We are a bit late on scene, even with our continuous-cover patrols*, he thought. The ships were desperately weaving, trying to make targeting them accurately more difficult for the enemy. One appeared to have been hit. There was oily, black smoke coming from its midship region.

'Control, Jonty patrol has sighted fifteen Stukas attacking the shipping. Tally-ho.'

The phrase 'Tally-ho' signified that an attack was underway.

'Red Section, attack in your pairs,' Smallbone called. 'One and two go for the Stukas targeting the vessel closest to shore. Three and four, take those after the ship at the south end of the group. Five and six, you chase the Stukas attacking the third vessel.'

What a difference! John thought, comparing the tactical decision-making and instruction from red one today with Bland's leadership efforts over Dunkirk. *Like chalk and bloody cheese.*

'Go after those preparing to attack first,' Smallbone transmitted as they got closer.

John understood there was little point in chasing after an aircraft that had already dropped its bombs. Better to stop what further bombing they could.

Three of the enemy aircraft were hit on the first pass by the Spitfires. One simply exploded in mid-air. Another dipped its nose when hit and slowly descended, trailing grey smoke. The third rolled onto its side, and then entered an ever-tightening spiral dive, clearly out of control. The remaining Stukas scattered, but John latched onto one of them as it tried to escape back towards France. Once on its tail, and within effective shooting distance, he fired. The gunner in the rear of the German aircraft must have died instantly, as a hail of bullets from John's eight machine guns converged on him.

The area around the gunner exploded, with large pieces of fuselage and cockpit flying off the damaged aircraft. Now on fire, it pitched over into a steep dive towards the sea below.

Back at Hornchurch after their successful interception of the Stukas, Smallbone reviewed the engagement with the pilots. He was keen that any lessons to be learned were duly noted. The encounter had been over quickly, and the debrief showed that five of the Stukas had been shot down. The rest had fled when confronted by the Spitfires. No Red Section aircraft had been hit by any enemy fire. Their action on this first patrol was about as successful as it could have been, John thought, as Smallbone summarised the facts.

'That went well, thank you, gentlemen,' Smallbone said, as he finished his summary. 'I'm very happy with five nil. How did you find your first encounter with the Luftwaffe, Pilot Office Bentley?'

'No issues, thank you, sir. It didn't seem difficult.'

'Today, that was true,' Smallbone said, 'but don't assume all your encounters will be like that. The Stukas have not been performing well against us. You will have seen the memo from Fighter Command regarding its assessment of capability. The Stukas are not getting the same opportunities over here as they had when they operated in Europe. Jerry has been suffering significant losses in its Stuka operations this side of the Channel. No match for the Spit, or the Hurricane. I think we will see them either withdrawn or perhaps given fighter cover.'

'Yes, sir, thank you for that,' Tim responded enthusiastically.

'When you have finished here, back out to dispersal, please, gentlemen,' Smallbone continued. 'Our next patrol is due out in fifty minutes.'

As the pilots were making their way back to their aircraft, John found himself walking alongside Tim.

'It's good that you got a relatively easy one for your first encounter, Tim,' he said.

'Yes, I keep being told that today could have been worse.'

'Stukas rely a lot on their rear-cockpit gunner. We have found them not to be that accurate in the past, but there's always a risk of being hit, so you need to stay aware as you position yourself behind them. If conditions suit, drop down below the enemy's height when you are coming in. Then, when you are in range, do your shooting as you pull up. It's harder for the rear gunner to draw a bead on you if you approach like that, from below his line of sight.'

'Thanks. Shall do. What will it be like with other German aircraft? Are the larger bombers better at defending themselves?'

'If they don't break out of their formation, they can concentrate the firepower of all the aircraft there, each with multiple gun stations, so that increases the risk for us. The real work, though, Tim, is dealing with the fighters that provide the cover for the bombers. Then your skill as a pilot and your knowledge and experience in war ops become very important.'

'Oh yes, I understand that's going to be more difficult for me. I have no encounters with the enemy, apart from this morning's Stukas, so my experience levels are not high,' Tim replied nervously.

'We all started out like you, Tim. All I can say is take some time when you are on the ground to have a preliminary think about how and where you will position your aircraft in different flight situations when engaging. Then try to fly what you have thought about, and been taught, instinctively. When you get busy in the air with Jerry, you will have no time to wonder about your next move, so it has to come to you quickly. You need to know where to put your aircraft, and how best to achieve that, without any hesitation. Pausing while you think, or failing to execute your manoeuvre properly, could see you taken out, not to put too fine a point on it.'

'Thank you, I understand what you are saying and appreciate your advice,' Tim said as they reached dispersal, and set about preparing themselves for their next operation.

CHAPTER TWO

'I thought we were much better organised in the air today,' John said, speaking loudly to be heard over the buzz of conversation in the dining room. Additional squadrons had been sent to RAF Hornchurch in recent days, as well as John's squadron, and the station's facilities were stretched as a result.

Despite the crowd, John and the usual group he associated with had managed to secure a table where they could sit together. Roger, Richard, Greg, and Charlie were there, together with the new chum, Tim Bentley. Craig Thomson, who, like Greg, had flown as a member of Sidey's patrol today, had also joined them. John liked Craig; he was from a farm, so he saw him as something of a kindred spirit. Craig's family farmed near Berwick. He was a friendly chap and a capable pilot, and had gone out of his way to welcome John and make him feel comfortable when John had first joined 415 Squadron. Craig had some amusing personality traits, particularly his tendency to dispense advice on life and its issues.

'No doubt about it,' John continued, 'we had a good day with Smallbone running things. We were working together so much better than in the past with Bland, especially when we were preparing to attack the Stukas on our first patrol this morning.'

'Yes, I thought so too, John,' Roger agreed. 'The tactics were spot on and the orders on engagement were appropriate. It all worked well.'

'Shows the importance of capable leadership, I think,' Richard noted. 'It also shows the importance of us doing something about it and getting a change made. We would have been a lot less effective today if Bland had not been sidelined by his latest medical issues.'

'Yes, it was the same for us with Sidey. Much better in the air than if Bland had been running it,' Greg confirmed.

'What happens if Bland is recertified as fit to fly?' asked Craig. 'He will be back at some stage. There is undeniable improvement without the CO leading us in the air, so I don't want to see that end if he returns.'

'I think the new leadership arrangements will be well embedded by the time he re-joins us, and they will be difficult to alter at some future time. Particularly if there is some resistance to any change, which I'm sure there will be,' Richard said, with a broad grin.

'How was your first day, Tim?' Greg asked the squadron's newest pilot, changing the subject.

'It all went well, thanks, and I learnt a lot. Probably picked up more pointers in my flying today than I did during my entire air warfare training course.'

'I bet you did,' Greg acknowledged. 'That's the difference between reality and theory. Mind you, the practical lessons have an additional edge to them.'

'Like when someone is trying to shoot you down,' said Charlie. 'That gets your attention.'

'I was red six on the patrol today. Being last in the formation line gave me a good position from which to observe actions by those ahead, and, of course, once we were attacking in our pairs, I followed my leader closely,' Tim said.

'Yes, I saw Smallbone had put you at the back. Good place to be for your first op,' said Richard, 'but it's a spot you have to be careful about.'

Tim looked at him enquiringly.

'The reason I say that,' Richard continued, 'is that you might be the first target for anyone coming on us from behind. We all have to keep an eye on what is happening on our tails. Don't want to look in the mirror and be surprised to see an Me one-o-nine closing in. The man at the back has a special responsibility to keep watch behind us.'

'Yes, of course, I do remember that from my training,' Tim replied, making it plain by his tone that it was not something Richard needed to point out to him.

'You'll be a father soon, I hear, Tim,' Greg cut in.

'Yes, our first baby is due next month,' he responded proudly. 'My wife and I are very excited. Hopefully I will be able to get a few days' leave so I'm at home after she gives birth.'

'I'm sure that will be possible, Tim, but I would suggest you get a note to the adjutant about it, with expected dates, so he can prioritise you for leave. You will certainly get it before John here does. He just wants time off to visit his girlfriend, Mary, and we know what that's all about.'

'Easy, Greg,' John said as the others chuckled, Tim included.

The group continued chatting over dinner, talking about everything except the war. No-one wanted to discuss that topic any more this evening. Instead, they all talked about their families, their plans for the future, and better times to come.

Some days later, John and the other squadron pilots were outside the dispersal hut, enjoying cheese sandwiches and cups of tea. Increased Luftwaffe activity meant their regular patrols had been discontinued. Now the squadron was in reactionary mode, launching in response to scramble alerts as inbound enemy aircraft were detected. The pilots had already scrambled earlier that morning, and were now back, trying to relax a little before their next call to action. They all knew that could come at any moment. Despite multiple encounters with the Luftwaffe in recent days, and the pressures they faced with constant calls to get airborne to meet yet more enemy aircraft, the pilots were all in remarkably good spirits as they chatted with one another.

'I have to say,' said John, 'if there wasn't a war on, sitting around between ops on these deckchairs in the summer sun would be damn pleasant.'

'I can see how comfortable you are, John. You've been asleep for the last five minutes,' Charlie commented.

'At least you didn't snore. That would've been unacceptable,' Roger added.

'How's the pregnancy going, Tim?' Charlie asked.

Since joining the squadron, Tim had become good friends with Charlie. He had also developed into one of the better performing pilots, with one probable and two possibles to his credit. With help from the rest of the squadron, Tim had learnt fast and survived.

'It's going well,' he replied. 'Doc has told us the baby's growth is normal, and Elsbeth herself is keeping healthy. So, all good, thanks.'

'Remind me what day the baby is due?' Charlie said.

'If all is on time, and if the calculations are correct, it looks like the twentieth of August.'

'You have been told about the squadron tradition, I presume?' Charlie asked.

'What's that?' Tim queried.

'First child requires you to take us to the pub when we are off tour, probably back at Catterick for our rest and recovery, and you pay for the first two rounds.'

'Does it? Ah, okay, sure,' Tim replied uncertainly.

'Don't worry, we will stay off the top shelf,' Charlie assured him, before starting to laugh. 'Sorry, old chap, just a joke,' he went on after a moment. 'We won't require you to pay for our drinks. You will need all your money for the new member of your family.'

The telephone rang.

'Red Section only, scramble!' shouted the airman in charge of the dispersal hut.

Today that section was a six-ship flight, comprising Richard, who was leading as red one, Roger, John, Charlie, Greg, and Tim. Squadron Leader Smallbone had asked Richard to lead this morning's operations, as he was caught up in a special meeting with someone from Fighter Command headquarters.

As they climbed away from the aerodrome at Hornchurch, the sector controller transmitted instructions to Richard. The section was coded "Shiner" for control's purposes this morning.

'Shiner, this is control. Climb to angels twenty. Heading one zero zero for an intercept of ten-plus bandits on an inbound track towards Dover.'

'Shiner, wilco, heading one zero zero, climbing to twenty thousand,' Richard repeated to the controller. 'Red Section, this is red one. Echelon right as we proceed, please, and space now, to maintain lookout,' he then transmitted, before going on to add, 'Red six, keep a *very* good watch behind'

Tim Bentley, red six, called his acknowledgement. 'Wilco. Red six is watching *very* carefully.'

John, remembering the exchange between Richard and Tim some days ago, grinned to himself.

As they crossed Dover, the controller called again.

'Shiner, your targets are at fifteen thousand, ten miles at your one o'clock. Looks like bombers. No fighter escort showing currently.'

'Roger, Control,' Richard responded. Then, 'Red section, this is red one — I don't see our bandits. Anyone see them?'

A chorus of negatives followed. None of them had picked up the inbound aircraft yet. A few minutes later, John saw movement against the backdrop of distant clouds. He focused his attention. Sure enough, there they were. It looked like a group of about fifteen Heinkels.

'Got them, direct ahead, Heinkels,' John called. A chorus of sighting confirmations followed. Everyone had seen them now.

'In we go. Follow me, maintaining current echelon and spacing. Fire at will. I don't see any fighters. Go to pairs to continue after first pass,' Richard radioed, before calling to advise control of the situation.

'Control, this is Shiner. Targets sighted. Tally-ho.'

As the six Spitfires raced down, the approaching Luftwaffe bombers started taking evasive action. They scattered in all directions, some left, some right, most diving and turning at the same time. It was a panicked reaction from pilots who did not like what they saw coming, John thought. He had seen similar behaviour on previous occasions when intercepting enemy aircraft, but it had not happened often, so he had decided it was likely to be related to the level of experience of the crews involved. Pilots new to battle might react in that way, but not those who had been hardened by past exposure to aerial warfare. John knew more experienced bomber crews would stay together, as that enhanced their defensive ability. Gunners in different aircraft close to each other could coordinate their fire to make it harder for attacking fighters.

'Go to pairs, shoot at will,' Richard called. He had decided there was no point in maintaining the six-aircraft echelon formation as they approached for their first pass, now the Heinkels had split up and gone different ways. It was time for individual engagements. He peeled away towards one of the bombers, followed by his wingman, Roger.

John, as red three, led the second pair into a diving turn, chasing a Heinkel that was manoeuvring violently to escape the Spitfires. Charlie clung to his tail as John descended. Near them, John saw Greg latch on to another bomber, with Tim close behind, flying as his wingman in that third pair. The sky was full of aircraft, climbing, diving, twisting, and turning as lumbering bombers tried to escape nimble Spitfires. It was an aerial melee.

John fired at a Heinkel that suddenly appeared in front of him, crossing his path about six hundred yards away. The range was too great for his shooting to be effective, and, in any event, the German had appeared so quickly he had not allowed any deflection in his aim, so a hit was never likely. John turned to follow the Heinkel.

Now the range was down to four hundred yards and reducing rapidly as he quickly overhauled the bomber. He fired again. This time he saw some results. Its port engine started smoking as it took a prolonged burst from the guns on John's Spitfire. Grey and wispy at first, the smoke soon turned black and started billowing from the engine nacelle. Then there were flames. Small at first, the fire soon grew into bright yellow and orange flames that streamed behind the engine.

'Got you,' John muttered to himself. At that moment the Heinkel's left wing exploded. The flames must have reached the fuel tank, he decided. The wing separated from the fuselage and the bomber began to roll to the left, its rate of roll increasing as John watched. It fell away towards the sea far below, rolling through a full three hundred and sixty degrees as it spiralled down.

John looked around for another target. There were two Heinkels at what he thought to be one mile's range. They were descending, trying to get as much speed as they could to reach the safety of France. Closing in on them quickly, John was preparing to shoot when he heard a warning call.

'Red Section, fighters, twenty plus Me one-o-nines, coming out of the sun.'

It was Tim, red six, calling the warning. John looked towards the sun. It was difficult to see anything against its glare, and he could not pick up the aircraft he had just been warned about. Then his aircraft shuddered violently, as if shaken by a giant hand. He had been hit by a concentrated burst of fire.

Instinctively, John rolled his aircraft into a steep bank to the left and pulled hard on his control stick to tighten his turn. After two or three seconds, he released his back pressure on the stick and pushed it forward and to the right, rolling his aircraft into a diving turn in the opposite direction. Not wanting to remain on a relatively straight course any longer than necessary, he then pulled his Spitfire into another steep turn to the left, before levelling his wings and looking around. He could not see any hostile aircraft. There was no sign of his wingman, Charlie, either. *Hopefully that's just because he couldn't stay with me when I was trying to get away from Jerry*, John thought. He did not want to contemplate the alternative, that the one-o-nines had got him. Suddenly another burst of fire raked his Spitfire.

'*Christ!*' John shouted, pulling his aircraft into a steep climb and rolling sharply to the right. He maintained that roll until he was inverted, and then pulled hard on the control stick to enter a dive. *Where the hell did that come from?* he wondered. He had seen no sign of any other aircraft when scanning the skies just a few moments ago. He again searched the sky around him, above, below, behind. No sign of an enemy aircraft. Then he saw smoke coming from his engine bay, and a few wisps were also beginning to emerge from behind his instrument panel, into the cockpit. He needed to get home quickly.

John was concerned that the smoke signalled the risk of a full fire developing. He turned west, towards England, lowering the Spitfire's nose to help build speed as he gingerly eased the throttle forward to low cruise boost. John had decided to be conservative with his power setting because of the potential effects of the damage to his aircraft. As he flew towards the British coast under partial power, his instruments showed him he was descending at a rate of one thousand feet per minute. His just-completed combat manoeuvring had cost him altitude, and he had been down to four thousand feet at the time he had set a heading to take him back to Hornchurch. *That is plenty of height to reach land*, he thought, *so long as all remains well with my aircraft.*

John had no desire to ditch, or worse still, to bale out. He had never wanted to have to use his parachute, although he had been forced into doing that some months ago, when he and Charlie had a mid-air collision during a training exercise. It had all been a blur, with no time for John to worry about jumping out of his aircraft, if he was to survive. He had been so low that if he had not got out immediately, he would have been killed. Unusually for a pilot, John had a fear of heights, but it was a phobia that never affected him sitting in his cockpit, happily flying thousands of feet above the ground. It was when he was doing something such as climbing a ladder, or standing at a cliff-edge, that he would feel the vertigo he dreaded. John did not know for sure, but he thought it would probably be the same if he baled out at altitude and was hanging in his parachute, looking at the ground thousands of feet below his dangling legs. He did not want to put that to the test today, unless he was forced to get out of the aircraft.

The smoke was not getting any worse in the cockpit at the moment, but John noticed the engine was beginning to run roughly, with an occasional misfire echoing from the exhausts. He could also feel the controls were not as responsive as normal. The aircraft, and its engine, had clearly suffered some damage that was affecting its performance.

John assessed his situation as he came down. *Looks like two miles to the coast. Passing through two thousand eight hundred feet now. Still high enough to glide to land if the engine fails.* As if in response to that thought, there was a sudden loud bang from the front of the aircraft. Then John saw he had no power; his engine had failed completely. Flames were now coming out of one side of the engine cowling. Fire was every pilot's nightmare.

John leapt into emergency procedure mode. Too low to have the luxury of time, his checks were abbreviated. He would be on the ground very soon, so he just recited the basics out loud. 'Fire: fuel off, switches off. Engine failure: convert excess speed to height, assume best glide speed. Forced landing: check where best to come down, and plan an approach.'

As the flames continued to grow, John realised he would have to get out. A forced landing was not a safe option. He might not have time to get the Spitfire down safely before the fire reached his fuel tanks, situated just in front of the cockpit.

Damn, I'm going to have to jump. John had rehearsed many times what he would do if he ever had to bale out. He quickly went through the process in his mind. *Unlatch the canopy and slide it*

31

back. Undo the straps. Roll inverted. Stick forward. Use legs to eject. Count to three. Pull the ripcord. Pray.

John realised he needed to be quick. If he took too long to get out, his height for parachute opening would be marginal. He reached for the cockpit canopy latch, his first step. It would not move. It had been damaged. As much as he struggled with it, he was unable to get it open. He knew that now he would have to land the aircraft. He felt the fear of being burnt alive as adrenaline flooded his body. *Stay calm, John,* he told himself.

He looked ahead. There was a large field immediately past the beach, now just a short distance in front of him. He would need to turn ninety degrees to the right when he got closer, to align his aircraft's approach with the length of the field he needed for landing. He thought the wind was fine for that direction, noticing the way some nearby trees were bending in response to what must have been a fresh breeze of about twenty miles per hour. *It's looking good for a forced landing,* he thought, *provided this fire doesn't blossom into something large in the next few minutes.* He decided to increase his airspeed, wanting a better margin for the manoeuvring he would have to undertake as he approached his chosen landing area. He lowered the Spitfire's nose some more, and was soon going faster, but his rate of descent had also increased markedly. *High rate of descent now, and you have no power. Careful, this could be dicey.*

When he reached the field in which he had decided to land, John planned to turn his aircraft through ninety degrees, to line up his final approach with the longest length available on that field. The increased speed he had created by lowering his aircraft's nose would be valuable when he made that turn with no power. The extra speed would also help him reduce the Spitfire's rate of descent when he got close to the ground, by allowing him to firmly round out his descent. *Field surface looks level and unobstructed*, John confirmed to himself. *Don't need to belly it — wheels down.*

The wounded Spitfire crossed the beach at two hundred feet above ground level, with one hundred and thirty-five miles per hour showing on its airspeed indicator. John pulled the aircraft into a steep, descending, ninety-degree turn to the right, to align himself with the longer length of the field lying just beyond the beach. That took some speed off, as John had planned. He applied some back pressure to his control stick as he completed the turn and rolled his wings level. *Perfect! Rate of descent reduced.* He was now nicely lined up with the longest part of the field, landing into wind, and his airspeed was reducing through one hundred miles per hour. John put his wing flaps down and felt their drag come in as they lowered. Then he applied more back pressure to his control stick, to raise the nose slightly. The Spitfire sank slowly towards the ground as its speed continued to wash off. John was happy with his approach and landing profile, and his speed was back through eighty-five miles per hour. *This should be okay*, he thought as he flared for landing. John held the aircraft just above the surface, keeping both the main wheels and the tailwheel from touching down on the grass for as long as he could, before finally letting them all come down at the same time, in a three-point landing. That gave him a lower touchdown speed than if he had landed on the mains alone, with his tailwheel still up. There was less risk of tipping over if the surface had been rougher than anticipated.

The Spitfire lurched and vibrated its way across the grass, but it stayed straight and did not tip onto its nose. John was pleased the field's surface had been okay, but he could see flames were now coming from the engine bay and getting bigger by the second. The panel was still smoking, but there were no flames coming out of it inside the cockpit. *Now to get out*, John thought, as his aircraft came to a halt. He knew that was easier said than done, given the jammed cockpit, but he would try everything he could.

He struggled with the latch. It still would not move, and the flames were now coming a long way out of the nose area. His escape axe, meant to help him hack his way from the aircraft in an emergency, had disappeared from its holder. *Somewhere in the front of the cockpit area*, he thought, *behind the rudder pedals, I suspect.* After all his operations against the enemy, and after successfully nursing his damaged aircraft back, John did not want to die just because he was unable to escape from his cockpit in a field in southeast England. Then it occurred to him there was something else he could try. He pulled his service revolver from under his parachute pack and put the muzzle up against the latch. He risked shooting himself with a ricochet, but he had to try. He shut his eyes and pulled the trigger.

The bang inside the small, enclosed cockpit was deafening. John could smell the cordite. He opened his eyes. Flames were now starting to envelope the front of the canopy, and the smoke was thick and black. John knew if he did not get out in the next few seconds, he would not be getting out at all.

John saw the latch had been broken in two by the shot from his revolver. He grabbed the frame and pulled. Free from the grip of the latch, the canopy slid back. Quickly unstrapping his harness, he clambered out. He moved fast, jumping off the rear of the wing and running at least thirty paces before stopping to turn and look at his aircraft. As he did so there was a dull *whoomph* as the fuel tank erupted into a fireball. Flames blossomed quickly, enveloping the entire cockpit area. John moved back, away from the intense heat.

He did not dwell on what might have been as he stood watching his Spitfire disappear in the conflagration. He knew he had been lucky. *Okay, need to organise myself and find my way back to Hornchurch*, he thought, looking across the field.

A policeman was running across the grass towards him. John could see the bicycle the constable had been riding leaning against the trunk of an elm tree, adjacent to the narrow country road bordering the field in which he had just made his forced landing.

'Great to see you, old chap,' Richard enthused when John walked back into the officers' mess at Hornchurch. 'To be honest, we thought you were a goner. Tim saw you take multiple hits and go down, smoking badly. He reported no parachute seen.'

'I couldn't open the bloody canopy,' John replied, 'but I'm not too unhappy about that — it meant the option of jumping out wasn't available. I would have been damn scared, leaping into space.'

Richard roared with laughter. 'Well, you made it, so that's all that matters,' he said. 'I hear your aircraft didn't survive, though.'

John nodded. 'Last I saw, it was a fireball in a field near Deal.'

'Did someone help get you out after you crash-landed with a jammed hood?'

'There was no-one there when I came to a rest, so I had to improvise.'

'What did you do?'

'I used my revolver to put a shot into the jammed latch mechanism. That fixed my problem.'

'Bloody hell!' Richard exclaimed. 'You risked the bullet deflecting and hitting you!'

'Taking the risk was infinitely preferable to the certainty of burning to death.'

'Of course. Well done on putting your Spit down safely and getting yourself out in one piece.'

John acknowledged Richard's words with a nod, before asking if the squadron had suffered any losses.

'No losses, apart from your machine. You won't be aware of this, John, but Tim took out the Jerry who shot you down.'

'Did he? I must thank him when I see him. I have to say he's developing into a very capable pilot. Seems to be picking up air warfare tactics quickly.'

'Yes,' Richard agreed, 'he is fast becoming one of our aces. He has four confirmed already.'

'I will buy the father-to-be a beer tonight,' John said.

'We are being given a spell away from front-line duties,' Richard went on. 'Dave Sidey says we're going back to Catterick tomorrow. We'll have some time to rest and recuperate before we come back down here for our next tour.'

'I'm very happy to hear that,' John replied with a smile.

That evening, in the mess bar, prior to dinner, the pilots of 415 Squadron celebrated completing their current tour of duty. They talked a lot about what they planned to do when back in north Yorkshire.

'I hadn't realised we would be back at Catterick so soon. My wife's going to come and stay at one of the local guest houses. It'll be a good chance to catch up. The baby's not far away now,' Tim said, beaming widely.

'Nice, Tim. Enjoy. By the way, thank you for getting the Hun that shot me down,' John said.

'Any time,' Tim replied. 'I am feeling good in the air now. My Spit and I have become close friends, and we understand each other.'

John laughed at that, but he knew what Tim meant about the bond that could form between a pilot and his aircraft, especially when flying as much as the squadron had been in recent weeks. John had felt it himself. Having seen others struggle with what air warfare required of them, he was pleased that Tim seemed to have the insight and instinctive responses that were necessary to make him a capable fighter pilot. *Good chap, too*, John thought, noting the way Tim, as the most recent joiner, was fitting into the squadron.

'What do you have planned when back in Yorkshire, John?' Tim asked.

'I'm going to relax and just enjoy not having to fly three or four missions every day. I'll probably contact my girlfriend, Mary, and see if we can meet up at some point.'

'All very well for you chaps with wives and girlfriends, but spare a thought for us singletons,' Charlie complained.

'Ah, Charlie, would you know how to behave even if you could find some poor woman prepared to befriend you?' Craig asked.

'I'm sure I would be fine, thank you,' Charlie responded, with a feigned air of hurt. 'The local bookshop is the place to go. It's a very easy place to start a conversation. You can discuss a book you've read, a book they're looking at, or even a book you've heard about. Then, depending on the time of day, what will follow will be either tea and cakes, or five o'clock drinks. If all goes especially well, maybe even supper.'

'I suppose being a Spitfire fighter ace makes it easier to impress a woman, Charlie?' Greg said, grinning.

'Greg, I will be anything she wants me to be if it means she will go out with me.'

'God, you are desperate, Charlie. Well, good luck to you,' Greg chuckled.

'Well, I'm going home to Norfolk,' said Richard. 'I called the adjutant. He thinks twenty-four hours' leave will be okay. He's going to confirm when we get back to Catterick tomorrow.'

'His Lordship needs some farming advice for the Norfolk acres, does he?' Roger asked.

'I could give him some, if you like,' Craig offered. The pilots all laughed at that. They knew it was just Craig's sense of humour, although he no doubt thought he could add value to any farm operation, if given the chance.

They all liked the Honourable Richard Cowles, to allow him his proper honorific, but often the pilots were keen to poke fun at him. John sometimes wondered if it was because they were really questioning the fairness of upper-class wealth and privilege. He was conscious that Richard was often a target for them.

'The family likes to keep me up to date with what's planned around the estate,' Richard said. 'They want me back there running things as soon as this war is over.'

His comment made John think about his own future. *Will I go back to the family farm in New Zealand? I have to survive this damn war first.* John had left home two years ago, and while farming was a fond memory, it was rapidly becoming a distant one. He probably wouldn't go back to that way of life, he decided.

Squadron Leader Sidey appeared at their table.

'Just to advise you, gentlemen, that we depart at o-ten-hundred tomorrow for RAF Catterick. Briefing and flight planning are at o-nine-hundred. Flying Officer Noble, you will take one of the spare aircraft up, since you destroyed the one that we gave you earlier.'

They all laughed. Some levity around the loss of an aircraft, which was unfortunately all too common these days, made it easier for them all to cope with what were dire times.

CHAPTER THREE

Repositioning the squadron the next day, a Sunday, went smoothly. The weather was benign, the aircraft in good working order, and, as Charlie proclaimed loudly when they were all back at Catterick, no-one had got lost.

John wasted no time telephoning Mary. Unfortunately, she could not see him for two days.

'Sorry, John, I'm heavily committed at the hospital tomorrow, and Tuesday too,' she said.

'All right, I appreciate it's short notice. Let me know when you have some time.'

'I shall ring you tomorrow night,' Mary responded.

John was disappointed he had to wait to see her, but he understood that as a nurse, she couldn't simply drop everything.

Things went better for Tim. His wife had already arrived in Catterick village, earlier than expected. He told John and the other pilots that they were off to supper that evening with "LG". John had discovered that LG stood for Little Guy or Little Gal, whichever the baby was to be.

'Last time I put my hand on Elsbeth's tummy, I could feel LG kicking,' he told the other pilots as they ate their lunch. 'Bloody amazing.' Tim was clearly going to be a doting dad.

'How long now, Tim? Three or four weeks?' Roger asked him.

'Three,' Tim replied. 'I have a pass to stay out until tomorrow morning, so I won't be back on the station until then.'

Richard grinned. 'Get going then. We know you want to.'

Richard's comment was followed by various remarks from the other squadron pilots sitting around the table, all smiling broadly as they spoke.

'See you. Give Mrs Bentley our love.'

'Enjoy yourself, Dad.'

Just as Tim stood up to leave, Bland entered the room and came across to them.

'You all got back safely then,' he said, to no-one in particular.

'Yes, sir. As you probably know, we are back for a short rest,' Richard responded.

'If all goes well, I may be going back to Hornchurch with you. I am hopeful the medics will have decided whether I'm fit to fly in the next few days.'

John caught Greg's eye. The last thing they wanted was the CO resuming leadership duties while on war operations.

'Very good, sir. Hopefully you will get some clarity soon,' said Richard.

The possibility of Bland resuming flying duties was a major problem for them all, John thought. Their demanding and dangerous patrols over southeast England were no place for inadequate leadership.

'Are you off somewhere?' Bland asked, turning to Tim.

'Yes, sir. I have a short leave pass and will be off the station tonight. I'm seeing my wife, who is staying in the village.'

'Is that appropriate right now, Pilot Officer?'

'Uh, I think so, sir. The adjutant approved my formal request.'

'I am the CO, and I haven't approved it. Didn't even know the request had been made.'

Tim looked crestfallen, clearly concerned by the direction the conversation was taking.

'Pilot Officer Bentley discussed it with me, sir,' Richard said suddenly. 'I told him that a short leave pass would probably be available and he should make an application to the adjutant. Pilot Officer Bentley has just completed an arduous tour of duty at Hornchurch and has flown multiple war operations in recent weeks. We have been sent back to Catterick by Fighter Command for a short rest. A pass to see his heavily pregnant wife overnight didn't seem inappropriate to me.'

'When you put it like that, Flight Lieutenant, I see no reason for leave being declined. Take your leave as planned, Pilot Officer,' Bland said. He then turned and walked out of the room with no further comment.

Everyone at the table breathed a sigh of relief. The CO always put great weight on what the Honourable Richard Cowles thought, since he was part of the aristocracy.

David Sidey came in at that point, but before he could join them the door flew open and Flight Lieutenant Michael Gardiner, the station adjutant, came running in, clearly agitated.

'I have just had a call from the commanding officer of Thirteen Group,' he announced, looking towards the group of pilots.

'What about?' Sidey asked, taking control as the senior officer present.

'One of his radio direction finding system operators has identified a large group of enemy aircraft approaching the coast from the northeast. He ignored the blips on the edge of his screen at first, thinking the system was ghosting, and nothing was likely to be there. But the signals did not disappear, and in fact they grew in intensity. I am advised that Thirteen Group now believes there are multiple aircraft at this moment approaching Newcastle upon Tyne. We've never had a raid this far north. They must have come out of Norway.'

'How many?' Sidey asked, looking worried.

'Not clear at their current range, but maybe fifty plus. It looks to be a big raid.'

'Bombers and fighters, do they know?'

'At this stage they think it's only bombers, but they will be able to confirm that soon, when the approaching aircraft are closer.'

John realised that the Germans may be trying a surprise raid. They probably think there isn't much fighter capability up here in the north, since the RAF spends most of its time confronting the Luftwaffe in the south. It's a good thing we have radar coverage here to give us some warning.

A few minutes later, after a quick telephone call to 13 Group, Sidey had all the information he needed, which he shared with the pilots.

'There are multiple hostile aircraft inbound from the northeast, tracking towards Newcastle. There's a lot of them, fifty plus have been confirmed, so Thirteen Group wants everything in the area up. The local standby squadrons are well outnumbered. We will scramble to assist with interception, getting our vectors when airborne. The code we have been allocated is "Mooney".'

John realised that getting everyone organised was going to be difficult.

'Adjutant, cancel all leave passes, and stop any pilots leaving the station,' Sidey instructed. 'We will scramble those pilots we can muster, but I suspect we will be too late to get everyone, given we are on rest and the short notice.'

Gardiner was on the nearby telephone immediately, talking to the station gatehouse.

'Sergeant, Adjutant here. Stop any squadron personnel leaving the station, please. Advise them all leave is cancelled and to report to briefing.'

Tim walked into the briefing room a few minutes later. John noted that his normally cheerful expression had been replaced with a scowl.

'What's up?' he snapped, surprising John with his sharpness.

'Inbound enemy aircraft heading to Newcastle. We've been asked to help. Sorry about your pass to see Elsbeth.'

'Oh, I see. Right then, let's get it done. The sooner it's over, sooner I can resume my leave. They haven't been this far north in force before, have they?'

John was pleased to see that Tim's scowl had disappeared. He was now back in professional mode.

'I think they are hoping we would have concentrated our aircraft in the southeast to meet all the attacks being continually launched against that part of the country. This raid is thought to have originated in Norway. Jerry probably thinks he can successfully attack by sneaking in on our flank. They wouldn't know that as well as maintaining a small ready-force, Fighter Command has a policy of resting squadrons here between tours. They will know soon, though,' John said.

'Everyone going up?' Tim asked.

'We have eight aircraft we can scramble to help the local ready-force,' John replied. 'Sidey told me four of our pilots had already left the base on leave before the alert came in, so that is why we go with just eight. I'm sorry, Tim. I can understand how hard this is for you, being called back to active duty when you were on your way to see your wife.'

Tim shrugged. 'Yes. I was just going out the gate when I got the news. Another minute and I would have been gone, enjoying my much-anticipated meeting with Elsbeth and LG.

That's life these days, I guess. No sense in complaining. We are at war, and if Jerry calls, we have to respond.'

John just nodded. He felt sorry for Tim, but he understood there had been no choice for Squadron Leader Sidey. The surprise raid had to be met, with as many aircraft as possible.

The pilots were all quickly into their flying kits and moving towards their aircraft. Ground crews were already starting the engines of some of the aircraft, as they awaited the arrival of the pilots.

As they climbed towards Newcastle, the sector controller was talking to Sidey, operating as red one. His wingman, red two, was Richard. Squadron Leader Sidey had put the eight aircraft into four pairs for this operation. Each pair had its own colour designator. Red, yellow, green, and blue. Yellow Section was led by Squadron Leader Smallbone, with Greg as his wingman. John was green one, with Charlie as his wingman. Roger led Blue Section, with Tim as his number two.

'Mooney squadron, Control. Your bandits are forty miles northeast of Tynemouth at angels twenty. Fly zero three zero to intercept. Height your discretion.'

The controller was not as experienced as those in the south, at 11 Group, so he had decided the Spitfire pilots themselves would be better placed to judge the optimum height for an attack, John guessed.

'Roger, Control. Mooney squadron will climb to angels twenty-two. Heading zero three zero. Will report with hostiles in sight,' Sidey replied.

'Split to wide pairs, echelon left, climbing twenty-two thousand,' he ordered. The eight aircraft positioned themselves in pairs, two wingspans' width separating one member of a pair from the other. The eight Spitfires formed a line out to the left of Sidey's aircraft, with wide spacing between each pair of sixty yards.

'Looking out, please. Report any sighting.'

They flew on, all eyes scanning ahead, trying to pick out the ominous black dots in the sky that would indicate approaching Luftwaffe aircraft.

'Mooney, Control.'

'Go ahead, Control,' Sidey responded.

'Confirming returns do not indicate any fighter escort. Bombers only. Fifty plus.'

Hearing the communication on the frequency confirmed John's thoughts. The Germans meant to catch the RAF off guard, coming in from Norway to attack much further north than usual. That had the advantage of surprise, but the disadvantage of being a longer flight to England than if coming out of their usual bases in France or Belgium. Fighters did not have sufficient range for the trip from Norway. It was a trade-off: use the element of surprise, but lose fighter cover. *There are only eight of us*, thought John, *but we should be able to do some damage with no fighters to interfere as we attack the bombers. And the local RAF squadrons based in the northeast will have been launched as well.*

'Got them. Twelve o'clock. Our height,' Smallbone called, interrupting John's thoughts.

'Roger, keep climbing,' Sidey responded. 'I want us at least two thousand above as we start running in to engage.'

John realised that Sidey wanted the value of some additional speed when they dived down on the German formation. Not only did that make it more difficult for gunners in the bombers to accurately track the Spitfires attacking them, but the speed and inertia from a dive enabled the Spitfires to zoom back up quickly to continue their attacks from below.

Within minutes the eight Spitfires were positioning to shoot at the bombers.

'Tally-ho,' Sidey called, as he entered a shallow dive towards the leading Luftwaffe aircraft.

The bombers did not scatter when the Spitfires attacked, as John had sometimes seen in previous engagements. They stayed in tight formation. With some fifty aircraft the Germans were well spread across the sky. John knew why they were staying close together. These bomber crews were obviously experienced, and they would also be conscious they had no fighter cover.

Sidey's aircraft, one of the first to attack, was hit by a hail of bullets from three different bombers as he closed in on the Luftwaffe formation. John saw pieces coming off the nose and fuselage of Sidey's aircraft, but the Spitfire seemed largely unaffected by the damage and flew on. At the same time, he saw red two, flown by Richard, get in a long burst on one of the bombers. The German aircraft rolled on to its back and plunged towards the sea.

John lined up a target in his sights. It was coming straight towards him, so he did not need a deflection shot. He fired a two-second burst and was delighted when the bomber's starboard engine burst into flames. *You are going no further, my friend*, he thought to himself as the wounded aircraft dropped out of the formation and began a slow descent. Then John saw Tim out to his right, close to his leader, Roger. As he watched, he saw tracer fire from three or four bombers intercept the path of Tim's aircraft. There were multiple hits on his nose and rear fuselage. Tim's aircraft entered a steep dive and soon disappeared. That did not look good for Tim, John thought, as he lined up another enemy bomber.

A few minutes later, John heard an anxious call from Tim.

'Blue two hit, lost a lot of altitude. I've recovered the aircraft now. Engine is failing. Heading back.'

No one replied. They were all too busy flying and fighting, trying to shoot down the bombers and stay alive. Jinking run-ins were being used to make it harder for the German gunners to be accurate with their fire. Some of the Spitfires were making steep climbing attacks from underneath the bombers. Coming up underneath meant an attacking Spitfire was harder for the German gunners to see and target en masse. Then John saw that the local aircraft had arrived and were joining the fray. The Germans were under pressure, with no fighter cover of their own, and it soon became clear that the raid had been successfully stopped. With no fighter cover to worry about, the Spitfires had decimated the Luftwaffe formation. A significant number had been shot down, and others were now turning back towards Norway. John decided to break off and escort Tim. He knew that with the damage Tim had suffered he should be able to quickly catch him. He called Sidey.

'Red one, this is green one. Jerry appears to be breaking off and tracking away to the northeast, presumably heading back to their base. Permission to vacate the area and form an escort for blue two, who is on his way back to Catterick with engine damage?'

'Affirmative, green one. Go and escort blue two. We will mop up here,' Sidey responded.

A few minutes later John was closing in on Tim's damaged aircraft.

'Blue two, this is green one coming up on your port side.'

'Oh, hi, John. What are you doing here?' Tim asked. John thought his informality was reasonable in the current situation.

'What's your state?' John asked.

'I lost control when first hit. Not sure what happened, but the aircraft went into a dive that I couldn't recover until through five thousand. I think there's damage to my elevator, but I've managed to control it now. My engine is not making its usual sweet and steady sound either. It's misfiring occasionally and running rough. I have it on reduced boost setting. There is still a lot of shaking through the aircraft, and I'm having trouble reading the instrument panel easily. Despite the vibrations, I can see the oil pressure gauge clearly enough, though, and it is nearly off the bottom of the scale. With no oil pressure, I expect the engine will fail completely at any moment. I'm surprised it has lasted this long. My descent rate has been relatively low since recovering from my dive, so I should make it back to dry land.'

John knew that would all change in an instant if Tim's elevator control gave him more problems, or if his engine failed from a lack of oil, as it no doubt soon would. Looking ahead, he could see the coastline was about three or four miles away.

'Maintain your reduced power, Tim. You are looking good to make land.'

'That's my plan. I'm not jumping. Don't want to risk being lost in the sea so long as the aeroplane is still flying.'

John smiled at that. He understood the dilemma. A pilot floating around in his Mae West in the cold North Sea would not last long if he was not found quickly and pulled out of the water.

Seconds later, Tim called again. His struggling Merlin engine had seized. John could see the aircraft's propellor had come to a complete halt, not even spinning in the wind. It was being held in a fixed position by an engine that must have itself seized up. With no power and the increased drag from his

49

jammed propellor, Tim's aircraft was starting to go down much faster than it had before.

John looked towards the shore. It was still some distance away, and now that Tim's rate of descent had increased, John was uncertain if Tim would make it to dry land.

'Get it on best glide speed,' John called. He was back at that speed himself now, one hundred miles per hour. 'Can you do that with your elevator damage?'

'Yep, I've got it. Busy on the trim wheel. That's helping.'

'Good. What rate of descent are you showing now, Tim?'

'One thousand nine hundred feet per minute,' came the reply.

John did some quick mental calculations. They were currently passing through three thousand eight hundred feet. Tim's descent rate meant he had no more than two minutes left in the air. Two minutes at one hundred miles per hour? Call that, say, three and a half miles. *How far out are we?* he wondered, as he peered ahead. It was going to be close.

As Tim's Spitfire continued to descend rapidly, through the mist and drizzle they were now encountering as they approached the coast, John saw a stony beach.

'Tim, there's a gravel beach ahead. Can you make a forced landing there?'

'I will give it my best shot,' Tim said.

Looking at his altimeter, John saw that both aircraft were now descending through fourteen hundred feet.

As he continued to watch, John realised that Tim would not reach the beach for a forced landing. He was going to come down in the surf, and there were some large rocks appearing intermittently on the surface of the sea, between the swells. John had not seen them previously, as the waves had been hiding their presence.

'I'm in the water,' Tim called, as he dropped through the last one hundred feet of his precious altitude.

'Slow as you can. Keep your nose up, and good luck,' John called.

Please don't let this go badly for Tim, he thought, as he applied power and began to climb away. He had been down to less than one hundred feet himself while accompanying Tim, and now it was time to lift his own aircraft up and away from the rocks and surf into which Tim was about to crash-land.

CHAPTER FOUR

John circled back over the beach, desperate to see what had happened to Tim. He saw the tail of Tim's Spitfire sticking up from the water, its cockpit submerged. The aircraft's tail swayed backwards and forwards, like some large animal wallowing, as it was moved around by the passing swells.

On his second orbit above the crash site, John saw that two people had appeared, and they were trying to make their way out to Tim's aircraft, fighting the constantly breaking surf. *Coastal observers?* he wondered. They were jumping as each incoming swell reached them, and from time to time they would swim a few strokes in the calmer areas, between waves. John could see that reaching the downed Spitfire was not going to be a quick exercise.

As he watched, John realised that he could not afford to linger overhead for too long. His fuel state would become marginal if he did not start back to Catterick soon. After completing another orbit, and with the would-be rescuers now just twenty yards from Tim's aircraft, John reluctantly turned for Catterick. He felt a heavy burden of despair as he flew away from his friend, not knowing if he had survived the crash-landing, or, if he had survived, whether he could be rescued from his Spitfire before it sank completely.

On landing, John went straight to the briefing room to give his report. Most of the other pilots were back now, after completing their fight with the Luftwaffe. Sidey was among them.

'I located Pilot Officer Bentley when he was about four miles off the coast. He had experienced some control problems, but had that sorted. Then his engine failed just after I joined him. He started gliding when he lost power, and his prop froze in a fixed position. Tim had reported zero oil pressure when I first caught up with him, so his engine failure was not unexpected. The additional drag from the jammed prop caused him to come down much more quickly than if in a normal glide. He couldn't make land, and crashed into the surf about one hundred yards offshore. I wasn't able to see if he was okay, but there was no sign of him exiting the cockpit, which was partially submerged. I saw a couple of people were in the water trying to reach the aircraft and get him out.'

'I don't like that you saw no attempt by Pilot Officer Bentley to escape the aircraft. I hope he wasn't trapped inside,' Sidey said, with a resigned look. 'Well, we will know soon enough. There is nothing further we can do at present.'

John felt wretched at the possibility that Tim had been killed. He just nodded his agreement with Sidey's comments, and sat down heavily on a nearby chair. He had decided he would wait in the briefing room until more information came in.

'Flying Officer Noble.'

An airman had appeared at the door. John had been sitting in the briefing room for the last thirty minutes, saying little as he glumly stared at the floor.

'Yes?'

'Visitor for you at the front gate, sir.'

'Not at the moment, Corporal. I'm caught up in operational matters.'

'It's Mrs Bentley, sir.'

John was stunned. Did she know Tim had crashed? How could she? 'Thank you, Corporal. I will accompany you to the gate.'

As he walked, John wondered what Elsbeth knew, if anything. He presumed she was aware that Tim had not returned from the mission. Otherwise, why would she ask for him, and not Tim himself?

A heavily pregnant woman was standing outside the gatehouse. John knew it would be Elsbeth, whom he had not previously met. Her head was down, but she looked up as he approached, her eyes red-rimmed and swollen.

'John? John Noble?'

'Yes,' John replied.

'Tim has talked a lot about you. I've just heard he has not returned from an operation. Do you know what has happened to him?'

'Can we use your office for a moment?' John asked the gate sergeant, who was watching on.

When they were inside, Elsbeth asked, 'Do you know anything?'

'Tim's aircraft was hit by enemy fire. He took a shot in his engine and decided to head back to Catterick before it failed completely. We were out over the North Sea at the time.'

Elsbeth waited for John to continue, her hands resting on her swollen belly, as if to comfort the child she was carrying.

'I was with him when he made a forced landing in the sea, just a hundred yards or so short of the beach. I saw his aircraft floating in the surf, and there were some rescuers moving out towards him, but I don't know what happened after that. I had to leave the scene because I was low on fuel.'

'So he might be all right? I thought he had been shot down, and there was little hope,' Elsbeth said.

John shook his head. 'There is no certainty about what happened to Tim when he came down. He may be fine. Who told you that there was little hope?'

'I had a call advising me that my husband had crashed into the sea and was presumed dead.'

'What?' John exclaimed. 'Who told you that?'

'He introduced himself as the officer in charge. I think he said his name was Bland. Yes, that was it, Wing Commander Christopher Bland.'

John could not believe his ears. What the hell was Bland playing at?

'Elsbeth, that should never have been said to you. We don't know what has happened at this stage. Please ignore what you were told. It's simply misinformation.'

'I hope you're right,' Elsbeth sniffed between sobs.

'I will organise a ride back to your guest house, and I will be in touch as soon as I know anything. Jot down your address and telephone number on this, would you?' John said, as he passed her a small notepad.

Holding the contact details Elsbeth had given him, John stormed back to the briefing room.

'Sir, a word, please,' he said to Sidey, who was still there, talking to Catterick's intelligence officer about the recently completed operation.

'Yes, Flying Officer?'

'Could we go somewhere private?' John asked.

Sidey gestured towards an empty room adjacent to the briefing area. 'What is it?' he asked.

John told him about Bland's call to Elsbeth Bentley. When he had finished, Sidey was quiet. He too, was obviously surprised by what had been said.

'Leave it with me,' he said to John, as he walked out of the room.

Back in the officers' mess, John encountered Richard, who was sitting in the lounge, quietly sipping a cup of tea.

'Hi, John, the tea's good. Fancy a cup yourself?' he asked.

'No thanks, but I do want to talk to you. It's about Tim.'

John explained what Bland had done, and how it had affected Elsbeth Bentley.

'Why would he do that?' Richard asked. 'None of us knows Tim's fate for sure, so what on earth was the CO thinking?'

'I wondered about that myself,' John responded. 'It could be that he was trying to reassert some authority, having been sidelined from operational leadership and now wanting to show that he was in control of all information. But that's a bloody clumsy and cruel way to go about it, while there is still uncertainty.'

'Whatever the reason, he should never have behaved in that way.'

'I have raised it with Dave Sidey. He will take it up with Bland, I'm sure. Elsbeth now understands that Tim is missing, but at this stage there is no basis for saying he is presumed dead. She's upset, as you will appreciate, but clinging to hope. She's waiting for me to let her know as soon as we hear something definite.'

'Bland needs to go.' Richard's voice was steely.

John was surprised, but he understood the depth of feeling some of the squadron pilots had about their Commanding Officer. This latest incident had simply exacerbated matters.

'He's arrogant, which is bad enough in itself, and he can't even attempt to claim any justification for it,' Richard continued. 'His aerial leadership is atrocious, and he might have got people killed. He has tried to blame others for our losses, including when he was shot down himself at Dunkirk. And no-one has forgotten how he set up the inquiry into the training accident that killed Jack Peters, with the principal objective of pinning the blame on you. That was not only a disgrace, but a serious breach of military protocol. Thank God we found a way to sideline him from war ops, temporarily, at least.'

John was taken aback by Richard's outpouring. He had not realised just how poorly he thought of him.

'I'm going back to the briefing room to see if there is any news on Tim,' said John. 'Coming?'

'A couple of fishermen have reported seeing a Spitfire come down in the surf off Tynemouth. They managed to retrieve an unconscious pilot before he drowned. He was lucky, apparently; he only just avoided hitting a nasty area of rocks.'

The flight sergeant relaying the message looked pleased. So was John, who guessed that it must be Tim, and he was alive.

Twenty minutes later the telephone rang. It was the Tyneside police. The sergeant passed the telephone to John, who was standing next to him.

'We have Pilot Officer Timothy Bentley here,' the policeman said, when John introduced himself. 'Apart from a large bump on the head, he appears to be fine. We will get him checked out at the hospital and arrange a ride back to RAF Catterick, if he's fit to travel.'

When that was repeated out loud by John to everyone in the room, there was a cheer, followed by some vigorous clapping. Most of the pilots had stayed while awaiting confirmation of what had happened to Tim, and they were pleased to get good news. John knew he had to let Elsbeth know about Tim as soon as possible. It was a message he would be pleased to give her. He dialled the number Elsbeth had given him.

'She's not here at the moment,' the landlady of the guest house in which Elsbeth was staying replied.

'Please ask her to call me when she gets in, on this number.' John gave the landlady the number for the officers' mess at RAF Catterick.

Just over two hours later, Tim walked into the mess. He had a bandage around his head and his clothes were coated in what looked like mud.

'Tim, you made it! Bloody wonderful!' John was on his feet, giving Tim a welcome hug. Richard and the other pilots joined in with the welcome.

'Good to see you back in one piece, Tim.'

'Knew you wouldn't let Jerry knock you over.'

Tim grinned at them. 'Thanks, chaps. I appreciate it. Got to run, though. I need to see Elsbeth.'

'Looking like that?'

'I will grab some clothes and go. I can clean myself up later. Don't want to waste time here when Elsbeth will be wondering where I am.'

She certainly will be, thought John, *thanks to that fool Bland*.

'I tried to telephone, but she was out, so I will just turn up at her door. It will be a surprise,' Tim said, beaming widely.

'I will take you in the squadron car,' John volunteered.

'Great, let's go,' Tim said. 'Let me just grab some gear. Meet you outside the door in five, okay?'

When John and Tim arrived at the guest house where Elsbeth was staying, the landlady met them at the door.

'I'm worried,' she said. 'Mrs Bentley went for a walk, but that was some hours ago, and she hasn't come back.'

John and Tim looked at each other with concern.

'She seemed very upset about something,' the landlady continued. 'She said she wanted to go for a walk up to the old mill ponds to clear her head. I told her she shouldn't walk near those ponds. They are deep, and the path is a bit precarious in places. Anway, quite apart from the dangerous path, I told her it was too far to go for someone in her condition, but she was determined.'

Thanking the landlady for the information, John and Tim turned and left. They walked as quickly as they could, heading for the mill ponds. They had decided to walk rather than use the car, assuming it may be easier to locate Elsbeth if they followed the actual path she had taken. John decided to tell Tim about Bland. Tim was furious.

'That idiot's message has caused Elsbeth unnecessary distress. Senior officer or not, I'm going to have words with him.'

They strode on quickly and reached the ponds in fifteen minutes. After a short time looking around, they could see no sign of Elsbeth. Reluctantly, they made their way back through the town and passed a tearoom, where two young women were closing up the premises. John decided to ask if they had seen a pregnant woman recently.

'A pregnant woman?' repeated one of the women. She had freckles and ginger hair. 'Oh yes, we know her all right, don't we, Em?'

Her friend, Em, agreed. 'We surely do. She stopped in for tea and a sandwich a while ago, and blow me, she went into labour, right here in the tearoom. We got her to the hospital, really quick. Why do you ask?'

She got no reply. Tim, with John close behind, was already running down the street towards the local hospital.

The morning after the raid, the pilots gathered in the briefing room, where they were addressed by Squadron Leader Sidey.

'Yesterday's raid was a surprise,' he began. 'No two ways about that, but luckily, because of Fighter Command's squadron rotation policy, we were here in the north and able to help the local Thirteen Group squadrons deal with Jerry's attempt to sneak in.

'The disadvantage for any raiders coming in from Norway is the distance. It makes fighter escort impossible. Hence, there were no fighters to deal with yesterday and we had good success against the bombers. We took down eight Heinkels and lost only one aircraft ourselves. Other squadrons got another nineteen between them, so not a good day for Jerry. The pilot of the aircraft we lost, Pilot Officer Bentley, is okay, and will be back later today. He is away at present, having been granted a short off-station pass.'

Murmurs and nods from several of the pilots followed.

'I might add,' Sidey continued, 'that he became a father for the first time last night, so no doubt that will be recognised in the mess this evening.'

More acknowledgement from the gathered pilots.

'Our focus now, prior to our return to Hornchurch, is to get ourselves rested and our aircraft and equipment ready. The maintenance sergeant has told me that all our machines are in good shape, subject to some minor work to be done on two of them, so we are looking good for our return south later this week. At present, we are scheduled to fly back to Hornchurch on the eighth. Our first operation will be early on the ninth.

'You will be wondering how things might develop in the south, in terms of both the level of Luftwaffe activity and their targets. We have received some intelligence about that,' Sidey continued. 'A captured Luftwaffe pilot has spoken about what he called *Adlertag*. That means "Eagle Day" in English. Fighter Command believes we might be facing a large-scale attack on that day, probably the first of many. Targets are uncertain at this time, but more work is being done to see if we can determine what they might be. In the meantime, as many squadrons as possible are being assembled in the Eleven Group sectors.'

'Do we know the date for Eagle Day?' Greg asked.

'Thirteenth of August is the date I have been given. That's five days after we return to Hornchurch,' Sidey replied. 'Are there any further questions?'

There were none, and the meeting ended.

As they walked back to the officers' mess, Richard, Greg, and John discussed what had been said.

'Based on previous intel reports, I suspect that Eagle Day will see Jerry coming in huge numbers and bombing our airfields, with the RAF being the principal target,' said Richard. 'And it won't be a one-off — it'll probably be the first of many similar days, as Sidey suggested. There have already been some attacks against the RAF, but now it looks like Jerry is going to scale it up.'

'I agree,' Greg replied. 'If they want air supremacy, they will keep attacking our facilities and will try to take out all the infrastructure we need to be able to keep operating. Coming in large numbers, staged so there are continuous waves throughout each day, will let them take advantage of the superior numbers we know the Luftwaffe has. We can scramble and stay airborne for finite periods only, so if they keep coming, they will know they can exhaust our ability to have anything in the air to meet them, at some point.'

'Exactly. That would be the tactic for them to adopt,' Richard said.

'How's Tim, John?' Greg asked, changing the subject.

'He's a very happy chap,' John answered. 'Delighted to be a father to a new baby boy, and, of course, very pleased to still be alive after crashing his damaged aircraft into the surf. Elsbeth's good too. No difficulties with the birth.'

'Excellent. Yesterday could have turned out rather differently. How awful would it have been for Elsbeth to have lost a husband on the day she gave birth?' said Greg, shaking his head at what might have occurred.

'The doctors say Elsbeth probably went into labour early due to shock,' John said. 'Bland should never have called her and told her Tim was presumed dead. Why would he do that before there was confirmation? The man's a bloody fool.'

'Let's hope Bland listens to Dave Sidey when he takes it up with him,' said Greg. 'We can't have anything like that happening again. There are procedures and protocols for reporting losses, people and aircraft, and it's vital, of course, to have accurate knowledge of what has happened.'

'The list of issues concerning our CO just continues to grow,' Richard said. 'It won't be long now until his medical checks are complete, and then he is going to want to reassert his position as our in-the-air commander. That's something that cannot happen.'

'I think we all agree, Richard,' said Greg, 'but how do we achieve that result?'

'I'm working on it,' Richard replied with a frown.

'The Germans seem to be coming in ever-increasing numbers,' Mary said to John as they were enjoying a drink together in the local pub, 'but from what I read in the papers, the RAF are shooting most of them down.'

Mary, knowing John would soon be returning to Hornchurch for another tour, had managed to swap some duties and get up to Catterick to see him before he left.

'We've had our successes, Mary, but you need to appreciate the stories about the Luftwaffe attacks and our defence are written with the morale of the British public in mind.'

'Of course, but the press wouldn't lie, would they?'

'Let's just say they are always keen to show we are successful in our encounters. That means the actual numbers of losses on each side are often just a best estimate, driven by wishful thinking.'

'Father says we are doing all right against the Germans.'

Mary's father was a senior officer on 13 Group staff, something John had not known when he had first met Mary and tried to impress her by buzzing her country home in his Spitfire. He had found out shortly after he had landed back at Catterick. Mary's father had made a complaint, and John had been reprimanded for unauthorised and unnecessary low flying.

'They are suffering more losses than us, true,' John replied, 'but then they have a lot more aircraft.'

'How are your fellow pilots faring?'

'They are fine. We have quiet moments when we lose someone, but we accept that's war, and we get on with it. They are all good men — well, apart from one who is a problem.'

'Is he not a good pilot?'

'No, he's not, and that's a major issue for us. In addition to being a poor pilot, he's also rather unpleasant and lacks judgment. Do you know what he did? He told a pilot's wife that her husband was missing, presumed dead, before we had accurate information about what had happened to him.'

'Oh, that's awful, John.'

'The pilot had crashed, but he returned safely to the station with nothing but a few bumps and bruises. Needless to say, he now has a very happy wife. For a few hours she thought she was a widow. And get this, Mary, she was pregnant, and therefore very vulnerable. The shock of being told her husband had been killed sent her into premature labour. At least she now has both a healthy husband and a healthy baby boy.'

'A happy ending,' Mary said, 'but what a dreadful situation. Your CO should come down on that person, so everyone gets the message about unacceptable behaviour and poor performance.'

'Well, Mary,' John responded with a glum look, 'that would be sensible, but the person concerned is in fact the CO himself.'

CHAPTER FIVE

It was raining lightly at Catterick as Richard and John walked quickly across the quadrangle that separated the officers' mess from the station's administration block. They were planning to see Bland, who they knew would be working in his office.

As they entered the block, they were met by Michael Gardiner, the adjutant.

'We would like to meet with the CO,' Richard told him. 'There's something we wish to discuss with him.'

A few moments later they all stood at the open door of the CO's office. 'Excuse me, Wing Commander,' said Gardiner, 'Flight Lieutenant Cowles and Flying Officer Noble wonder if you have a moment? A private matter.'

John saw Bland smile in response to the adjutant's query. *Yes*, thought John, *of course you are pleased to see Richard*. Richard's father, Lord Cowles, was the head of a wealthy family that owned huge tracts of prime farmland in Norfolk. John knew that Richard's title and family wealth counted with Bland.

'Gentlemen, what can I do for you? I can only give you a few minutes, as I'm rather busy with this material sent out by Fighter Command,' Bland said, gesturing towards the pile of paper on his desk. 'You will be interested in what it says — it's a discussion paper on variations being considered for our current engagement strategies. The paper's writer seems to favour adopting some of the techniques the Luftwaffe used in Spain. I know the Germans learnt a lot during their recent war experience there, when they were helping Franco. Looks like Fighter Command might now change some of our procedures to take advantage of those tactics.'

John was pleased to hear the RAF hierarchy had recognised that a change to aerial warfare tactics may be useful. He had suggested something similar himself months ago, and had suffered a lot of criticism from Bland for his trouble. John could see Richard thought it was a good idea too. He was nodding his head in agreement.

'A worthwhile exercise, sir,' John said.

'I agree, it could be valuable, sir,' Richard added, glancing at John with a wry smile.

'Yes, I think so,' Bland responded. 'I see from the paper that operating in pairs on an engagement, with a leader and wingman, may now be an officially favoured technique for the Royal Air Force. This squadron, of course, adopted pairing for offensive operations some time ago, so we are ahead of the game.'

John stared at Bland. He was thinking about Bland's resistance to fighting in pairs when he had originally suggested it for use by the squadron. *Mind you*, he thought, *Sidey opposed it too, early on*. The difference was that Sidey had the pilots adopt it shortly afterwards, at Dunkirk, whereas Bland was only now starting to think of it as an official strategy because it had the blessing of Fighter Command.

'Anyway, enough of all that,' Bland said. 'Why do you want to see me?'

'Sir,' Richard responded, 'my father has asked if I could visit him on the estate. I have told him I could make a quick trip, an overnight stay only. I thought tomorrow night would suit. That would ensure no clash with our preparations to get us down to Hornchurch at the end of the week.'

'I see. You want my permission for a short-leave pass?' Bland asked.

'Well, yes, sir, but additionally, Father would like to meet my Commanding Officer. He has asked if you would like to come with me, as his guest for the night.'

John thought that Bland was about to purr with pleasure. He was clearly very pleased to receive the invitation.

'Very kind of His Lordship. I'm sure we would be able to manage a night away. So, yes, on both counts. Yes, you may have a leave pass, and yes, I would be delighted to accept His Lordship's kind invitation.'

'Thank you, sir. I will let them know down in Norfolk. Father has also asked me to bring any of my fellow pilots I want, so I have asked Flying Officer Noble to come as well.'

When he next spoke, Bland's voice was a lot cooler. 'Of course, if that is what His Lordship would like. Your leave is approved too, Flying Officer Noble,' he said, briefly glancing at John. Then he stood up, came around the desk, and held out his hand to Richard.

'I look forward to this visit very much, Flight Lieutenant Cowles. Thank you.'

He shook Richard's hand firmly, holding it for longer than normal, John saw, noting Richard's discomfort.

Over dinner in the mess that evening, Richard told the others what he was planning.

'I spoke with Dave Sidey today. He told me Doc Berryman has indicated the CO will probably get his medical clearance back any day now. That means when we go south to Hornchurch, Bland will come with us, and he will probably want to reassume the lead on war ops.'

'His uncertain medical status was only ever our temporary saviour,' John noted.

'Yes, but what we have with Dave Sidey and Tony Smallbone is working well, so we should try all avenues to make that continue. Consequently, I have been looking for some way we might be able to keep Bland away from the role.'

'Have you come up with anything?'

'Possibly. When I was speaking with Father, I told him about the problem with our Commanding Officer. A man with no idea about aerial warfare strategy, a poor tactician in the air, and zero leadership skills, but he wants to lead us in battle with the Luftwaffe. I gave Father some examples of incidents that had not gone well as a direct result of Bland's incompetence. He agreed it was a recipe for disaster but wasn't sure how he could help. So, I told him about Bland's personality — self-centred, arrogant, and a terrible snob — and suggested we could use that to our advantage.'

'I can see you didn't hold back,' Charlie commented with a grin.

'Well, it gave Father an idea. We agreed we would try to get Bland into a situation where the man's own nature could help us.'

The pilots listened expectantly.

'We are going to have him down to the estate for an overnight stay. Ostensibly it's about Father meeting the CO, nothing more, but obviously that will lead to discussions about the squadron. John is coming down as well, and we will steer the conversation towards operations against the Luftwaffe, the squadron's strategies, and air warfare tactics. It should offer the opportunity for some points to be raised, which Bland may just listen to and act upon, especially if he hears Father supporting something we discuss. We have nothing to lose, really. I can tolerate him on an overnight stay for that.'

'It's worth a try, no question,' John added.

'Indeed. Father has worked up something that he will raise with Bland. John has been briefed by me on what is planned. If it goes well, it may result in Bland deciding there's a better way to run operations than him acting as in-air leader against Jerry.'

'Well, all the best with that project,' Craig said. 'You've set yourself a hard task.'

'Perhaps, but we need to try. The plan is to go down to the estate tomorrow,' Richard went on. 'Father will be well briefed and will be careful in the way he deals with the CO. Bland will not even realise he has been manoeuvred into a position that makes him think the war operation leadership in the squadron might be better to continue as it is, with him playing a slightly different role.'

'Hope you are right,' said Greg, 'because if we can't dissuade Bland from taking over as our leader in combat, then a hard job is going to become a lot harder for us all, and life more dangerous.'

There was general agreement with that sentiment. Just then Tim appeared.

'Chaps,' he said, by way of greeting. He had a huge smile on his face.

'Tim, good to see you,' said Greg. 'How are mother and baby?'

'They are doing well, thanks. Elsbeth said the actual birth was quick. Onset of labour to delivery was about ninety minutes. And my son, Peter, is fine. Seven pounds two ounces, and a slick of dark hair. Elsbeth is going to be in the maternity ward for some days, according to the matron. There wasn't much point in my staying at the guest house on my own, so I thought I would spend some quality time with you fellows instead,' he said cheerfully. 'I will be able to see Elsbeth on the ward every day until we leave for our next tour. She will be discharged in just over a week if everything goes well. Then the plan is that she'll go home with her mother and father, who are coming up tomorrow. They live in Chelmsford. We will be close by, operating out of Hornchurch then, although I've told Elsbeth it's unlikely I will get any time to visit. It's good she will be getting some help during her first few weeks of motherhood, though.'

'All's well that ends well, Tim. Baby arrived safely. Wife in good shape. You survived your encounter with Jerry. You had a big day,' John said.

'I'm certainly glad to have got through it now,' Tim replied.

'I'm sorry Bland upset things, telling Elsbeth you hadn't made it,' Richard said.

'Yes, I was surprised. I thought our procedures were better than that.'

'They are,' Richard replied. 'It was another example of Bland's incompetence.'

'No-one's planning to go into town this evening, so after dinner we should retire to the mess bar and wet your son's head,' Charlie suggested.

They all thought that a good idea.

On arrival at the Cowles family estate in Norfolk, Richard introduced Bland and John to his father.

'How do you do, Wing Commander?' Lord Cowles said, as he greeted his son's commanding officer. They were at the front entrance to the estate's manor house. Richard had told John that his father preferred the smaller manor house. It was warmer and not as dank and gloomy as the property's main building, the old castle.

'I am very pleased to meet you, sir,' Bland replied, with a slight dip of his head.

God, he's bowing, John thought.

'And this is John Noble, one of my friends in the squadron. He is from New Zealand and was a farmer before joining the RAF.'

'Pleased to meet you, John. A Kiwi, eh? We can spend some time over dinner talking about your country's rugby team, the All Blacks. I am a huge rugby fan.'

'How do you do, sir?' John responded with a smile. 'I'm always happy to talk rugby.'

Lord Cowles turned to Bland. 'I am very pleased you were able to get down with Richard. Thank you for accepting my invitation. Please, come in.'

An hour later, after the guests from RAF Catterick had installed themselves in their rooms and freshened up, they met in the library for pre-dinner drinks.

'Richard tells me your squadron was caught up in the evacuation from France, Wing Commander.'

'We were, and please, Your Lordship, Christopher is fine. No need for rank.'

'Certainly, Christopher. And here in my home, please call me Patrick. "Your Lordship" is for the public realm. Same for you, John,' said Lord Cowles, smiling at John.

Bland beamed with pleasure, obviously delighted to be invited to address a lord informally.

Over several gin and tonics, well-iced and with the obligatory slice of lemon, the two men got to know each other better. They covered a wide range of topics, including schooling, flying, and Lord Cowles' intentions for the farm, but they avoided talking directly about the war. John and Richard spent most of that time making little more than an occasional comment.

They adjourned to the dining room for dinner, and towards the end of what John thought was one of the best meals he had had since leaving the family farm back in New Zealand, the general conversation moved on to sport. Lord Cowles told them that he was an avid cricket fan and went on to share several anecdotes, including one about the former principal England cricket selector, an old friend.

'I told him we needed a pace attack, to startle and unsettle. He declared he wanted more spin. Maybe, if we were playing in India, I said, but here, in England, we have pitches best suited to seamers, at least for the initial two or three days of a match. I think he was just kidding me about favouring spin, because he selected a ferocious seam attack for the test at Headingley, and we routed the opposition.'

'Interesting to be that involved and then to see it play out, Patrick,' Bland responded. 'Myself, I am at my happiest watching a football team perform. The teamwork is always first-rate, and watching the game strategy unfold is very satisfying.'

'True,' responded Lord Cowles, 'but I'm a rugby man. I'm grateful to that fellow Ellis, who picked up the ball and ran with it during a game of football at Rugby School. He gave us the game we have today. It has become the national sport of New Zealand, I understand — is that right, John?'

'Yes, that is a fair assessment. Our national team, the All Blacks, were quite successful at rugby, and I think they will be again, once the war is over.'

As the evening continued, John observed Bland. He had never seen him so relaxed and affable, happy to chat amiably about every topic raised. *An ideal starting point for when we get to the sharp end of our discussions later*, John thought.

'This is a good brandy,' Lord Cowles said as he poured a glass for each of his guests after dinner. He had just opened a new bottle. 'I'm not spoiling it with ice or ginger. That all right with you all?'

'That's fine, Patrick. The way I always like it, thank you,' Bland said quickly, keen to agree.

After some further discussion on sport, and after a quick foray into the effectiveness of the news services in keeping the British public advised about the state of the war, the conversation turned to the squadron and its operations.

'Christopher, I have often wondered how the method of attack is decided when your squadron of Spitfires is approaching a formation of enemy aircraft with which you will engage. The different dynamics in the various situations must give rise to a myriad of options. How do you quickly decide what the squadron should do on each occasion?'

John wondered how Bland would answer the question. In the past, the CO had said the predetermined Royal Air Force attack plans were the only options when engaging the enemy. John had come in for some criticism from Bland for suggesting it was less than optimum to have fixed plans to address the dynamics of an aerial engagement.

'The Royal Air Force has different protocols for different situations, Patrick. They have devised various air-attack plans to be used, each dependent on particular factors — how many of our aircraft are involved, the number of enemy aircraft we will encounter, their type, the formation they are flying in, their height and position relative to us, and other matters, such as the position of the sun, cloud in the area, that sort of thing.'

'I see,' said Lord Cowles. 'It seems to me that despite the fixed air-attack responses that have been promulgated by Fighter Command, the decision on how to proceed should always be based on the unique circumstances you encounter. That may mean using something other than one of the set-piece responses could be a better approach?'

'Once the variables have been assessed by the in-air leader, he chooses which of the plans is best for the circumstances he has observed. The actual tactics to be used will be part of whichever plan the leader assesses as best meeting the circumstances. There are six plans to choose from, so that provides scope.'

'Well, you would hope so. Tell me, Christopher, once an engagement begins, are you normally able to continue with the tactics of the plan chosen, or does manoeuvring and counterattack by enemy aircraft require a variation?'

'Depends on the type of engagement we are in. Enemy bombers normally stay together, as that helps their defence, so no change is usually required in that situation. On the other hand, if covering fighters engage us, and they usually do, we soon end up in a series of individual dogfights.'

'So, your initial formations and attack plans don't last long when your squadron begins engaging with the fighters there to protect the bombers?'

'No, they don't. At that point the fighters usually dictate our engagement method, which is often one-on-one.'

'So, if I understand you correctly, Christopher, the leader of the squadron chooses one of the available attack plans for initial engagement, but whatever is decided is usually replaced by individual initiatives as soon as enemy fighters join the fray?'

'Yes, that's a fair summary of what normally occurs.'

'I see. There are two things here, it seems to me. First, it's important the person calling the initial engagement tactics in the air is experienced and insightful. He has to be able to ensure the standard plan he chooses is the correct one with regards to the circumstances applicable?'

'No doubt about that,' Bland replied. 'He has to choose the appropriate attack plan based on what best suits whatever he is seeing in the air at the time.'

'And second, the fixed plan chosen usually has a short life when implemented, because you have to be able to react to what the enemy does?'

'Yes, it can start to become a bit of a free-for-all, quite quickly sometimes, certainly when fighters arrive on the scene.'

'So, leadership is important at the outset, when you first engage and choose an attack plan? And then again, once the air battle develops, so that the pilots know when they are free to engage with the enemy in response to what is happening around them?'

'Correct. The leader of the squadron instructs on an attack plan for the initial engagement, and will then signal when individual initiatives should begin. Pilots are not free to take off on their own until given that signal, unless they have no choice as a result of enemy action affecting them directly.'

'To me, this all highlights the value of having someone with good tactical insight in charge of the squadron in the air.'

'No question about that, Patrick.'

'I find myself wondering if there would be an advantage in a leader being able to use his experience and insight to develop a tactical response to the circumstances he encounters, rather than him simply choosing one of the promulgated standard plans. You see the difference? The leader's skill and experience are applied to assessing the best way to actually engage the enemy, rather than assessing which of the standard air-attack plans best fits the circumstances.'

'I agree there is value in having the person with the best experience and capability making the in-air decisions. Whether we are ready to abandon our standard air-attack plans at this stage, and simply rely on intuition based on experience, I am not sure,' Bland replied.

For the next twenty minutes, and over a further brandy each, Lord Cowles and Bland continued talking about air warfare strategies and tactics. Occasionally, either Richard or John was asked for their view, but the main conversation was between the two older men.

'It's complex, I can see that,' Lord Cowles said, nodding sagely, 'but answer me this, please, Christopher. Can you be confident that whatever promulgated plan you apply, it is the optimum? You are obliged to select your tactics from a range of specific options that have been given to you previously by Fighter Command. If an experienced in-air commander saw another course of action he would prefer to take, what could he do? To be clear, my question is about the initial attack plan chosen, before you might become reactive to the arrival of enemy fighters. I understand tactics are completely within the flight leader's discretion from that time.'

'As I said, there are general parameters that dictate how we might respond initially, as per the air-attack plans. They cover most situations that would be encountered, and so provide us with all necessary options, I think.'

John noted that Bland had not answered Lord Cowles' question. John's own view, which he had unsuccessfully tried to raise at the time of Dunkirk, was that a system that involved choosing between different, pre-ordained attack plans was not good enough. He did not think it mattered that there were several plans to choose from. In his opinion, that could not be as effective as a skilled assessment by an experienced fighter pilot in the air, on the day, responding to what he saw in front of him.

'Richard mentioned you have been grounded for a while?' Lord Cowles asked.

'Yes, minor medical matters. I expect to be flying again in the coming days.'

'Who led the squadron on war operations when you weren't flying?'

'There are two other experienced pilots in the squadron: Squadron Leaders Sidey and Smallbone. They both have top-level expertise in air warfare strategies and techniques. Valuable chaps.'

'Are they well-placed to order a unique reactive response, once an engagement with, say, some bombers is past its initial stages, and the air-attack plan chosen is no longer optimum?' Lord Cowles asked.

'Yes.'

'So, could they not also order an initial response that involves something other than as provided by one of the pre-determined plans, if they saw a better way to respond at the outset?'

John saw what Lord Cowles had done. It was the same question he had asked earlier, about individual initiative supplanting the choice of a fixed plan on the day, but he had phrased it differently.

'I prefer the squadron to stick to one of Fighter Command's fixed plans, to reduce the risk of a non-standard attack plan being developed and it not working as hoped.'

'I am surprised by that view, Christopher. You said earlier that the in-flight leader will call for the reactive response that will displace the fixed response as soon as things change, such as when you are attacking bombers and then the fighters arrive.

You are happy the leader calls a unique alternative response at that point, but seem to be suggesting it is better they don't do that initially. I am wondering why that should be?'

Bland did not reply immediately, and John could see he was mentally wrestling with the point Lord Cowles had made. This was confirmed when he spoke. 'When you lay it out like that, yes, I do find myself questioning if there is a better way to use our skill and resources. Perhaps air-attack plans are best used only when a leader is unsure.'

'You are happy with the abilities of Sidey and Smallbone in every respect?' Lord Cowles asked.

'Absolutely. I have complete confidence in them.'

'Do you have that same specialist capability, Christopher?'

'I have enough to lead the squadron, but I accept I'm probably not at the level they are. I do not have the war operations experience they have, and for that reason I would certainly stay with one of the established air-attack plans when leading the squadron.'

'So, if they were leading the squadron in the air when you were not available, their skill and experience would allow additional options, beyond the fixed plans, if they thought that valuable?'

'Ah, yes, I suppose that might be so.'

'That might be worth considering then, Christopher, to give your squadron more options?'

'Perhaps.'

John could see Bland was wavering.

'Have you considered leaving Sidey and Smallbone as the in-air leaders once you are back on operations? You accept they may be able to offer additional options, you have absolute confidence in them, and you acknowledged they call the engagement mode anyway, once an encounter develops beyond its initial stages.'

'As the commanding officer, I think it appropriate that I take the lead, so that is what I will do when I am back in the air.'

'Have you ever considered leading via governance arrangements rather than operationally?'

'I'm not sure what you mean by that, Patrick.'

'Let me explain. It's a concept that's just starting to become established in commercial life. No reason why it wouldn't be valuable to use in the squadron. It involves a person taking an oversight role, separate from actually running a particular activity. That person governs an operation by setting overall policy and then maintaining oversight on how the policy is adopted and used by those charged with implementing it — the managers, if you like. The people managing the operation day to day must do it in a way that complies with the governance expectations placed on them by their overseer. It has been very successful in some of the commercial areas in which it has been tried, with improved performance noted.'

'I would be keen to try anything that improved our performance in the air, Patrick, but as CO I must carry on as the person in charge, with ultimate responsibility. What you describe is very similar to my command responsibility in any event, and that is tried and trusted.'

John and Richard exchanged glances.

'Of course,' Lord Cowles responded, 'but the difference is that on any squadron operation that you lead in the air, you are then also acting as a manager. Your oversight role becomes part of the operational role in that case, because the governance function is subsumed into the operational function. The two roles are merged into one. I think there is room for some separation of function.'

Bland said nothing, but John could see he was listening intently.

'Consider this, Christopher,' Lord Cowles continued. 'You have said Squadron Leaders Sidey and Smallbone are the best qualified and most experienced to lead operations in the air. They would be able to offer a valuable alternative to the fixed plans where they saw the opportunity and thought it appropriate to do so. As the Commanding Officer, all the outcomes achieved by the squadron are your responsibility, and you have a duty to oversee everything is being done to ensure best outcome. If I were you, I would be using the people most qualified to lead the squadron's war operations, and I would act as their governor, overseeing what they did and how they did it. They would be required to operate within the policies I set for the squadron, but on the day, in battle, the actual tactical decisions made would be theirs.'

'I see,' said Bland. 'You are suggesting that while I'm in charge overall, my senior pilots make the decisions in the air, but always taking into account the parameters I have established?'

'Exactly, that's what this new concept of governance is about. You have oversight and govern; they manage and operate while taking into account what you have required as governor. It's the best of both worlds. You get your top pilots making decisions in the air when confronted by the enemy, but they make their decisions within a framework you have established as their commanding officer, and it's specific to your squadron and its needs. It's different from treating Fighter Command as the squadron's governor. The people there can only set general policies. You can avoid any gaps in effectiveness arising from those general policies, as the commanding officer of a squadron with its own characteristics and operations. For example, you could allow them the freedom to select an alternative engagement plan rather than a fixed attack plan, where they saw an advantage in doing so in any particular encounter.'

Bland clearly liked what he heard. 'I do see how that methodology may well be useful, and I am very grateful to you, Patrick, for raising it for my consideration. You obviously think it is a good way to operate.'

'I do indeed, Christopher, and I am pleased you are going to think about it, as in my opinion it could have real value for you and your squadron.'

Bland gave him an unctuous smile. 'Yes, and having heard it from you, with your knowledge and experience, I know the idea is sound. You have given me a lot to think about. Be assured that I will follow it up.'

Lord Cowles smiled. 'Wonderful. Now, goodnight, everyone. I'm going to retire.'

CHAPTER SIX

Thursday, 8th of August 1940 dawned fine at RAF Catterick as the squadron prepared to move to Hornchurch. Multiple concerted attacks by the Luftwaffe on various aerodromes throughout 11 Group's area the previous day had left most feeling grim. John knew the pilots of 415 Squadron would be in for a particularly difficult time when they were back at Hornchurch, as the Germans concentrated on targeting the Royal Air Force and its facilities in the southeast of England.

Bland had told the squadron pilots at a briefing the previous evening that he was flying again, having received medical clearance. John had not been surprised when he had gone on to say that he had developed a new method for managing the squadron's air operations. His plan, he had told the assembled pilots, was for Squadron Leaders Sidey and Smallbone to continue to lead in the air on war operations, whilst he maintained oversight and established parameters within which they would make their operational decisions day to day.

'I had a meeting recently with an important person who has a great deal of insight into how operations are best controlled to ensure optimum results. He has used it in controlling business operations, but the principles he uses would be just as effective for us in running the squadron. It is a system that has real merit,' Bland had said. 'I think it is a good way forward as our engagements with the Luftwaffe increase, both in number and, I expect, in intensity. Göring thinks he has a job to do, and I am determined that we will be in the best form we can be to disrupt his plans.'

John smiled to himself as Bland went on to explain the new way he would lead the squadron, using a concept known as governance. John was pleased that the CO's overnight stay with His Lordship in Norfolk appeared to have produced a satisfactory result.

Though the squadron's trip back to Hornchurch was just a repositioning flight, all the Spitfires had been fully armed. Luftwaffe activity in the area to which they were going was extensive, so Sidey, who would lead today, had taken the view that they should be prepared and able to engage if they met any enemy aircraft while transiting.

'Pairs, please, line astern with step-ups,' he had called once they were all airborne.

The squadron moved into seven pairs of aircraft, each pair about sixty yards behind the pair in front, but two hundred feet higher. There were fourteen aircraft instead of the normal twelve. The squadron was taking two spares to Hornchurch. Aircraft damage and losses were anticipated.

They had been cruising at sixteen thousand feet for forty minutes when control called. Today's radio code allocated for the squadron's transit flight from its home base, as they relocated from Catterick to Hornchurch, was "Mover". John thought someone at control was attempting to be funny.

'Mover, this is Control. We have bandits for you, approaching the Debden and Duxford area. Resident squadrons are already up on other missions, so we are putting you in. Climb to angels twenty, turn onto heading one two zero.'

'Control, this is Mover, climbing angels twenty on one two zero,' Sidey responded as he led the squadron into a gentle turn to the left to pick up the required heading.

'Call with bandits in sight, Mover. Expect one hundred plus.'

'Mover, wilco,' Sidey responded, using the usual short form radio transmission that meant "will comply", to tell control the squadron was doing as requested.

Five minutes later Sidey called again.

'Control, this is Mover. Have bandits in sight. Confirm one hundred plus. Estimate sixty bombers and forty fighters above.'

'Move to wide echelon right,' he transmitted to the squadron pilots. That would provide a better shooting position for the Spitfires than the current stepped up line astern as they approached the enemy formations. John noted that Sidey was not bothering with any of the formal air-attack plans. He was making his own decisions regarding positioning and profile to meet the enemy aircraft, and John agreed it was a better way to proceed.

'Target the bombers on your first pass. They are our priority at this stage, but the fighters will come down on us, so watch out for them.'

As they closed in on the bombers, the Spitfires began shooting. The eight machine guns on each aircraft chattered, causing their airframes to vibrate as they fired. The Germans did not scatter in response, their aircraft continuing in a relatively tight formation. John could see the tracer rounds from various Luftwaffe gunners streaming towards the squadron, painting their lines of fire through the sky. The tracer looked slow and graceful as it arced through the air, but John knew that if it should suddenly appear to accelerate directly towards him, his aircraft would be shredded by the brutal and deadly barrage the elegant tracer lines disguised.

John felt his Spitfire shake as he loosed off multiple deadly rounds in just a few seconds. The port engine of the bomber in his sights began to smoke, and soon there were flames coming out from under the engine's cowling. Then the German aircraft started to slowly roll to the left as it fell out of its formation, in an ever-increasing angle of dive.

'One-o-nines attacking, one o'clock high,' someone called.

John saw them. They were coming very fast. Too fast. He knew they would only have a second or so to fire a burst as they got close enough to shoot at the Spitfires. After that, their speed would take them quickly past. The Messerschmitts would then have to turn and climb back up to make a second attack.

John realised that one of the Luftwaffe pilots had picked his Spitfire as his target. John saw him coming and pulled into a steep turn towards the Messerschmitt's line of approach. He was trying to manoeuvre into the blind spot created by the Me 109's nose as it dived, but the German pilot was experienced. He rolled his 109 inverted so that he would not lose sight of John's aircraft under his nose.

John glanced up as he released the back pressure he had applied to his control stick to haul his Spitfire into the required tight turn. He saw immediately what the Luftwaffe pilot had done, just as a burst of fire from the 109 struck his aircraft. John felt and heard the rounds impacting behind him, at the rear of the fuselage. He realised he was up against a capable flier. Then the German was past him, so fast he had only had time for a short burst at John's Spitfire.

Looking around, John saw the sky was full of numerous one-on-one battles. Aircraft were wheeling and peeling through the air. The bombers were still there, although the tight formation they previously had was gone. Apart from the odd single bomber, they seemed to have formed into numerous smaller groups, with perhaps six or seven aircraft in each. The occasional Spitfire could be seen making an attack on some of the bombers, but most were engaged with the Luftwaffe fighters.

John swung his aircraft around to chase some nearby Heinkels. There were six of them. As he approached, gunners in the bombers concentrated their fire at him. The air was full of tracer. John went into an extended series of barrel rolls, hoping to spoil their aim. It seemed to work. None of the tracer fire came directly towards him. When he was close enough, John started firing. It was a bit hit and miss, he realised, because he was still rolling his aircraft as he approached, impairing his ability to accurately line up any one bomber in his sights. While not precision-shooting, John thought he would score some hits somewhere among the group of enemy aircraft. Sure enough, he saw pieces coming off the cockpit of one of them. Then he hit another Heinkel in its tail. Both of the damaged Luftwaffe aircraft started flying erratically. John decided he must have incapacitated the pilot of the Heinkel he had hit in its cockpit area. The other German aircraft seemed to be having control problems. He was wondering if either aircraft would succumb to the damage he had inflicted when the Heinkel with the damaged cockpit suddenly swerved through the air, into the other bomber. It was a mid-air collision. Fuselages crumpled together, and wings enveloped one another. The two aircraft became one twisted lump of metal before falling from the sky.

John broke away and quickly looked around. There was nothing to be seen. Ahead, the bombers had dispersed. He could not see any of the German fighters that had been everywhere just a few minutes ago. Time to set a heading for Hornchurch. *What a bloody welcome back to our Eleven Group tour of duty*, he thought to himself.

That evening, shortly before going into dinner, John and Richard were talking about the operational techniques that might now be used by the squadron. They were conscious of the advice from Fighter Command that the Luftwaffe was likely to begin intensifying its attacks soon, specifically targeting the RAF and its infrastructure.

'A chap based at Duxford told me Bader is well advanced in finalising a new defensive strategy that he's calling the Big Wing,' John said.

'Yes, I've heard the same,' Richard acknowledged. 'Apparently, it involves four or five squadrons flying together as one group when intercepting Jerry. I understand Leigh-Mallory at Twelve Group is very keen the strategy be adopted by Eleven Group. He's pushing Park to use Big Wings, but the suggestion is that Park is not keen.'

'I don't get it,' John said. 'Multiple squadrons flying together is hardly new. During Dunkirk we joined up with other squadrons on several occasions to form what was effectively a Big Wing for our ops over France. I know the idea was to give us additional firepower on engagement, but it wasn't a successful tactic, so why this push now for a so-called new strategy? Does Bader's plan provide something extra?'

'I think Twelve Group leadership must see their Big Wing proposal as different from what we did at Dunkirk. They wouldn't be promoting the idea otherwise,' Richard suggested.

'There will need to be something clever in the new plan then, if it's to be better than what happened when we operated several squadrons together during Dynamo,' John said, still unconvinced.

'I'm wondering what will happen if Park is not convinced of the value of this *Big Wing* idea, and there is a disagreement between him and Leigh-Mallory. That's something we can do without as Jerry ramps up its offensive operations against us.'

John nodded. He understood it could be a serious issue if there was conflict between the leaders of the two fighter groups. 'I'm not surprised Park hasn't agreed to adopt the idea at this point,' John said. 'He will know what happened at Dunkirk. I might ask Sidey about it at briefing. He should be able to tell us what's happening.'

Operating from Hornchurch, the pilots of 415 Squadron were soon experiencing the unrelenting pressure of continuous German attacks. In their first two days there, they had to scramble on seven separate occasions. The waves of Luftwaffe aircraft they went up to meet seemed never-ending. John and his fellow pilots felt exhausted, both physically and mentally, and four of the squadron's Spitfires had already been lost in air battles with the enemy. Only one of the pilots shot down had returned. The other three were missing, presumed to have died in their aircraft.

At dawn on the squadron's third day of operations from Hornchurch, the pilots were in their briefing room listening to Sidey. He was outlining who would fly, and in what position, on the next mission.

'We have had to utilise our reserve aircraft as a result of the last two days of war ops. It is clear Jerry is throwing everything at the RAF, but not without suffering significant losses. While we have lost some aircraft, our squadron can be proud of the fact we have claimed six destroyed and five possibles. Our success ratio is currently the highest in Fighter Command, so take some comfort from your success.'

A murmur rippled around the room as Sidey continued.

'Fighter Command has decided that we will be used, initially at least, on a supernumerary basis. This means that when enemy aircraft are to be intercepted, we will be sent in, either as a full squadron or just as an additional six aircraft, to join other squadrons being utilised for that intercept. Where just six of us are committed, our remaining squadron aircraft will stay at full readiness but will not take off until instructed.' Sidey paused and looked around at the puzzled faces in the room.

'You may be wondering why the squadron would be deployed at less than full strength. Command's position is this: the RAF has far fewer aircraft than the Luftwaffe, and if too many are put into the air at the same time, then apart from any squadrons not already committed, we may be exposed to a lack of reserves. The view at the top is that using fifty per cent of the capacity of what they are calling a supernumerary squadron will be a useful strategy. The important driver for deciding to operate some squadrons in this way is that the RAF will be better able to manage its limited resources. It can add part of a squadron to an intercept, and it can keep the other part of that squadron in reserve, along with any other available full squadrons. The additional flexibility this approach provides is considered very valuable by Fighter Command. In particular, it will lower the risk of having insufficient aircraft available to put up against a later wave of Luftwaffe aircraft. There will, of course, still be occasions when all squadron aircraft go up together. Command may even drop the supernumerary squadron reserve approach completely, with more experience, but it is to be trialled for a period.'

John glanced across at Greg and raised his eyebrows in an unspoken question. Greg responded with a nod. He clearly agreed with the proposed strategy. There was one issue, however, that John wanted to clarify. He raised his hand.

'Yes, Flying Officer Noble?' Sidey asked.

'That makes sense, sir, given the number of separate raids we are seeing every day. The ability of the RAF to successfully intercept inbound enemy aircraft should be largely unaffected, even with the new reserve policy of holding part of squadrons back where appropriate. The only thing I think we need to be clear about, sir, is how we identify the proposed target of an approaching enemy formation. That might dictate a change in response.'

'Could you explain what you mean, Flying Officer?'

'Well, sir, we have seen the Luftwaffe targeting RAF aerodromes in recent days. They want to damage the infrastructure necessary for us to operate our aerodromes, maintenance facilities, ammunition caches, and fuel supply. Serious damage to any of those facilities would set us back. But what would really delight Jerry, would be to catch our aircraft on the ground. If control detects an inbound raid, how can they be sure what the target is? If it's an attack on an airfield, half of any resident supernumerary squadrons could be sitting on the ground as a result of this new policy. If an airfield attack is identified, everything should be up from that aerodrome as soon as possible. Otherwise, the reserves become easy targets and are wasted as an additional available resource.'

'You make a good point, Flying Officer,' replied Sidey, 'and the view is that our Chain Home system can be used to give the main control centre at Bentley Priory sufficient information to enable identification of the probable target of any inbound raid. The radar information will also be supported by others — Anti-Aircraft Command, the Observer Corps, and Coastal Command. All the information received will be filtered and analysed before being conveyed to Sector Controllers, so we think we will have a fairly good idea of a raid's proposed target before the enemy arrives overhead. If it's an aerodrome, we will have time to scramble any reserve aircraft being held there on the ground.'

'Thank you, sir. I see the rationale for holding reserves on the ground, but care will be needed to ensure adequate warning if a particular aerodrome is targeted.'

David Sidey nodded his acknowledgement, then continued with his briefing. 'When we are called, the first off will be A Flight, comprising Red and Yellow Sections. I will be red one, with Flying Officers Noble and Ross as red two and three respectively. Flight Lieutenant Cowles will lead Yellow Section, with Flying Officers Barton and Somerville as yellow two and three.'

John was pleased. That was a good group to fly into battle with. All experienced in war ops, and capable in the air.

'B Flight, while being held in reserve, will reposition to our forward operating base at Manston. There are two reasons for this. First, a sizeable amount of fuel is stored there, and Fighter Command wants it utilised as soon as possible. Second, when the squadron's reserves are brought in, they will be available from a position closer to the action than at Hornchurch. Time to engagement will be reduced. The plan is for B Flight to transit to Manston shortly, with existing fuel, and to top up there after landing.'

Sidey proceeded to designate the membership and formation positions for B Flight, which comprised Blue and Green Sections. Smallbone was to be blue one, with Tim as blue two, and a new pilot, whom John had not yet met, was to fly as blue three. Craig was green one, another new joiner was green two, and Bland was to be green three, at the very rear of B Flight. John understood Bland had requested that position, thinking it fitted his new leadership style. It allowed the CO to sit at the back of the formation, where he could better observe how the flight performed in an engagement.

'Thank you, gentlemen,' Sidey said. 'Please go and organise yourselves as required for today's ops. Blue and Green Sections should reposition to Manston as soon as they're ready — say, forty-five minutes?' he queried, looking towards Smallbone.

'Yes, we will be airborne in forty-five. Thanks, chaps,' he responded.

'Here we go again,' John said, as he and Greg walked to the dispersal hut.

'We just have to keep launching ourselves at these bastards and shooting them down,' Greg responded.

John was surprised by the depth of feeling in his voice. *It's the pressure we are all under*, he decided. 'Well, it's good that Command's detection and control system is working well, getting us to the right place at the right time. Jerry must wonder why we are always up waiting for him when he approaches England, and you heard Sidey — early target identification will be a priority.'

'I understand all that, John, but I worry about the huge imbalance in numbers. The Luftwaffe has plenty of aircraft to throw at us, and we are just a few. The odds are definitely against us.'

John shrugged. 'We keep at it. We must.'

As A Flight crossed Canterbury at twenty-two thousand feet, the sun was climbing above the horizon ahead of them. They had been scrambled just minutes after Blue and Green Sections had taken off for Manston, where they would top up their fuel and stand by as the reserve flight.

'Fifty plus, inbound for Dover, and you will be joining other squadrons being vectored to intercept this raid,' had been the advice from the controller as they got airborne.

Soon the six Spitfires received their instructions from the sector controller, giving them a heading to intercept the German aircraft. He was happy with their current height, he confirmed, so they remained at twenty-two thousand feet.

They were flying in three pairs, in echelon right off Sidey's aircraft, with about sixty yards between each pair. The individual aircraft in each of the pairs were some thirty yards apart, with the second aircraft of each pair positioned a few aeroplane lengths behind his leader. It was quite a wide formation, John thought.

'Call a sighting when made,' Sidey transmitted as they approached Dover. 'I don't see them yet.'

Six sets of eyes scanned the sky, not just those of the two leaders, as it would have been had they been flying in two Vic formations. The limitations of those formations had been another concern John had raised with the squadron's senior hierarchy in the past. He had received short shrift then.

No one reported anything for some minutes, then the radio crackled to life.

'Heinkels,' Greg called. 'Ten o'clock low, at about twenty thousand. I count eighteen. Don't see any fighter cover.'

Eighteen? John thought. *Control said fifty plus earlier. Where are the others?*

'Red one, this is red two,' said John. 'Fifty plus were reported. Have they split?' While he knew that precise aircraft numbers were not easily discerned from a radar screen, normally the controllers were reasonably accurate.

'Control, this is Muscat,' Sidey said, using the code given to them for this mission. 'We have eighteen bandits in sight. Can you update us on the height and position of the remainder?' he transmitted, in response to John's query.

'Muscat, we have identified a formation split, with thirty plus bandits making a late heading change, and now tracking towards Ramsgate. They are maintaining twenty thousand. For your information, we have called your reserves at Manston to scramble.'

Christ, I hope they have finished their refuelling, John thought.

In response to the controller's advice, John looked out to his left, straining to see the group of enemy aircraft now tracking to Ramsgate. Then he saw them.

'Red one, this is red two. I have them. Nine o'clock low. It's our missing Heinkels.'

'Roger, red two. Our reserves from Manston won't be on the scene in time,' Sidey called. 'We will have to split. Yellow Section, take on the aircraft targeting Dover. Red Section, follow me — we will take on the Ramsgate attackers.'

Sidey rolled his aircraft to the left and started to dive towards Ramsgate. John and Charlie followed, increasing their engine power as they turned and dived. The chasing Spitfires were soon closing in on the Heinkels tracking towards Ramsgate, but John could see they might not reach the bombers before their bombs were dropped on the town. *Probably going for the port area,* he decided. *Wonder why they made such a late split? Perhaps it's a deliberate tactic to fool us?*

The leading Luftwaffe bombers were now over the port at Ramsgate, but no bombs could be seen falling from the bellies of the enemy aircraft. Then, in a moment of cold realisation, John understood what was happening. Ramsgate was not the target.

'Red one, this is red two. They aren't bombing Ramsgate. I think they are after Manston.'

John knew B Flight would probably still be on the ground there, unable to scramble until they'd finished topping up the aircraft fuel tanks. *Oh my God, they're sitting ducks*, he thought.

John followed Sidey's aircraft as he dived at the leading Heinkels, now starting to bomb Manston aerodrome. Charlie was close behind. Each of the three Spitfires scored hits as they made their first pass. One of the Luftwaffe aircraft suffered severe damage and started to lose altitude as it slowly turned back towards the English Channel. John managed to get an extended shot at another bomber, and both its engines began smoking before it entered a dive that became progressively steeper, until vertical. *He will not be pulling out of that*, John thought, as he looked around for another target. Glancing down at Manston aerodrome below, he could see bombs exploding along the length of the aerodrome's operational area. He could also see some aircraft trying to take off to escape the bombs carpeting the airfield. John renewed his attack on the German bombers.

He loosed off a long burst, raking two bombers as he made another pass. One started smoking, but the other appeared unaffected. He wheeled around for another shot. This time he concentrated his fire on each of the aircraft for a bit longer. Success! The first of the bombers rolled steeply to the right and began descending rapidly in a spiral dive. The second bomber caught fire. Within seconds bodies were plummeting from the mortally wounded Heinkel as the crew baled out. John saw their parachutes blossoming open a few seconds after they exited the doomed aircraft.

Other Spitfires now joined the attack. John recognised Smallbone's aircraft. The Manston reserves had arrived. *Good, they got off*, John thought. The Germans had had enough. They began turning for France, even those that had not yet dropped their bombs. The Spitfires continued to harry them as they fled, and John saw three more Heinkels go down before Sidey called a halt when they were about ten miles out over the Channel.

'Break off, lads. Fuel will be getting marginal. Set a heading for Hornchurch. See you on the ground.'

John was angry. He stomped into the debrief, glaring at everyone.

'Well, that was a major screw-up,' he said, looking around as if willing someone to challenge him. No-one said anything, but Sidey moved up beside him and spoke quietly.

'Maybe it was. Maybe it wasn't. We will discuss and analyse. Ranting won't help.'

John stared at him. What had happened was exactly the sort of risk he had raised at the pre-flight briefing. True, he had been satisfied with what Sidey had said at the time, but now it was clear the risk had not been adequately mitigated. The Germans had outfoxed them with a last-minute split, and squadron members had been caught on the ground at Manston.

Squadron Leader Smallbone came in. He looked upset. 'Gentlemen,' he said, 'B Flight was bombed as we were taking off from Manston, and I regret to tell you we suffered the loss of an aircraft. Pilot Officer Bentley was in his take-off roll when a bomb landed in front of his aircraft. He was too close and couldn't avoid crashing into the crater it created. His Spitfire exploded on impact. He was unable to get out.'

Oh, Christ, thought John. *Not Tim. Not the brand-new father.* He turned and walked out of the room, kicking a chair in anger and frustration as he went. He hurried to the officers' mess, longing for the privacy of his room.

There was a quiet knock on John's door.

'Yes?'

'Flying Officer Noble, it's Squadron Leader Smallbone. May we speak?'

It was an hour since John had stormed out of the briefing room. He had finished crying, but continued to wrestle with the what-ifs and whys regarding the bombing of Manston and the loss of Tim. He opened the door.

'Come in, sir.'

'I understand Pilot Officer Bentley's wife is staying in the area with her parents, so I'm going out to see her. As you know her, I thought it may help if you were there too, when I tell her what has happened.'

John was pleased Smallbone had thought of taking him when he went to see Elsbeth. It was going to be a difficult moment. Elsbeth would appreciate Tim's friend and fellow pilot being there with one of the squadron's senior officers.

'Yes, I will come with you,' John replied, taking some comfort from the fact that Elsbeth was staying with her parents. At least she would have their support.

As they drove to see Elsbeth, Smallbone told John what had happened at Manston.

'We got a call from control to scramble. We were to intercept enemy aircraft inbound to Ramsgate. They didn't know at the time that it was actually Manston that the Germans were targeting. I had started my take-off roll when the first bombs began landing. Tim was my number two, out to my right and about thirty yards behind me.'

John noticed Smallbone had adopted an informal tone, using Tim's first name.

'I was through fifty miles per hour, tail up, and soon to be airborne, when the grass about sixty yards ahead of me virtually erupted. One moment it was a flat green surface, the next a mix of brown earth and grass, lifted at least forty feet into the air by an exploding bomb. It created a huge crater that I just managed to avoid by swerving to the left. My right undercarriage leg must have missed it by no more than twenty feet. Because Tim was in his take-off roll to my right, the crater created by the bomb was directly in front of his aircraft. He did not have the same opportunity as me to swerve past it, and consequently he went into it and his aircraft was destroyed.'

It was Elsbeth who opened the front door of the small cottage on the outskirts of Chelmsford when John knocked about ninety minutes later.

'Oh, hi, John, what are you…'

She trailed off when she saw another officer standing behind John, and took in the look on his face. She knew straight away why they were there.

'No. No. Oh God, no!' she screamed as she started pummelling John's chest with her fists.

John put his arms around her shoulders and pulled her towards him. 'I'm so sorry, Elsbeth. I'm so terribly sorry,' was all he could say as he held her, struggling to hold back his own tears as she sobbed.

CHAPTER SEVEN

Weather conditions over southeast England on Tuesday the thirteenth of August, 1940, were poor. Not impossible for flight operations, but enough to make flying difficult. Looking at the forecast, John thought it would curtail at least some of the day's anticipated Luftwaffe activity. He and the other pilots had been briefed on the possibility of significant offensive operations by the Luftwaffe today. If Britain's intelligence was correct, an all-out effort was about to occur, as the Luftwaffe embarked on a mass attack aimed at seriously debilitating Britain's air force. The Germans had called it *Adlertag* — Eagle Day.

Sidey addressed the pilots in the briefing room. 'Gentlemen, despite the weather, we still think there is a possibility of some major attacks today. The likely targets are our airfields, and, perhaps, the Chain Home radar stations. We know Hitler's objective is to overcome the Royal Air Force. Fighter Command is going to continue its policy of holding back part of the so-called supernumerary squadrons as a reserve to give us a better chance of meeting all inbound hostile flights.' Sidey paused. 'Before continuing the briefing, I want to talk about yesterday's operations.'

The room was silent as every pilot listened expectantly.

'Yesterday, the enemy did something we did not expect. The last-minute redirection of part of an attacking formation, from Dover to Manston, meant we were left with squadron aircraft exposed on the ground. By the time control had identified the true target, there was insufficient time to get our aircraft safely into the air before the bombers arrived overhead. To avoid such a situation in the future, a change of policy has been developed for the use of forward bases.'

I should bloody well think so, John thought. He was still angry that Tim had been caught on the ground in the surprise attack. He wished he had pushed Sidey harder when he had questioned the risk of enemy formations splitting off to targets not previously identified by sector controllers, particularly when that target was an RAF aerodrome.

'Fighter Command is no longer going to hold Eleven Group reserves on the ground at any station within thirty miles of the coast in Sectors C and D,' Sidey continued. 'First responders may be positioned there initially, to go up to meet enemy aircraft detected approaching over the Channel. However, once any Luftwaffe aircraft get close to England, we don't want a situation like the one we had yesterday. The plan now is to keep reserves back at main bases, such as here at Hornchurch, and at Biggin Hill, Kenley, and Croydon. That will ensure we maximise the time we have to warn and scramble those reserves if there is late identification of an aerodrome as a target. Command thinks the late change yesterday was a deliberate tactic to prevent us recognising Manston aerodrome as the target for as long as possible. The new policy won't stop the Germans doing something similar again, but we hope that the consequences for us will be different.'

The pilots remained silent. Everyone had been affected by Tim's loss, and there was some concern, certainly in John's mind, that the Germans had outwitted those at Fighter Command who used Britain's radar defences to plot where an attack was likely.

An airman appeared at the door to the briefing room. He had been running and was breathless. 'It's a scramble, sir!'

'Thank you, Corporal,' Sidey said, before turning back to the squadron members. 'We will resume this later. Now go — same groupings as yesterday. Red and Yellow Sections off first. Green and Blue will hold here in reserve. Pilot Officer Ridley, take the blue two position.'

Blue two had been Tim's operating position the previous day, John recalled.

Red and Yellow Sections were soon airborne. It seemed to John, flying as red two behind the flight's leader, Sidey, that they were becoming very adept at getting into the air quickly.

The six Spitfires climbed to the east, awaiting instructions from control. Sidey and his accompanying pilots did not yet know their target detail.

'Gussy, this is Control.'

Gussy was the flight's code for this mission.

'Control, this is Gussy leader, read you strength five. Currently passing angels seven, and our heading is one two zero,' Sidey responded.

'Roger, Gussy. Climb angels twelve and turn right onto one eight zero. We have thirty bandits approaching Beachy Head.'

'Gussy, wilco, climbing to twelve thousand on one eight zero,' Sidey acknowledged.

Control called again. 'Gussy, speed indicates they are probably Stukas. We anticipate attacks on Chain Home sites, most likely at Beachy Head and Pevensey, but possibly also Truleigh and Fairlight.'

'Roger,' Sidey replied.

As the Spitfires approached the town of Polegate, Sidey called a sighting.

'Bandits, eleven o'clock low, estimate two thousand feet below our level.'

En route, the Spitfires had found it necessary to pick their way around some cloud build-ups. In the prevailing weather conditions, the enemy aircraft had not been easy to see, but now they had located them. John was pleased with the controller positioning them at twelve thousand feet, a perfect height above the Stukas to begin an attack. Red and Yellow Sections had about six miles to run before crossing the coast to intercept them.

As he watched, John saw the Stuka formation split into three groups, ten aircraft in each. One group turned to their left, flying parallel to the coast on a westerly heading. *They are after the Truleigh station*, he decided. Another group turned right. *Yep, Pevensey*, John thought. The remaining Stukas continued on their course, heading directly towards the Beachy Head station.

'In pairs please, gentlemen,' Sidey called, before issuing instructions that indicated he had reached the same conclusion as John regarding the Stukas' targets. 'Red one and two will continue directly to Beachy Head to meet the inbound hostiles. Red three and yellow three, go left and intercept the Stukas threatening Pevensey. Yellow one and two, go right and intercept those moving along the coast towards Truleigh.'

The others peeled away as instructed. Sidey and John, red one and two respectively, continued towards the group of Stukas now preparing to start their dive-bombing runs against the station at Beachy Head.

'Control, this is Gussy leader. Identified targets are Truleigh, Beachy, and Pevensey,' Sidey transmitted. Then, as he lined up the first Stuka about to commence its attack, he made the standard "tally-ho" call to ensure control understood the enemy aircraft had been intercepted and an attack was underway.

John saw Sidey fire a long burst at a Stuka, which rolled away, smoking. Positioned out to Sidey's right, John fired at another Stuka. It reared up into a short, steep climb, before falling onto its back and plummeting earthwards. *Must have hit the pilot*, John decided. He looked around. Control had not detected any fighter escort, but you never knew. John swept the sky again. There were no other enemy aircraft to be seen. He turned to line up another Stuka and fired. It turned and dived towards the east. Normally, John would have pursued the fleeing aircraft, but today he thought it more important he try to stop those still trying to attack the radar site.

John wheeled around, looking for fresh targets. He saw a Stuka spinning to the ground. *Sidey must have got it*, he thought. Just then, another Stuka he had not seen coming passed across in front of him, about six hundred yards away. It still had a bomb slung under its belly. John set off in pursuit, the Spitfire's superior speed soon closing the distance so he could fire effectively. At a range of three hundred yards John fired a long burst. He would normally not have fired until he was two hundred yards out, but he was keen to interfere with the German's attack as soon as he could. Some tracer passing nearby, even if none hit, might put the pilot off.

Suddenly, there was a huge explosion in front of him. The aircraft he had been shooting at disintegrated. *My God, I must have hit his bomb and triggered it*, he thought, as he pulled his control column hard to the left and added power in a maximum rate turn to avoid flying through any airborne debris.

Soon the engagement was over. The radar station at Beachy Head had not been hit. There were some craters near the masts and engineering hut, but no direct hits nor any damage to any of the antennae that John could see.

Sidey called. 'Red two, this is red one. Job done. Good work. Setting a heading for Hornchurch.'

John slipped into his position as wingman and followed Sidey back to base.

On landing back at Hornchurch, John found the other members of Red and Yellow Sections had landed not long before them. Blue and Green Sections were not on the ground, having been scrambled to meet a different enemy threat. As their aircraft were being refuelled and re-armed, the pilots waited at dispersal, discussing the mission. It had been a successful intercept. No losses to the squadron, no material damage to any of the three stations they had been called to protect, and a total of five Luftwaffe aircraft destroyed, plus four probables and two possibles.

'The Stukas just aren't up to it this side of the Channel, despite the reputation they built when supporting attacks by German troops and armour in Europe. When we meet them, they have no answer to the capability of the Spitfire,' Greg commented.

'That's right,' said Sidey. 'Today they were, again, relatively easy targets. Six Spitfire defenders thwarted the plans of thirty Stuka attackers. I think they will either be withdrawn from ops over England, or only sent with fighter cover in future. I suppose they had to use them today as a precursor to the mass raids we are expecting. They were trying to knock out our ability to detect approaching aircraft.'

'Scramble!'

The call came from the dispersal hut. A young airman was leaning through the doorway, shouting the order he had just been given on the telephone. The pilots ran to their aircraft. Engines spluttered to life, with smoke and flames coming out of their large exhausts, before settling into the regular grumble of an idling Merlin. It was a relatively quick turnaround. Since landing just a short time ago, the Spitfires had been rearmed and refuelled, and had had their oxygen cylinders replaced. Hardworking ground crews had all the aircraft ready when the call to scramble came in.

As John climbed into his cockpit, he saw that the Blue and Green Sections were landing. *Hopefully they will get more time on the ground than we have had*, he thought.

As he taxied for take-off, John noticed that aircraft from the other squadrons at the aerodrome had also started their engines and were getting ready to depart. *So many going up at the same time? What's inbound?* he wondered. It was not long before he found out.

'Gussy, this is control. We have twelve bandits inbound across the Channel, high speed at low level, tracking towards you. Fighters. There are also another forty plus inbound, at medium speed, five miles behind at angels eighteen. Bombers, by their radar signatures. There looks to be some fighter cover above and behind those bombers. The signal being returned is weak, but our best guess is another twenty plus fighters at angels twenty-four, some eight miles behind. Will clarify as soon as able. Target is assumed to be your aerodrome. Intercept the low-level inbound fighters. Others from Hornchurch are meeting those at higher level.'

John immediately realised what the Germans were doing. Their fighters were going to make a fast, low-level attack on the airfield, shooting at everything they could catch on the ground as they crossed. The warning they had received was timely. John appreciated that without Chain Home to alert them, their aircraft would have been caught on the ground. The first they would have known about the threat was when Me 109s snarled in, flashing over the aerodrome boundary hedges and starting to shoot. Then, a few minutes later, bombs would have begun falling from the bombers passing overhead at eighteen thousand feet, seeking to destroy any exposed aircraft, equipment, and infrastructure. *Hope Green and Blue Sections are quick with their turnaround,* John thought.

'Red and Yellow Sections, level off at three thousand,' Sidey called. 'Control has reported our bandits have just crossed the coast at Sandwich. They are tracking directly towards Hornchurch, low and fast. We are flying the reciprocal of their track to intercept. I expect we will meet them around Faversham.'

A few minutes later, he called again.

'Got them at eleven o'clock, about one mile south of the marshes. Look to be hedge-hopping. Three *Schwärme*, one behind the other, about one hundred yards apart.'

John knew he was referring to the flight formation the Luftwaffe had been known to use.

'Get into the same pairs as earlier, with lateral spacing sufficient for independent shooting. Red one and two will attack the first *Schwarm*. Yellow one and two take the second. The threes can take the third. Tally-ho.'

The six Spitfires rolled left and divided into three separate pairs, each aircraft in a pair about thirty yards out from his partner so they could fire freely at their rapidly approaching targets.

The Me 109s did not respond to the approaching Spitfires. *They haven't seen us yet*, John thought as he dived towards them. *Too busy ensuring their safe clearance over those hedges, focused on their planned low-level attack.*

As Sidey and John, the first pair to get close, opened up with their guns, the Germans saw them for the first time. Their reaction was to climb steeply and turn towards the approaching Spitfires, but not before two of the 109s in the first *Schwarm* had been shot down. One of the Luftwaffe aircraft appeared to simply fall out of the sky. The other began trailing a mixture of black and white smoke. Oil and glycol, John knew, as he saw it descend, unable to maintain height. It landed in a field, with its wheels still up, and slid to a stop.

Focusing on the remaining 109s, John saw there were now several dogfights underway. As he watched, Sidey began an attack on another Luftwaffe aircraft. John followed Sidey, as his wingman. The German pilot twisted and turned his machine through the air. He rolled and looped. He tried everything, but he could not shake off his pursuer. A long burst from Sidey's eight machine guns brought the uneven contest to an end. *Well*, John thought as he saw the Luftwaffe aeroplane go down, *you died not knowing you had been facing one of the Royal Air Force's top aerial warfare exponents.*

It soon became apparent to the pilots of the remaining 109s that they were not going to make a successful low-level attack on RAF Hornchurch today. They had been intercepted thirty miles out and lost four aircraft, with three more being badly damaged and only just able to limp back across the Channel. The remaining Luftwaffe fighters vacated the area as fast as they could.

'Let's help with the bombers,' Sidey called, when he saw the 109s were leaving. He called control.

'Control, this is Gussy leader. We have broken up the low-level fighter attack, and they are either down or heading back to France. Request vectors to intercept the bombers inbound to Hornchurch.'

'Gussy, Control. Confirm your fuel state for further engagement.'

'Control, Gussy leader. We have over one hour. We can engage.'

'Roger, Gussy leader. Interception detail available in a moment.'

They were at sixteen thousand feet and still climbing when Sidey called his sighting of the bombers to which they had been vectored. The Germans were in a tight formation and putting up a solid curtain of protective fire. Some Spitfires were attacking them, but most were busy dogfighting with the fighter protection that accompanied the bombers. The air was swarming with Messerschmitts and Spitfires, turning and rolling as they battled with each other.

'Red and Yellow Sections, echelon left off me and target the bombers. Our priority is to stop them. Watch for fighters. They are busy with some of ours now, but will no doubt intervene when they see us arrive and engage the bombers.'

The six Spitfires quickly repositioned. Soon, each member of Sidey's flight had started firing as they closed in on the bombers. John appreciated that for a crew member in one of the bombers, it would have been unsettling to be confronted by a line of six Spitfires spread out in front of him, each unleashing the firepower of eight machine guns.

John saw the upper fuselage gunner's canopy on one aircraft, half open in the usual way for combat, explode into fragments as it received multiple hits. The gunner's position was just two or three yards behind the cockpit, so a slight variation in aim would have spelt the end of that aircraft. As it was, he could see the gunner had not survived. After passing over the top of the bomber formation, the Spitfires turned for another attack, but some of the Me 109s were not going to let them do that. John saw a group of four Luftwaffe fighters diving out of the aerial melee above.

'One-o-nines attacking from eleven o'clock high,' he warned with a quick radio transmission.

None of the Spitfires reacted immediately. They maintained their line of approach on the bombers, each pilot determined that his aerodrome would not be attacked. Three of the bombers were hit and dropped out of the formation. Two turned for home and the third started to turn, but its left wing kept dropping, its angle to the horizontal quickly becoming steeper and steeper. With no effective lift, it fell into a steep nose-down attitude and started to rotate around its longitudinal axis as it went down. *He's gone*, John confirmed to himself. *There's no coming out of that loss of control.*

Looking up, John saw that the four German fighters that had broken away from the general dogfighting were now close. He saw the tracer coming and rolled hard to the right, almost inverted, then dived. He kept his dive steep to avoid the power loss some manoeuvres could cause in a Spitfire's Merlin engine as normal fuel flow was affected. There was no sign of Jerry in his mirror, he confirmed, when he was established in his dive. Then his aircraft shuddered and bucked as rounds hit it. John took his aircraft from its steep dive into a tight spiralling descent, then he levelled his wings and pulled back hard on the stick to begin a climb, at the same time banking steeply to the left.

The Messerschmitt that had just shot at him flashed past. John rolled his own aircraft and dived after the German. The hunter had become the hunted. The Luftwaffe aircraft gently eased out of its dive and began climbing straight ahead. Its slower speed in the climb, and its straight track, presented John with a relatively easy shot. He fired a long burst from three hundred yards and saw the German's rear fuselage and tailplane take rounds from his guns. Seconds later, the 109's tailplane appeared to collapse. The Luftwaffe aircraft pitched down sharply and plummeted towards the fields of southeast England far below.

John saw that the bomber formation they had been attacking had now broken up. Some Spitfires were chasing individual bombers, although many were still caught up, dogfighting with the 109s. He saw Bland's aircraft lining up to attack a bomber. Blue and Green Sections must have been scrambled in time to get off Hornchurch before the German bombers had arrived overhead, he realised. As he watched, two more Me 109s broke away from the dogfighting melee above and swooped towards Bland's aircraft. He called a warning.

'Green three, fighters on your six, high.'

There was no response from Bland. *Too intent on a kill*, John thought. As he watched, he saw the bomber in front of the CO's plane explode into flames. Bland had got in a long burst from a range of only two hundred yards, but the pursuing 109s had now caught up with him. They opened fire. He could see Bland's Spitfire being hit.

John repositioned his aircraft and began firing at the closest 109. His shooting did not cause any damage, but it did distract the pilot from his attack on the CO's aircraft. The two

Luftwaffe pilots turned towards the Channel. John started to pursue them, but then broke off after a few moments. He would not be able to catch them quickly, and he knew his fuel was getting low. Looking around, he saw a Spitfire descending rapidly and trailing smoke. *Looks like Bland. He should be okay. His plane is under control and he has plenty of choices for a successful forced landing*, thought John, noting some large, flat fields below through a gap in the cloud.

David Sidey surveyed the briefing room. His pilots had all survived. There had been some damage to the squadron's aircraft, but apart from the CO's Spitfire, there was nothing serious that would not be possible to fix overnight.

'Gentlemen, well done. You all did your job,' Sidey said. 'I have just had a call from the CO confirming that he got down safely and was uninjured. His Spitfire has suffered some damage, though, and will be grounded for a while. We were able to stop Jerry taking out the Chain Home stations around the Beachy Head area. And when the Luftwaffe tried to attack this aerodrome, none got through. Raids on Biggin Hill and Kenley did get past Fighter Command's defences, but the damage there is not extensive. No aircraft were caught on the ground at either Biggin or Kenley.

'The Germans did have moderate success with some of their other attacks against Chain Home stations, namely at Dover and Foreness, but the damage is not extensive and the sites should be fully operational again by morning. The station at Ventnor, on the Isle of Wight, also took a hammering. Command couldn't get fighters there soon enough to intercept the Stukas. Nevertheless, the damage is fixable and I understand the station will be fully operational again within thirty-six hours.

'All in all, Fighter Command's detection and interception capability is proving incredibly valuable for us. We know what's coming, what the likely target is, and how many bandits we are facing. Today, we successfully disrupted most of Jerry's attacks. Before we disperse, does anyone have anything they wish to say regarding today's ops?'

John raised his hand. 'Just an observation, sir, but I was surprised we faced Jerry in such numbers given the weather conditions this morning. I would have thought their planned grand event, *Adlertag*, would have waited for a day when the weather was better. That suggests that either they decided to push on despite the conditions, or that today was simply poorly executed, with local commanders making their own individual operational decisions and no centralised control of the overall Luftwaffe effort. Or perhaps today wasn't *Adlertag*. It wasn't that big.'

'We don't know what happened on the German side, Flying Officer,' Sidey responded, 'but early intelligence from Fighter Command is that the morning attacks originated principally from the areas around Pas-de-Calais. The full German strength didn't appear until early afternoon, when aircraft coming out of airfields further north, particularly in Belgium, joined the attacks. Why they staged their forces in that way is unclear. Maybe there were weather issues, or maybe they were just disorganised for their first mass effort, and their force got split because of poor command and control procedures. We don't know, but let's see what happens in future. Today was just the beginning, I think. We should expect more large raids.'

No question about that, John thought. *They will come every day now, in huge numbers. Hitler wants to cross the Channel, so we need to be resolute.*

John decided he would ask Sidey about 12 Group's Big Wing proposal. 'Are we going to use multiple squadrons operating together in one large group to meet enemy aircraft, sir, as we did on several occasions at Dunkirk? I understand Twelve Group is pushing for the use of what it is calling a Big Wing.'

'No, Eleven Group will not be operating in that way. Air Vice-Marshall Park does not propose that we adopt it.'

'Will Twelve Group use the tactic, do you know, sir?'

Sidey hesitated. 'As you know,' he finally said, 'we had experience operating wings comprising more squadrons than standard during Dynamo. That occurred when Fighter Command decided to reduce frequency in favour of intensity over Dunkirk, because of the numbers of Luftwaffe aircraft attacking our troops. There were times, as you will recall, when we had three or four other squadrons operating with us. Those larger formations were intended to provide a greater presence on engagement. That meant stronger patrols, but it also meant that we could only put our aircraft up at less frequent intervals. Unfortunately, the greater force represented by various squadrons grouping together didn't work that well. We were taking too long to rendezvous and establish ourselves, and there were other issues as well. All in all, the view was that forming up multiple squadrons to transit to Dunkirk, to engage *en masse*, was not the answer.'

John nodded his acknowledgement. He had heard that the effort to create greater intensity during Operation Dynamo, the evacuation from Dunkirk, had meant there were periods when there was little RAF fighter cover available to protect the troops on the beaches. The commitment to operating the expanded wings had soaked up resources and left available cover too thin at times. Also, as Sidey had noted, there were operational difficulties if a Big Wing was to be used. Delays in meeting up with other squadrons, as well as the loss of cohesion once an engagement began, were just two of the problems.

'As a consequence of the multiple squadron experience at Dunkirk, Air Vice-Marshall Park does not want to use a similar technique now,' Sidey continued. 'He thinks we will put timely and adequate defence of our airfields at risk if we use Twelve Group's Big Wing strategy against attacking Luftwaffe aircraft. He wants us to remain nimble, able to respond quickly and precisely to Britain's defensive requirements.'

'Understood, sir,' John replied, pleased to hear that 11 Group was not going to use that tactic again.

CHAPTER EIGHT

John and Richard were sitting in the lounge of the officers' mess at Hornchurch.

'Bland is lucky he's still here after being shot down today,' John said.

Richard looked at him quizzically.

'I saw what happened. It was another example of his inability to see the bigger picture,' John continued.

'What makes you say that?' Richard asked.

'We were attacking the bombers. Then the fighter cover arrived, and we had to defend ourselves. I got caught up with a couple of Me one-o-nines, but they broke off quite quickly and headed back to France.'

'Running, were they?'

'No. I think it more likely they were getting low on fuel and did not want to get caught up in an extended dogfight.'

Richard nodded. 'I see.'

'Bland was chasing a single bomber, and two one-o-nines started following him. I called a warning that there was someone on his tail, but he did nothing. He flew on after his target, and made no attempt to deal with the fighters closing in on him from behind. They took him out easily. I saw him going down, heading for a forced landing somewhere below. What surprised me was his apparent inability to process information under pressure. He was so focused on positioning himself and attacking the bomber he was following, he seemed to shut out everything else. He didn't appear to have any awareness of his situation. I can't think of any other reason for his lack of evasive action when I warned him about the Jerry on his tail.'

'I've heard about that sort of behaviour in pilots who are not experienced in what they are doing,' Richard responded. 'Doesn't normally occur with the more experienced chaps. Doc Berryman calls it tunnel vision; you put so much concentration on one particular thing that you ignore other important matters going on around you. You lose awareness of everything outside of your target.'

'Maybe that's what it was, but he's an experienced pilot, not a newbie to war ops.'

'I've said it before: the man's not a capable fighter pilot,' Richard replied. 'It's great he has decided to let Sidey and Smallbone lead now, applying his newfound love for what he calls governance oversight. But he's still a risk, to himself at least, as you saw again today.'

'Now that we know there seems to be a continuing problem with the CO, it's important we keep an eye on him,' said John. 'I want everyone around me to be on their best game when we are up against Jerry. Substandard performance from one of the team during battle is simply not on when it affects us all.'

'I agree,' said Richard. 'Sidey and Smallbone are both aware of the issues around Bland, certainly as a leader, but we should ensure they understand he still has moments in the air where he doesn't do things well. In the meantime, we keep ourselves ready for more busy days, meeting and greeting our German friends.'

John laughed, before telling Richard that he would be off operations the next morning. 'Sidey wants someone from the squadron to visit sector control in Uxbridge. The objective is to give pilots a better understanding of the information Chain Home provides, and how the sector controllers operate.'

'That's a good gig, John. How did you pull that off?'

'Apparently, Fighter Command has mandated that one person from each fighter squadron is to attend and observe at sector control for a few hours, and when back at the squadron he is to talk to his fellow pilots about what he has seen. The thinking is that if those in the air are completely *au fait* with what happens in the control room, that will lead to enhanced communication and performance when Chain Home is helping us to intercept Jerry.'

'Fair enough. That might be useful,' Richard said with a nod.

'Yes, I think it will be. I'm going early tomorrow, to be there as ops start. There'll be a briefing first, and then an hour or so observing, so I expect to be back by midday.'

It was only 5.30 a.m., but in the 11 Group Operations Room the next day, Thursday, 15th of August, the plots were already beginning to build. The officer in charge, a squadron leader, was sitting at a desk placed on the highest of a series of seating tiers, overlooking a large map table in the centre of the room. John had been invited to sit next to him. The table carried markers showing the position of enemy aircraft, and John could see there were several markers in place already.

'Something going on here,' the squadron leader said to John, before calling down to a sergeant sitting near the map table. 'Fetch Wing Commander Peters, please. Tell him there is an unusual build-up over the French coast.'

Ten minutes later, a sleepy-looking man showing the rank of Wing Commander came in and clambered up the steep stairs to where John and the squadron leader were sitting.

'What's up?' Peters asked, as he surveyed the markers below on the table. The markers were being moved by young women using long sticks. The sticks reminded John of the billiard cues in the officers' mess at Catterick.

'Not sure, sir, but we are seeing groups of German aircraft forming in three separate areas. There are one hundred plus assembled northwest of Amiens. They have just started towards Britain at eighteen thousand feet. Present track will have them crossing the coast at Dungeness. A similar number has formed up near Calais. No track from there to calculate yet. Then, south of Bruges, we have what looks like fifty aircraft setting up formation. They are currently climbing through seventeen thousand. We have never had two hundred and fifty aircraft coming in this early in the day,' the squadron leader said.

'Right,' came the response, as the wing commander stared down at the markers. 'Thank you, Squadron Leader. You were right to alert me. I think those aircraft coming in from the Amiens area, with their projected entry point at Dungeness, are likely to be targeting aerodromes in Sector C: Lympne, West Malling and Biggin. Perhaps also Croydon and Kenley, if they come in a bit further. We should also treat Hawkinge in Sector D as a potential target for this group. It's relatively close to Lympne.'

John found himself agreeing with the senior officer. Fighter Command's advice had been that the RAF and its facilities would be prime targets. As he was thinking about that, the squadron leader introduced him.

'Wing Commander, this is Flying Officer Noble, here for the four-one-five familiarisation visit. Flying Officer Noble, Wing Commander Peters.' Peters and John shook hands, before the wing commander returned his attention to the map table as they heard a call from the floor. It was one of the WAAFs, busy repositioning some markers.

'Fifty plus hostiles at position niner alpha setting heading this time. Calculated entry point is the Thames Estuary.'

As John watched, a young woman, her dark hair pulled back into a bun, used her stick to move a marker forward. The marker had a small plaque attached to it, showing "50+" and "18", above a large, red arrow.

John knew that signified the fifty Luftwaffe aircraft inbound, at eighteen thousand feet, and the arrow on the plaque showed the direction in which the aircraft were tracking. The colour of the plaque indicated the currency of the plot, and the marker's position on the large map corresponded to the estimated position of the aircraft at present, something coded *Nine Alpha*. John realised it was the enemy aircraft that had been assembling near Bruges, and they were now on their way to Britain.

'Right-oh, Squadron Leader,' Peters said, 'I think this lot could be for Rochford and Hornchurch. Possibly also Manston, Detling, or Gravesend. We will be clearer about this when they get closer and we can be more precise about their track.'

'Call for you, sir. Fighter Command, Bentley Priory, Group Captain Davidson.'

The flight sergeant passed the telephone receiver to the squadron leader.

John knew the group captain calling from Bentley Priory would be Michael Davidson, the officer in charge of the main control centre for Fighter Command. He had heard about him from Richard, who knew his family.

The squadron leader spent the next few minutes talking with Davidson about the attacks being mounted. It appeared, from what John could hear, that the group captain had the same information as they did, and had reached the same conclusions regarding likely targets.

'Yes, sir, that's how we see it here, too,' the squadron leader said, before finishing the call with an acknowledgement about what would be done.

'Group Captain Davidson agrees, sir — it's aerodromes,' he said to Peters. 'He has instructed that we establish and manage the response of Eleven Group from here. He will maintain an overview and contact us if anything comes up that he wants to discuss.'

'Very well. We'll plan our response when we see how it develops,' Peters responded. 'Everyone is available, I see.'

John looked across the room to the tote board on the wall that showed the squadrons that were available. He could see from the illuminated discs showing under each squadron's number that they were all ready. Not surprising, of course, given the time of day, but he knew the aircraft based at any of the likely aerodrome targets would need to get airborne soon. Having aircraft still on the airfield when Jerry arrived overhead would not be good. He knew what could happen if the Germans surprised the RAF on the ground. Manston was still fresh in his memory.

Another call from a WAAF working the operations table interrupted John's thoughts.

'One hundred plus hostiles at position seven tango, setting heading this time, angels twenty. Calculated entry point is Dover.'

John looked at the markers on the table. They were being moved as the positions of enemy aircraft were updated. The Luftwaffe formations were building. *Looks like there will need to be a full response today, no half-squadron reserves*, he concluded.

'Squadron Leader,' said Wing Commander Peters, 'it does indeed seem that they are going to have a go at our aerodromes.'

'I think that's right, sir. We will get a better indication soon, as they get closer. I suggest we scramble full squadrons from all the possible target aerodromes, starting with those most easterly, closest to the attacking aircraft. Keep the squadrons operating from possible target aerodromes further west on full readiness, as reserves when needed.'

'Very good. I agree,' Peters responded. 'Scramble all aircraft at Manston, Hawkinge, and Lympne, now. Others to full readiness.'

Within minutes the lit discs on the tote board showed the squadrons scrambled, and soon to be climbing up to meet the Luftwaffe aircraft, to which they would be directed by the operations room controller.

'Shall we launch West Malling, Detling, Gravesend, and Rochford shortly?' the squadron leader asked Peters.

'Yes,' he replied, 'but let's hold Kenley, Croydon, Biggin, and Hornchurch until we see what spacing we have between the first and second waves.'

Christ, John thought. *A second wave, thirty or so minutes behind the first. The numbers are stacking up against us.* He could see that the Luftwaffe was mounting an enormous attack. There were several plots on the operations table, and each one showed a sizeable enemy force inbound.

'Full readiness,' the airman manning the telephone in dispersal called to the pilots of 415 Squadron. John and the others had been waiting at the dispersal hut at Hornchurch, expecting a call to scramble at any time. It was midday, and John was not long back from his sector control room familiarisation visit. He had known, having seen the plots building earlier, that the squadron would be busy today. Sure enough, that was proving to be the case. The squadron had already been up that morning to intercept multiple inbound enemy aircraft, along with every other squadron in the sector. When he had got back to Hornchurch after his visit to the control centre, a couple of the pilots had jokingly asked him if he was sorry to have missed the morning's fun while he had been "gallivanting" around Uxbridge.

With the call to full readiness, the pilots were required to sit in their aircraft, ready to go as soon as they were called. They had been warned in recent days that they should expect the whole squadron to have go up, rather than committing part only as a supernumerary squadron. John understood why that was so, after his early morning visit to sector control. *Now I'll see the reality of what the markers were showing*, he thought, as he sat in his Spitfire. He knew there would be a lot of German aircraft coming his way.

As he waited for the order to get airborne, John thought about Mary. He had not spent as much time as he would have liked with her over recent weeks. A quick cup of tea one afternoon and a hurried brunch late one morning was all they had managed. It was made all the harder by being away from Catterick, down at Hornchurch, with only short rest periods back at Catterick between tours. And when he did get back, Mary was often too busy at the hospital to get away easily.

John's thoughts were interrupted by the call to prepare for take-off.

'Clear,' one of his maintenance crew shouted. That meant John could be confident that all the ground crew were well away from the prop, and it was safe for the engine to be started. It was soon rumbling contentedly as he quickly completed some abbreviated pre-flight checks and began to taxi into take-off position. War-time scrambles only allowed abbreviated checks. There was insufficient time for a pilot to run through a comprehensive check-list.

John was green two, behind Greg as green one. Bland was green three, flying as the flight's tail-end Charlie, his preferred position these days. Though he was no longer leading any air engagements, the squadron pilots all understood they were still in Bland's hands to a certain extent. As tail-end Charlie, he was best placed to warn them of any enemy aircraft mounting an attack on them from behind. Not a perfect situation, John thought, given Bland's operational reputation.

As they climbed towards the east, John heard the controller calling Sidey, leading today as red one. They were coded "Hambo" for this operation.

'Hambo leader, climb angels twenty-five on heading one one zero. Thirty plus hostiles at angels twenty-one, twenty plus hostiles at angels twenty-five, four miles behind.'

John understood that his new friends in the 11 Group operations room would be busy planning the allocation of their limited defensive resources to meet the incoming formations of Luftwaffe aircraft.

As they approached the coast, John could see smoke rising from where he knew Manston aerodrome was situated, out to his left. Some bombers had been successful, he realised, as he looked at the smoke. There were dogfighting contrails criss-crossing the sky above Manston, so he knew RAF fighters were there, battling the Luftwaffe.

Looking ahead, towards Dover, John saw a similar scene. Dense black smoke was pluming up from what he guessed was Hawkinge airfield, and there were a lot of high-level contrails.

'Bandits sighted,' Sidey called. 'Thirty plus Dorniers at twenty thousand, I estimate. Can't see the fighter escort yet, but control reported twenty plus at five thousand feet above and four miles behind the bombers. We will split. Red and Yellow Sections, attack the bombers. Green and Blue, take on the fighters. With me, Red and Yellow Sections, echelon right, in pairs, attack spacing.' With that, Sidey called 'tally-ho' to control and started diving towards the oncoming Dorniers.

Tony Smallbone, leading the remainder of the squadron as blue one, called his instructions.

'Move to pairs.'

The six Spitfires repositioned quickly.

'Got them. Me one-o-nines. One o'clock, same height as us,' Greg, as green one, called.

'I see them,' Smallbone responded.

John searched the sky and located the approaching aircraft himself. He quickly glanced towards where Red and Yellow Sections were positioning to attack the bombers. *They might get in one pass before the fighters arrive*, he thought, as he looked up at the Me 109s diving down to protect the bombers. John prepared to engage the fighters, and for the free-for-all that would develop as the dogfighting began.

Within minutes, Blue and Green Sections were heavily involved with the fighters. Aircraft on both sides were wheeling and turning, diving, climbing, rolling, and pitching, as they fought to outmanoeuvre each other and get into a position to shoot. It was chaotic, as always.

After no more than fifteen minutes, it was over. The Me 109s melted away, back to France. Fifteen minutes of full-power combat had soon drained their fuel down to a level that made it necessary for them to return to their base. John knew that none of the German pilots would want to risk running out of fuel and having to ditch in the inhospitable waters of the English Channel.

As John descended towards Hornchurch, he passed by Detling and then Gravesend aerodromes. He could see aircraft landing at both, but he also saw numerous bomb craters on the operational surfaces of the stations. *Careful lads*, he thought, as he watched the RAF aircraft landing between adjacent craters. It looked like Jerry had got a few bombers through.

Approaching Hornchurch, John saw similar scenes. One of the maintenance hangars had been destroyed as well. When he landed, he was careful to pick a line that kept him well clear of the huge holes and piles of earth on the runway.

Sidey was in the briefing room when John walked in.

'You chaps in Green and Blue Sections did a good job keeping the fighters off us for as long as you did, while we went after the bombers,' Sidey said to him. 'It gave us a few minutes to have a good go at them before the one-o-nines arrived.'

'I'm not sure how many we got,' John replied. 'We'll have to wait for intelligence to collate the reported numbers. I didn't see any of us go down, so I'm hoping our losses against the one-o-nines are nil.'

'Victories against their fighters are one thing, but what I really care about is that we stop the bombers,' Sidey said. 'The damage they did here, and at Gravesend and Detling, won't impede operations, but I can't say the same for Manston, Hawkinge and Lympne. I hear they took a pounding, but it's all repairable over the next forty-eight hours, I understand, and Jerry lost a lot of aircraft in those attacks.'

'They are coming in their waves, which makes tactical sense,' John said. 'I saw it starting first thing this morning, when I was on my familiarisation visit at Uxbridge.'

'Yes, the first wave started coming through at about o-five-fifty,' said Sidey, 'followed by a second about forty-five minutes later. What we just encountered was the third lot today.'

'So, if a fourth wave comes in now, are we ready?' John asked.

'I can't answer for the other squadrons, but our own aircraft are being turned around and will be ready to go within the next fifteen minutes. My flight sergeant tells me he can refuel, re-arm, and fit new oxygen in ten minutes.' Sidey grinned. 'I was giving him some leeway when I told him he should be ready in fifteen.'

John thought that Wing Commander Peters, in the 11 Group control room, would be reasonably pleased with the way the day had gone so far. He had seen the squadrons scrambled off the aerodromes closest to the Channel as the first Luftwaffe aircraft had approached. Then, when a second wave had come, more aircraft had been launched from the aerodromes further west, including John's squadron from Hornchurch.

The reports indicated that the Spitfires and Hurricanes of the RAF had been relatively successful in breaking up the momentum of the three distinct waves of Luftwaffe aircraft that had come in so far today. A good number of bombers had been shot down, and some had turned for home early when faced with the aircraft scrambled to meet them. John was pleased to have been back in time to help with the third wave, and he was also pleased that the bombers that had got through and hit their targets had not caused any telling damage. *Attacks like that will not affect our ability to maintain a steadfast defence against the Luftwaffe*, he decided. *While it's hard for us, Chain Home is helping us enormously, alerting us to attacks and positioning us to meet them.*

A short time later, the intelligence officer gave an update to the squadron pilots.

'As it stands, we have eight Dorniers down, plus four probables and three possibles. Regarding the fighters, three possibles. No losses to Four-one-five Squadron. A good result. So far, the enemy attacks have been well and truly disrupted.'

The pilots had just started to breathe a sigh of relief, when they were dragged back into operational mode.

'Squadron to full readiness,' was the call.

Damn, thought John, as he turned to run out to his waiting Spitfire with the other pilots of 415 Squadron, *they're still coming*.

CHAPTER NINE

Two weeks later, and after an intense period of fighting that had involved multiple scrambles every day, John was enjoying the early-morning stillness as he walked towards the dispersal area. He was wondering what today would bring when his thoughts were interrupted.

'Flying Officer Noble, a moment please.'

It was Bland, standing at the door of the administration block. John turned and walked over to him.

'Sir?'

'When you get to dispersal, would you tell Squadron Leaders Sidey and Smallbone that I want them, together with one of the squadron's more experienced pilots, whom they should bring along, to come to my office at seventeen fifteen hours this evening. I want to brief them about a meeting we are going to be having there at seventeen thirty. There are some special visitors coming to the station at that time. I can't say who at this stage, as it's all very hush-hush. Please apologise on my behalf for the short notice and the secrecy, but they will understand why in due course.'

'Certainly, sir. I will pass that information on when I see them.'

'Thank you, Flying Officer. I understand Command is expecting Jerry over in large numbers again today. Another busy day for us, I expect. Let's hope both the squadron leaders are still available this evening, eh?'

John smiled thinly but did not reply. He understood it was just more classic Bland crassness.

When he reached dispersal, John could not see Sidey or Smallbone, but he knew they would appear shortly. All the squadron pilots were to be at readiness by o-seven-hundred. That was in five minutes, so John knew they would not be far away.

A few moments later Sidey and Smallbone emerged from the briefing room and joined the pilots waiting around the dispersal hut.

'Excuse me, sir,' John said to Sidey, 'the CO has asked that you and Squadron Leader Smallbone meet with him in his office at seventeen fifteen hours. He wants to brief you on a meeting you're to attend with him, and some visitors, at seventeen thirty. He also asked that you bring with you an experienced member of the squadron.'

'What's it about?'

'He didn't say, sir, but he did ask me to apologise for the short notice and the secrecy, saying it was all very hush-hush.'

'Very well, thank you, Flying Officer. We will meet with him at that time. Hopefully, the day's ops will be over by then. You may as well come along with us. You fit the bill for his request that we bring an experienced pilot to the meeting.'

The day was already warm as John and the other squadron pilots lounged about on a variety of chairs and couches outside the dispersal hut, waiting for the inevitable call to action. The summer of 1940 had been mostly fine. In any other circumstances that would have been wonderful, but in the current situation, with multiple Luftwaffe raids every day, poor weather was always welcome. It provided some relief from the constant aerial attacks. John was lying back in an old deckchair that was on its last legs. He relaxed and closed his eyes. *Give me clear blue sea, gentle surf and white sand, and I could be at Kaka Point,* he thought as he basked in the morning sun. Kaka Point had been John's favourite local beach when living on the farm back in New Zealand.

He could have easily fallen asleep, but he knew he should not do that. There could be a call to scramble at any minute.

As if on cue, the telephone in the dispersal hut rang, interrupting John's meandering thoughts. It only rang once, before being quickly snatched off its cradle by the airman in charge. Everyone was on edge, not just the pilots.

'Red and Yellow Sections, scramble.'

The call to battle was shouted from the dispersal hut window. John got up, grabbed his parachute bag, and began running to his aircraft.

'Bolter, this is Control,' John heard on his radio.

'Control, Bolter red one,' Tony Smallbone, today's flight leader, responded, using the codename for the squadron on this mission.

'Bolter, we have some business for you,' the controller responded. 'Fifteen plus hostiles have been identified. They are coming in at twenty-two thousand feet.'

Smallbone and his flight climbed to meet the Luftwaffe aircraft. As they passed through twenty-one thousand feet, he called a sighting.

'I have them. One o'clock. I count twenty, about one thousand feet above our height. Me one-o-nines. Don't see any bombers.'

Why send a bunch of fighters over Britain, and no bombers? John wondered, when he heard Smallbone's call.

The Spitfires were in echelon right formation, running off Smallbone's aircraft. While John knew their current formation would soon fragment once they started dogfighting, he thought it the best formation to use in their initial approach. It was a formation from which all the Spitfires could fire an opening salvo, at the same time if they wished.

The Me 109s looked to John to be about five miles from the approaching Spitfires, when Smallbone called a change in tactics.

'Red Section is going forty-five left; Yellow Section, go forty-five right. Hold the resulting heading for the count of ten, then swing back to face Jerry. We will attack them from two different angles.'

Ah, he's planning a pincer movement, John thought. *That's new.*

Three of the Spitfires turned left forty-five degrees; the other three turned right forty-five degrees. The manoeuvre seemed to perplex the German pilots. For a few moments they did nothing, but then the pilots responded. Half of them turned left, and the other half, right, effectively mirroring what the Spitfires had done.

John saw that Smallbone, red one, and Greg, yellow one, must have reached ten in their respective counts. Now they were both turning back towards the approaching Luftwaffe aircraft. Range was down to less than three thousand yards, and decreasing rapidly as the aircraft closed in on each other. Seconds later the Spitfires began shooting. The Me 109s reacted with return fire. The air was full of tracer. Aircraft of both sides began turning and twisting as they passed each other and tried to get around on an opponent's tail.

John pulled his Spitfire into a steep turn to follow a 109 passing close by. He was unable to get onto the tail of the German pilot, whose aircraft had entered a steep turn back towards John, trying, in turn, to get behind the Spitfire. It was a stalemate, with neither pilot able to gain ascendancy over the other. *I need to break this*, John thought to himself, allowing his aircraft's nose to drop out of the turn, causing it to enter the beginning of a spiral dive. The Me 109 followed. In an attempt to shake it off, John suddenly rolled his Spitfire into a steep bank in the opposite direction, towards the outside of his spiral dive. The 109 followed.

John continued his roll to the right until he was inverted, then pulled back on the control stick, putting his Spitfire into a vertical dive. He glanced in his cockpit mirror. The Me 109 remained behind him, its yellow nose looking ominous. Pulling out of his dive, John increased his engine boost and banked steeply to the left, into a maximum rate turn. His vision started to grey out as the gravitational loading in the turn took him close to blacking out completely. He held the aircraft hard in its turn, hoping he did not lose consciousness. After what seemed like forever, but which was, in reality, only a few seconds, he released some of the back pressure on the stick. His vision cleared immediately, but he could not see the German aircraft. He checked his mirror again. Nothing. He twisted in his seat and peered back over his shoulder. Nothing. Glancing down, he saw an Me 109 about one thousand feet directly below him. It was in a violent spin. *He's lost control. A high-speed stall in the turn would have flicked him into a spin like that*, thought John.

But he had no time to ponder why the 109 had spun out of its steep turn. He was now closely engaged with another Me 109. It came at him from his three o'clock, diving towards him and unleashing a long barrage of fire, but it missed. John pulled up into a steep climb and then rolled into a tight turn to his right, the side from which the 109 was attacking. That quickly put him closer to the 109, and above it. It would have been easier for the Luftwaffe pilot if John had turned his Spitfire left, away from the 109, but John was too experienced to make that mistake. John tightened his turn even more and started diving towards his attacker, who had turned and was climbing back towards him. They were head-on. The Luftwaffe pilot broke away at the last moment, giving John an opportunity. He steep-turned after the German and was soon behind him, in a good firing position. A three-second burst sent the 109 tumbling out of the sky.

A Spitfire dived past John, about three hundred yards away. He recognised it was Tony Smallbone's aircraft. Close behind Tony were two 109s, side by side, chasing him and firing when they could. There was some light smoke coming from the Spitfire's engine cowling. John followed them down, trying to get within firing range of the German aircraft in hot pursuit of Tony. He could not close the gap. The 109s were diving at high speed. *Tony won't be able to escape; they are too fast.* The smoke from Tony's aircraft had become dense and black, and some flame was now showing. The pursuing Luftwaffe fighters unleashed more rounds at the wounded Spitfire. The result was inevitable. John watched in horror as Tony's aircraft rolled onto its back and plummeted towards the sea.

As the two Luftwaffe fighters came out of their dives, John was finally able to get close enough to shoot. He fired a two-second burst into the first 109, which pulled up sharply and stalled, before spiralling down, out of control. He then fired at the second aircraft. It started to jink and dive, trying to avoid the attack, but John scored numerous hits. The German aircraft remained under control despite the damage, but the pilot must have decided he had had enough, because he put his aircraft into a steep, fast dive towards the French coast. John turned and climbed back towards the dogfights he could see going on above him. He hoped that Tony was all right. He had not seen a parachute.

As John approached, he saw Roger Barton's aircraft in a furious battle with three Me 109s. As he watched, Roger entered a steep climb that continued into a loop with a roll off the top. From that position, he went into a descending steep turn to the left, which positioned him behind one of the 109s. John saw him firing at that aircraft, but then another 109 swept in behind Roger and positioned itself on his tail. John turned towards that 109, intending to help Roger. He saw Roger's aircraft suddenly lose altitude while still turning. John knew what was happening. Letting his aircraft effectively fall sideways during a steep turn, slipping down while his wings remained nearly vertical in a steep bank attitude, was one of Roger's special escape manoeuvres. It usually fooled a pursuing pilot.

An Me 109 flying two hundred feet below Roger, which John knew would have been hidden from Roger's view, in his blind spot, collided with Roger's Spitfire as he slipped down on top of it. John saw the two aircraft appear to wrap their wings around one another, as if in an embrace. He knew the collision would have killed both pilots instantly.

Then, the dogfighting was suddenly over. It was almost as if the horrific sight of two aircraft colliding had brought the battle to an end. The remaining Luftwaffe aircraft turned east and made for their base in France. The Spitfires turned west, heading for Hornchurch. As he made his way back to base, John was in shock, having just seen his friend die.

The pilots were sombre as they gave their engagement reports to the intelligence officer. Only John had seen the actual collision that had killed Roger, but others had seen the aftermath, as tangled and twisted airframes had fallen from the sky.

There was no word on Tony Smallbone, who was last seen going down with a badly damaged aircraft, trailing smoke and flame. No-one had seen the surface impact. That had been too far below to observe. Nobody had reported any sign of a parachute, either.

Sidey came in. He had just heard the news. Two pilots missing, believed killed in action.

The intelligence officer updated him. 'It's not good, I'm afraid. Squadron Leader Smallbone is missing after being seen going down near Cliffsend, and Flying Officer Barton has been killed in a mid-air collision with a German aircraft. We have asked the Observer Corps for any sightings of Squadron Leader Smallbone. Nothing yet.'

'Thank you,' Sidey acknowledged, before turning to John, who had been standing nearby. 'You saw what happened to Roger and Tony?' he asked, using the pilots' first names, rather than rank and surname. John understood that. It was too formal in the circumstances for him to do otherwise.

'Yes, I saw both incidents. Squadron Leader Smallbone went down first, on fire. No parachute that I saw. I was watching until he was through, about, twelve thousand feet. So there was still time to get out after that if he could. Roger collided with an Me 109. It was in his blind spot, underneath him. He slipped right down on top of it during a descending steep turn. Total destruction of both aircraft. Neither pilot had any chance.'

'I'm very sorry to hear that. Let's hope that Squadron Leader Smallbone got out and is unhurt.'

'Sir, it was unusual today. The German fighters were on their own. Why weren't they covering any bombers?'

'I wondered about that myself, Flying Officer. Something similar was reported yesterday. A group of twelve fighters

135

crossed the coast near Folkestone — no bombers. Seems to be a new tactic by the Luftwaffe. Groups of fighters only. Perhaps Göring has decided he needs his fighters to focus on destroying RAF Spitfires and Hurricanes, rather than simply protecting his bombers. If he thinks we don't have many aircraft available to respond, he may see that tactic as a quicker route to air supremacy.'

'Excuse me, sir,' said the flight sergeant, who had just come in.

'Yes?'

'Observers near Cliffsend have reported a Spitfire going down on the beach, sir. Aircraft was destroyed on impact. Time and place fits Squadron Leader Smallbone's aircraft. There will be confirmation when the wreckage can be inspected. It's no longer burning, but it will have to be left for a while until it has cooled.'

'Thank you.' Sidey turned to John. 'I will speak some more about today's events at the full pilot briefing later.' With that he turned on his heel and left the room.

CHAPTER TEN

That evening, John and Sidey made their way to Bland's office for the meeting he had requested.

'Squadron Leader,' Bland said breezily as they entered his office, 'how has the day been?'

'Terrible, sir. We lost Flying Officer Barton in a mid-air collision with an enemy aircraft, and Squadron Leader Smallbone has been shot down and is reported missing.'

The smile on Bland's face vanished. 'That's terrible news. I was at headquarters this afternoon and have not caught up with the day's operational outcomes.'

There was silence in the CO's office for some seconds, and then the telephone rang.

'Bland speaking,' he said into the receiver. He listened in silence for a few moments, and then said, 'Thank you for letting me know. Please advise as soon as anything further is known.' Bland hung up and turned to Sidey. 'Good news, Squadron Leader. The Spitfire that crashed near Cliffsend has been identified as Squadron Leader Smallbone's aircraft. An inspection of the wreckage has shown there are no human remains inside. He got out.'

Sidey grinned. 'That's fantastic news, sir. The best I could hear,' he said.

'They have patrols out searching for him,' Bland said. 'Anyway, there is nothing we can do now but wait. Hopefully he's somewhere in Kent, and not in the Channel. We will hear soon enough, I'm sure.'

'Yes, sir,' Sidey acknowledged.

'Turning to tonight's meeting, I see you have brought along Flying Officer Noble?'

'Yes, sir. Flying Officer Noble is here as the capable and experienced pilot you requested I bring along.'

'I see.' Bland ignored John and went straight into his introduction concerning the meeting they were to have with some visitors to the station. 'Two operatives from Military Intelligence, Section Six to be precise, are coming in to see us shortly. I wasn't given any details regarding the purpose of their visit, but I was asked to have three of my most experienced flyers present. Squadron Leader Smallbone obviously cannot be here tonight, so it's just us.'

Sidey and John exchanged glances. *Why on earth is the Secret Service coming here?* John thought. Sidey obviously thought the same.

'Do you have any idea what it could be about, sir?' the squadron leader asked.

'No, none, but the fact they want you both at the meeting makes me suspect that it's something to do with flying operations. Whatever it is, we can't say anything about it; I've been asked for absolute confidentiality. They don't even want the fact they are coming to see us to be known by anyone else.'

'Of course,' Sidey responded. 'We will ensure confidentiality is maintained.' He glanced at John, who nodded his acknowledgement.

'Whatever it is, I'm sure it's going to be interesting,' Bland said. 'The Secret Service doesn't often come out to see an operational squadron.'

Just then the adjutant, Michael Gardiner, appeared at the door.

'Sir, just had a call. A patrol has located Squadron Leader Smallbone. They found him in a wood; his parachute was snagged on the top of a tree. He had been hanging there for a while, unable to climb down. No serious injury, though he has hurt his shoulder, and is likely to be off flying for at least a week, according to the doctor who has seen him. He will be back in the morning. He's going to spend the night at Hawkinge.'

'Excellent news, Adjutant. Thank you for letting us know,' Bland said. 'Please advise the other squadron members. We are going to be caught up here for a while.'

Gardiner left to take the news to the others. John was relieved to hear that Smallbone had been found alive and well, but he knew it would only partially alleviate the sorrow the pilots were feeling at the loss of Roger. While a pilot failing to return from a mission was not uncommon, it still hurt. You never got used to a friend not returning.

'How do you do, Wing Commander? I am Robert Adams and this is Geoffrey Stockton. We are from Military Intelligence. Our IDs,' he said, proffering identity cards to Bland.

The two men were both wearing navy-blue trench coats and carrying identical black fedora hats. *They look like twins*, John thought.

'How do you do?' Bland responded, before introducing Sidey and John. 'What can we do for you?' he went on when the introductions were complete and all the men were seated.

Robert responded. He was a man of about fifty, with a hawk-like nose and close-set eyes. 'To be clear, everything you are about to hear is subject to the Official Secrets Act. Whatever I tell you is covered by the provisions of that Act. A breach of confidentiality will have serious repercussions.'

Robert looked at Bland, Sidey, and John in turn, holding their respective gazes for a moment to emphasise how serious he was, before continuing.

'We have a source close to Luftwaffe High Command. That source has reported growing concern there, at senior level, regarding the resistance the RAF is putting up.'

That's good, thought John. *If they're concerned, it means we're doing something right.*

'This doesn't include Göring himself,' Robert went on, 'who thinks his air force is having great success in its attempts to destroy RAF capability.' He paused. 'Some of the senior staff close to Göring have raised their concerns outside the Luftwaffe. That concern has been picked up by the Reich's Ministry of Propaganda — the Ministry of Public Enlightenment and Propaganda, to give it its full name. That title tells you something about its role.'

Everyone nodded. The Ministry had an ugly reputation, particularly for its anti-Semitic jingoism.

'The Ministry's leader, Joseph Goebbels, wants to show that the Luftwaffe is dynamic and successful, to counter some of the criticisms around its performance against the RAF. To that end, he has advised Göring to organise a display day at an airfield in northern France. The event will be attended by senior officers from the Wehrmacht, and there will be a considerable number of Luftwaffe aircraft present, together with a demonstration model of a new type of fighter, said to be a step up in performance and firepower on the Me one-o-nine.'

'A new fighter, superior to the one-o-nine?' Bland asked, looking concerned.

'Yes. It's being developed by Focke-Wulf. They have allocated it a model number: one-ninety. We understand the

Luftwaffe plan to introduce it as a new frontline aircraft in four to five months.'

Sidey and John exchanged glances. A German fighter better than the Me one-o-nine? That could become a real issue for the RAF.

Robert went on. 'The whole objective of the display day is to boost morale, showing senior German military, and the German people themselves once Goebbels gets his newsreels and stories out, that the Luftwaffe is a force to be reckoned with and of which they can be proud. The message is this: *we are powerful, with capable aircraft and pilots, and we are well organised, so have confidence the RAF will be overcome.*'

'How does this affect my squadron?' Bland asked, coming straight to the point.

'We want to run a special mission and disrupt the event. We think three Spitfires, sneaking in at low level, completing one strafing run each along the lines of aircraft on display, is the way to proceed. If the new Focke-Wulf one-ninety is hit, that's a bonus, but the objective is to deliver our own message — that the RAF will not be subjugated, and the Luftwaffe is not safe anywhere. If the attack is successful, uncertainty regarding the capability of the Luftwaffe in Germany's High Command will continue. Göring will suffer increased pressure to ensure an outcome he is struggling to deliver, and Goebbels' Ministry of Propaganda will have nothing to publish.

'You may be wondering why we don't just go in with bombers, and specifically target the aerodrome on the day of the display,' Robert continued. 'Briefly, Bomber Command is not yet ready to organise a precise strike of that nature, particularly within the next few days. Also, we think a large force would cost us the element of surprise, and that would put the plan's success at risk.'

'I agree,' Sidey responded. 'A larger force would undoubtedly be seen and intercepted by the Luftwaffe before getting near the target. I like the idea of going in and out quickly, with just three Spitfires. That minimises any potential loss, and it also changes the whole attack dynamic.'

John understood the thinking behind the strategy. A surprise attack, mounting an operation where the worst-case scenario was the loss of three Spitfires — not enough for Goebbels to claim any real success, particularly if those Spitfires had been successful before being caught.

'This isn't an operation seeking mass destruction of Luftwaffe aircraft on the ground,' Robert went on. 'It's an operation aimed at embarrassing Göring and Goebbels, spoiling their plans to lift the image of the Luftwaffe with their special day. Damaging some of the parked display aircraft will achieve that. And if we get the Focke-Wulf one-ninety at the same time, so much the better. Wing Commander Bland, is your squadron able to plan and execute such a surprise attack?'

'Of course. We can put something together.'

'Geoffrey, would you come in at this point?'

Geoffrey Stockton got straight to the heart of the matter. 'I have responsibility for our agents on the ground in northern France, agents who work with local Resistance networks. When Robert's source in Berlin conveyed the information regarding the planned display day, we used my people to see if we could determine when and where the event would take place. Robert's source couldn't help with location, as the aerodrome had been given a codename. All that was known about the date was that it was soon, and somewhere in the northwest of France. Consequently, members of the Resistance have spent the last few days cycling, or driving their tractors and farm vehicles, through the French countryside, past the various aerodromes used by the Luftwaffe in that area. They were looking out for a reasonably large airfield that showed signs of preparation for an event.

'Unfortunately, they saw nothing of interest. It may have been too early to see any preparation. But then we had a stroke of luck. A contact of one of the Resistance leaders in Amiens has a contract agricultural support business. He has told them the Luftwaffe has requisitioned his services to mow some grassy areas at the Amiens-Glisy aerodrome on Thursday this week — that's the fifth. When he offered to do it a day later, because he had another commitment on the Thursday, the German officer involved insisted the mowing be done on the date he had specified. That was necessary, apparently, to avoid any clash with a lot of aircraft arriving on the sixth to participate in a display the following day. Consequently, we are reasonably confident the display day is to be held at the Amiens-Glisy aerodrome, and that it's going to take place this Saturday, the seventh of September. We will confirm the target aerodrome once the Resistance confirm they are seeing increased aircraft arrivals there on Friday. In the meantime, we want you to plan and prepare as if that aerodrome is going to be your target.'

Geoffrey paused, then began to describe the layout. 'The aerodrome has two main runway vectors. The longer vector is sixteen hundred yards in length and has a northeast-southwest axis. The other has a northwest-southeast axis and is twelve hundred yards long. They are laid out in a T shape, with the longer one forming the stalk of the T. We are hopeful the Resistance will be able to let us know, either late on Friday, or early on Saturday, which runway vector the Germans have used to line up their aircraft. Also, there are two anti-aircraft sites. One is on the north-western boundary and the other is on the north-eastern boundary of the aerodrome. They provide light ack-ack, probably forty-millimetre.'

'That's all we can give you today,' said Robert. 'Are there any questions?'

'I have nothing at present,' Bland said.

'As I understand it,' Sidey noted, 'this is an operation aimed at disrupting the Luftwaffe's claims of air superiority. This is not a mission intended to simply damage enemy aircraft and facilities in the normal course. The idea is to make it difficult for the Luftwaffe, faced with our attack, to get any benefit from the day for the purposes of its self-promotion.'

'Got it in one, Squadron Leader,' Robert said, nodding at him. 'You should know, also, that the Prime Minister is very keen that this attack take place. He thinks it will be a wonderful knock to the enemy's confidence.'

'Oh, yes, I see it in the way Squadron Leader Sidey described, too. It's a very good plan,' Bland said. It was clear to everyone in the room that he wanted to be seen to fully understand the ramifications of the proposal as well.

A few minutes later the agents from MI6 left, after giving Bland a contact number in case there should be any further matters he wished to discuss with them. When they had gone, Bland pushed back his chair and let out a long sigh.

'Bloody hell, what a task,' he said.

'We need to start planning soon, sir. Time is very tight,' Sidey said.

'Agreed, Squadron Leader. Let's have a preliminary scoping exercise now, to get some of the headline issues sorted out. I have to say, I still wonder why Bomber Command doesn't just take the aerodrome and its display aircraft out,' Bland said.

'Well, sir, the short lead-in time would make planning and initiating a mass bombing attack difficult, and it might affect our chances of success, given the heightened interception risk. So, it has to be the three Spits, in and out quickly, as we discussed,' Sidey responded.

John was not surprised that Bland had not fully understood the strategy involving the use of just three Spitfires, in a quick sneak attack. He also thought that Bland's inability to recall and use the information that had been discussed with the MI6 officers just a short time ago, was telling. It confirmed to him once again that Bland was well out of his depth in leading an operational fighter squadron in the current environment.

'Very well. Do we agree, just three aircraft?' Bland queried.

'From what was said, it seems to me as if someone from Fighter Command might have been present when this plan was discussed, probably in a dimly lit, smoky room somewhere in Whitehall,' Sidey said, with a smile. 'The use of three aircraft is optimum. One or two aircraft wouldn't make much of a statement — they could almost be claimed to be some lost aircraft stumbling across the aerodrome by accident. Five or more aircraft, and it's starting to look like a regular attacking force, which is not what is wanted, as I understood it. I think three aircraft, as suggested, is compelling for what Command is seeking here.'

'I agree, sir,' John said.

'All right,' Bland replied. 'We plan for three participating aircraft. Now, who goes? You will have a view on that, Squadron Leader,' he added, looking at Sidey.

Sidey was silent for a moment before responding, obviously weighing up all the relevant factors.

'This operation will be very demanding on the pilots. There can be no failure. We therefore need to send in our best. That is, experienced pilots who are capable of carrying out low-level ground attacks.'

'Well, who do you recommend?' Bland asked.

'I should lead, as the senior pilot in the squadron,' Sidey said. 'I would have suggested Squadron Leader Smallbone, but his shoulder injury rules him out. Flying Officer Noble meets all the criteria and has the added advantage of low-flying expertise. He oversaw many of the squadron pilots in their low-level operational training. As for a —'

'Very well. I will take the third slot,' Bland interrupted.

'With respect, sir, I was thinking of Flight Lieutenant Cowles as the third pilot. He is very experienced, and I would prefer to have your skills available as part of the planning and management of the mission, sir. I know Flight Lieutenant Cowles considers the oversight role you currently play in war ops has added value. We all think that it works very well, and it could apply here too.'

John could see that Sidey was trying to find a way for Bland to exit this situation without any embarrassment.

Bland was silent for a moment. Then he spoke. 'I know Flight Lieutenant Cowles has good war operations experience. With my medical groundings, I have not had the same opportunities, so consequently I have had a lot less exposure to those operations. In the circumstances I accept it may be better if he goes rather than me, so I will participate via my established governance arrangements. I'm pleased to hear that the squadron consider they are working well. The team of three we have discussed will execute this mission, and I will be OC for its planning.'

'Thank you, sir,' Sidey replied. 'I'm pleased we both see it the same way.'

It was a good outcome, John thought. He was perfectly happy for Bland to be Officer Commanding for planning purposes. It would be a group effort in any event, and it was not as if they would be relying on Bland in the air, during the mission.

CHAPTER ELEVEN

Early the next morning, Sidey was hunched over a large table in the corner of the operations planning room. John and Richard were with him. Spread out in front of the three pilots was a map of northwest France. Sidey had used a black pen to underline the name of a town, Amiens, and to circle nearby Glisy aerodrome, approximately five miles to the east.

'There it is, gentlemen, the site of Herr Göring's big day,' he said, stabbing his finger on the circled aerodrome. 'This is where he hopes to raise the reputation of the Luftwaffe in the minds of his senior brass. And where we will bring that to an end. We just need to get in without being intercepted. While there's some risk we could be spotted by German aircraft on our way across the Channel, I don't think it's a high risk. We will only be three aircraft, and we will be low — not above fifty feet. Any enemy aircraft on their way to or from Britain will be around twenty thousand feet, searching the sky for any RAF fighters threatening them at that level. I don't expect they will be looking down, thousands of feet, for three Spitfires at wave-top height, and the Luftwaffe certainly won't be expecting us to come into France.'

'I agree, sir,' John responded, 'but I wonder if there would be value in avoiding the standard corridor, between Britain and the Continent, used by the Luftwaffe. Why don't we adopt another route? That, together with our low altitude, would make it highly unlikely we would be seen on our way over.'

'What do you have in mind?'

'If we depart from Tangmere, our track to Glisy will be well south of the normal corridors used by German aircraft.'

'That has got merit, Flying Officer. Tangmere may suit. It will certainly improve our chance of not being sighted. But what about our range if we depart from Tangmere? Would you check that, please?'

'Already done, sir,' replied John. He and Richard had looked over maps of the area the previous night, in anticipation of this morning's discussion.

'Excellent, let's have it then,' said Sidey.

'Tangmere to Glisy is one hundred and sixty miles, so a return flight will be three hundred and twenty. That is getting near our maximum safe endurance, when we allow for increased consumption while operating at high-power in the target area, and on the way home, because we will no doubt be chased after the attack. Jerry will be upset and will want to catch us.'

'Agreed, and as I want to stay low on the way over, that will also mean an increase in the standard consumption rate,' Sidey acknowledged.

'My suggestion,' John continued, 'is that we don't go back via Tangmere on the way home. After we reach Glisy, the element of surprise is gone. After making our attack we should return to the nearest UK aerodrome, sir. That's RAF Lympne. It's closer than Tangmere by about sixty-five miles. Not much, I know, but it all counts when we are into our reserves.'

'Good work, Flying Officer. We'll depart out of Tangmere to reduce the chance of being seen by the enemy before we get to France. We can use a low power setting outbound to help preserve fuel and then return via Lympne to reduce overall distance. Let's proceed with our planning on that basis. I am conscious of the view expressed by the MI6 officers that the important issue is to successfully reach Glisy and make the attack. It isn't the *degree* of damage we inflict that's important;

it's the fact that there *is* an attack by RAF Spitfires against the Luftwaffe, on an aerodrome in Europe where they claim to control the skies, and whilst they are attempting to exhibit their power and presence to senior members of the Wehrmacht. It will ensure that the German propaganda machine does not get what it wants from the day, and contribute to continuing uncertainty about Luftwaffe success in the minds of those in the senior German ranks.'

'Agreed, sir. What Göring and Goebbels want to achieve from their day will be gone in a flash, the moment three Spitfires make it clear that the RAF is far from being subdued.'

Sidey grinned widely at that, nodding his head in affirmation.

'I've had a look at the map, and to avoid built-up areas and key infrastructure, which will be defended with anti-aircraft weapons, we should enter France at the mouth of the Somme River,' John continued. 'From the estuary, we follow the river's course inland, remaining at low level. There are marshlands for the first five miles. After that we will be over arable land with a slightly higher elevation. Glisy aerodrome is on the south side of the river, just past Amiens, forty-two miles up the river from the coast.'

Sidey and Richard leant over the map, scanning the length of the Somme River from its mouth to the aerodrome at Glisy.

'Terrain on each side of the Somme valley is relatively low at the river mouth, but begins to rise from about fourteen miles inland. The increasing elevation starts here,' said John, pointing at the map, 'near the town of Abbeville.'

'It looks to be about two hundred feet in elevation, on both sides of the river valley from there,' Richard noted as he peered at the map. 'Not much, but enough for us to tuck down into the valley.'

'Any obstructions — cableways, power lines and so on — must be identified as part of our planning. We would be in trouble if we flew into a wire strung across the river,' Sidey commented.

'Quite,' agreed Richard.

'With that in mind, I asked the adjutant to see what aerial photos we have of the Somme River valley,' John said. 'He didn't ask why I wanted them, but he knew MI6 had been here. I think he understood an important mission was on, so he ensured his enquiry was given priority at the Air Ministry. He designated his call *flash priority* despite that normally being reserved for discretionary use on behalf of Ministers of the Crown, and Air Ranks. We will get what we need delivered by motorcycle courier late this afternoon.'

'Nevertheless, in case the aerials don't give us all the information we need, I want you to spend some time with the map to see what you can identify, please, Flight Lieutenant Cowles,' Sidey noted.

'Sir,' Richard acknowledged.

'What is the brief for the actual attack?' John asked. He had his own ideas, but he knew that the proper procedure was to start by asking the view of the senior officer involved. John could add his thoughts once discussion had started.

'One strafing run each down the line of aircraft parked up on display, operating in line astern, and then home. That's all that's needed. We don't need to spend much time over the target,' Sidey replied. 'I certainly don't want anyone turning for a second run. That would increase our exposure unnecessarily. In any event, our principal objective is simply to embarrass the Luftwaffe with an attack on their special day. Three aircraft making one strafing run each can achieve what is sought, so that's all we will do.

'Glisy aerodrome is at an elevation of two hundred and eight feet,' he continued, 'and I propose that we come in at five hundred feet to commence our attack. We will begin strafing as we approach the aerodrome boundary. I think a ten per cent nose-down angle will be optimum for shooting at our parked targets. Because we will only be three hundred feet above ground level at commencement, I don't want to adopt an angle much greater than that, otherwise we'll get too low as we move along the length of the runway vector.'

'The intelligence chap with the Resistance contacts in France, Geoffrey, said he would be receiving information on Friday evening, or early Saturday morning at the latest, advising where aircraft are parked at Glisy,' John noted.

'Yes, the plan is he will pass that information to us well before we take off, and the earlier we have it, the better,' Sidey said, before going on to share his thoughts on an attack plan. 'We need to identify a final approach fix somewhere near Glisy from where we can commence a run-in for our attack. That fix will of course be dependent on where Jerry parks his aircraft, as that will dictate the direction from which we attack. As I said, I have in mind a line astern profile, and I think six hundred yards between each aircraft would be best.'

'Will line astern give defenders more time to respond than we should allow, sir?' John asked. 'If the third aircraft is following numbers one and two, at the same height and on same track, then anti-aircraft guns might be ready for him.'

'I think it has to be line astern, or near to it, given our targets are parked alongside a runway,' Sidey replied. 'If we approach in a lateral formation, I agree that we would complete our pass more quickly, but our tracks would cover an area substantially wider than that occupied by the parked target aircraft. I take your point, Flying Officer, but while maximising damage is not the priority, we need to ensure our shooting is effective.'

'I understand, sir. It concentrates our shooting and avoids lateral dispersal of our fire. But it increases the risk from ground defences for later aircraft, particularly number three. Perhaps we should consider sequencing our strafing runs from different directions? That would delay any German defenders who identify an attack pattern.'

John stepped up to an adjacent blackboard. He sketched the layout of Glisy aerodrome, showing the two runway vectors. The diagram he drew showed the T shape of the vectors on the ground.

'The cap of the "T", along here, is the vector orientated northwest-southeast. The longer of the two runway vectors forming the stalk is here, orientated northeast-southwest,' John said, pointing to what he had drawn. 'Let's assume the Luftwaffe is displaying its aircraft by parking them along the length of the stalk, here.' John made some chalk marks along the eastern side of the northeast-southwest runway.

'When we attack, number one comes in first from the northeast, and runs southwest. Number two is six hundred yards behind. One strafing run is made by each aircraft as they pass along here.' He pointed to some hatched chalk marks he had drawn to represent the parked Luftwaffe aircraft. 'At the end of their runs, numbers one and two vacate, making a right-hand turn out, staying low, and head back towards the coast. As number two completes, and enters his turn, number three comes in from the opposite direction and strafes, running southwest to northeast. To a German defender, it begins as a sudden attack from the northeast. One fast pass by two aircraft in relatively quick succession. Then, within moments, there is another attack, this time from the opposite direction, delivered by our third aircraft coming in from the southwest. There will be less risk, to number three in particular, if we sequence like this, sir, than if we all come in from one direction, in line astern.'

Sidey contemplated the diagram. 'Agreed. That makes sense tactically. It would delay recognition by defenders of the attack profile, and delay their response, momentarily at least. We only need a few seconds each to make our strafing runs, so sequencing an attack from different directions, as you suggest, Flying Officer, could provide us with some additional time before the Germans can organise their anti-aircraft fire. So, let's proceed on the basis that that's how we will make our attack. On that basis, we need to establish a final fix to the northeast of Glisy from which aircraft one and two will commence their attack runs, and to the southwest for number three. Could you identify and calculate those fixes please, Flying Officer? I propose we commence our final run-ins at a higher speed than we will have been using for our transit, by increasing our boost and rpm to the level necessary to give us three hundred indicated.'

'In and out quickly — they won't know what hit them,' Richard said with a grin.

'We should assume that when the first aircraft gets close to the aerodrome boundary, the ground defences will spot it. Nevertheless, at our speed and with the differential attack directions we just discussed, I expect we will get through before there is any substantive response from Jerry. We need to keep our time over the aerodrome as tight as we can, to limit their opportunity to respond. If they are well-trained, there might be some anti-aircraft fire by the time our third aircraft comes through, but I doubt they will be that quick. In any event, gentlemen, I will fly the number three position.

Flying Officer Noble, you will lead us in. Flight Lieutenant Cowles, you are number two.

'Can we reconvene at seventeen hundred? I want you to have the plan for the attack ready by then, please. And don't forget, we need to have thought about alternative scenarios to accommodate the Germans parking their aircraft alongside the other runway vector, or maybe alongside both. We have assumed for the purposes of this morning's discussion that it's a northeast-southwest strafing axis. It may be something else on the day. All right, that's it for now, thank you. Oh, by the way, I've told ops that you won't be flying any squadron operations until after Saturday. I just told them you were on a special planning detail.'

John smiled and looked again at the map of France spread out on the table. It was clear that some careful and complex work was going to be required.

'One last thing,' said Sidey. 'I have decided to call this mission "Operation Sneaker". It's a nod to the gentlemen from MI6, who described the operation as a quick sneak attack into occupied France.'

'It's important that we choose final fix points easily recognisable from the air,' Richard said, biting into his cheese sandwich. He and John were having a quick lunch in the officers' mess. 'I saw a number of large towns near Amiens we could use, and —'

'Not here, Richard,' John interrupted sternly. He was surprised Richard was talking so openly about their mission in the mess. Mentioning fixes over French towns would garner interest from those within earshot. Of course, John did not think anyone there would be a security risk, but nevertheless, the fewer who knew, the better. Operation Sneaker had to be treated as a top-secret mission.

'Oh, sorry, of course.' Richard was clearly embarrassed by his mistake.

They ate in silence, John feeling slightly awkward.

Back in the ops room after lunch, John and Richard were carefully looking at the map, trying to identify the towns they could use as position fixes for Operation Sneaker.

'This village, Sains-en-Amiénois, south of Glisy, looks to be a good point for Dave Sidey's final fix,' John noted. 'It's five miles from Glisy aerodrome, so ideal as the position from which he begins his run-in to attack from the southwest. It's a minute out, at three hundred. For us, coming in from the northeast, our final position fix could be the town of Cardonnette, here.' He pointed to a position on the map. 'It's also five miles out.'

Richard looked at the map, quickly identifying the towns. 'I agree,' he said. 'They're good for our run-in fixes.'

'I plan that we split tracks with Dave at Hangest-sur-Somme. It's on the river, as you will have guessed from its name, twelve miles short of Amiens. From Hangest, we fly east, to Cardonnette, and Dave turns southeast, to Sains-en-Amiénois. It will take you and I four minutes to overhead our fix. Dave will need four minutes and twenty seconds to reach his at Sains-en-Amiénois. Unless it's blowing a gale, the wind won't affect timing to any real extent over the short distances involved. We maintain our low en route cruise settings until we cross our respective fixes. The use of reduced power will have us cruising at two hundred indicated. When we turn inbound to Glisy for our strafing runs, it's power up, and three hundred indicated. Our run-in time from Cardonnette to the target is one minute. It will take each of us eight seconds to complete a strafing run along the length of the runway. The spacing of six hundred yards between me as number one, and you as number two, will add another four seconds to our time. That means, from when I cross Cardonnette, inbound to attack the aerodrome, until your strafing run as number two is complete, one minute twelve seconds will elapse.'

'Got it. One minute running in from our fix, eight seconds to strafe, and I am four seconds behind you. We strafe simultaneously for part of our runs, with you four seconds in front of me. One minute twelve seconds in total,' Richard said.

'Dave should reach Sains-en-Amiénois twenty seconds after we start our run-in from Cardonnette. At that stage we will be fifty-two seconds from finishing. As his run-in will also take one minute, he should arrive on scene eight seconds after we complete our strafing.'

'Might that be cutting things a bit fine? There would only need to be a few seconds' variation to risk a conflict between me finishing and Dave starting.'

'We do need to be careful,' John said, 'but the less time between us completing our strafing runs and Dave beginning his, the better. If we have a final check call as we start in towards target, that would signal to Dave if there was the risk of a conflict with you. He could then make any adjustments necessary to his timing.'

'What are you thinking, John?'

'As I cross Cardonnette, inbound for our attack, I call Dave. When I do that, he will know we will be clear one minute twelve seconds later. It's a last check on timing. So long as Dave doesn't start in from his fix at Sains-en-Amiénois any sooner than twenty seconds after my call, his time margin from us will be around eight seconds. My call would alert Dave to any discrepancy that had developed in the planned timing, and he could make minor adjustments to his approach to compensate if necessary.'

'Fine, I'm happy with that,' Richard said.

'All right, let's work up the detail now, so we have it ready for Dave at five. He will test our rationale, and I don't want to overlook anything,' John responded.

'Quite,' said Richard.

John was well aware of the implications of an error. Besides the personal consequences for all of them in the air, it could also result in Herren Göring and Goebbels getting what they wanted from their special day. John was determined that would not happen.

CHAPTER TWELVE

Right on time, at seventeen hundred hours, Richard and John arrived at Squadron Leader Sidey's office.

'Good evening, gentlemen. Have you got something that will give us a good chance of upsetting Herr Göring's plans for his day at Glisy?'

'I believe we have, sir, yes,' said John.

'Excellent. Come in and have a seat, and take me through it.'

'We have developed three attack scenarios. The one we use will depend on where the Germans have parked their aircraft on the day. Different positions will require different attack profiles. Our three scenarios are named A, B, and C,' John said.

Sidey chuckled.

'Each of the scenarios has the same entry point into France,' John continued, 'the mouth of the Somme. They also all use the same form of attack: a low-level strafing run. As number one, I will run in first, followed by Flight Lieutenant Cowles as number two, six hundred yards behind me. We will strafe along the principal line formed by the parked aircraft. When our runs are complete, sir, you, as number three, will come in from the opposite direction. We have calculated the time between number two finishing and number three commencing as eight seconds.'

'That's tight, but I accept it has to be if the split attack profile is to be effective. Let's have the detail on positioning and timing.'

'If the Luftwaffe aircraft are parked alongside the main runway vector, then scenario A applies. That scenario has

Flight Lieutenant Cowles and me attacking from the northeast, beginning our run-in from the town of Cardonnette. It's five miles north of Glisy aerodrome.' John indicated the town's position on the map on the desk.

'On reaching Glisy aerodrome, we strafe at a six-hundred yard spacing in line astern along the length of the main runway. At runway end, we make a turn out to the right, through forty-five degrees. The resulting heading is held for two minutes before another right turn is made to track direct to the mouth of the Somme. We don't track to the mouth immediately after the attack because we don't want to show our departure route to observers on the airfield. They will be alerting their own fighter control as to our presence and direction once we appear over Glisy, so we delay our turn to the northwest for two minutes. That will have us out of their sight as we make our track adjustment.'

Sidey nodded as John laid out the details he had worked on with Richard.

'As Flight Lieutenant Cowles completes his attack as number two, and turns out, you, sir, as number three, come in and strafe from the opposite direction. Your run-in commences from Sains-en-Amiénois, five miles southwest of Glisy.' John pointed it out on the map.

'After completing your strafing run, you hold runway heading for sixty seconds, then turn left and track to Hangest-sur-Somme, and follow the river valley from there to the mouth. You can turn earlier than us for the river mouth, sixty seconds instead of two minutes, because the terrain to the northeast of Glisy will have you out of sight sooner. That timing also ensures you don't go any further north than necessary. I'm conscious of the Luftwaffe fighter bases in that direction.'

'That's good, thank you, Flying Officer,' Sidey said. 'I have a couple of questions. First, after the attack, why do you suggest a track to the mouth of the Somme, rather than direct to Lympne?'

'Tracking to the Somme river mouth will keep us further south of the Luftwaffe fighter bases at Fressin and Beussent. They will be alerted after our attack, so we thought there would be value in staying a bit further south, at least until we reach the coast.'

'Okay, I understand that, and I agree. And my second question concerns timing. As number three, I attack from the opposite direction immediately after Flight Lieutenant Cowles has finished. Too early, and we risk a conflict. Too late, and Jerry has time to better organise a response. Timing is critical. Are we able to check that no-one is early, or late, as the attack develops?'

'Inbound, we split at Hangest-sur-Somme. As one and two, we will track direct to our final position fix for our run-in, which, as I noted, is the town of Cardonnette. You will turn to the southeast as we split, and track direct towards your run-in position fix, Sains-en-Amiénois. We will take four minutes to reach our fix. It will take you four minutes twenty to reach yours; it's slightly further. After that, we will each take the same time, one minute, to reach Glisy aerodrome from our respective fixes. So, the timing works like this: we will be over Cardonnette and commencing our run-in to strafe twenty seconds before you reach Sains-en-Amiénois. The elapsed time from our final position fix at Cardonnette, to the completion of our attacks, is one minute twelve seconds. That time is based on one minute for me and Flight Lieutenant Cowles to reach Glisy aerodrome from our fix, and twelve seconds for both of us to complete our strafing runs. That's an eight-second strafing run by each of us, with an additional four seconds allowed for the six-hundred yard spacing between our aircraft.'

Sidey nodded his understanding.

John continued, 'As I cross Cardonnette, I will call "inbound". When you hear that, you will know we will be complete one minute twelve seconds later. To ensure there is no conflict between us, you should ensure you do not cross Sains-en-Amiénois and begin your run-in any sooner than twenty seconds after my call. That will have you crossing the southern aerodrome boundary at Glisy some eight seconds after we have completed our attacks from the opposite direction and vacated the area.'

Sidey said nothing for a few moments as he processed all the tracks and timing. John stole a glance at Richard, raising his eyebrows in an unspoken question. *Have we got something wrong?* Finally, Sidey spoke.

'I agree with what you propose.'

John was pleased and grinned widely.

'We will need to ensure speeds are observed, and tracks are flown accurately, for the timing to work,' Sidey continued.

'Flying Officer Noble's calculations are correct in my view, sir,' Richard interjected, 'and the inbound call he will make ensures a last opportunity for you to consider any adjustment to your speed or track if timing is looking to be out.'

Sidey nodded. 'Now, that's scenario A. Tell me about B and C.'

'We use scenario B if the Germans park their aircraft alongside the runway vector that runs northwest-southeast. In B, we follow a similar attack sequence to A, two in from one direction, the third from the opposite, but we use different approach fixes to line us up. Timing will be the same; we will just use different commencement points.'

'And if Jerry scatters his parked aircraft around both runway vectors?'

'We use C if they park along both runways. That scenario has aircraft one and two strafing first from northeast to southwest, along the vector forming the stalk of the T, same as in A. But then three comes in from the southeast, and strafes as he flies northwest, along the cap of the T.'

'Good work, gentlemen. I'm happy with what you've planned,' Sidey said when John finished his outline of scenarios B and C. 'I agree timing is going to be a critical issue. As number three, the singleton flying a reciprocal attack track, I will need to be actively assessing my position and timing against yours. The only other question I have is, what other risks are there to the success of this operation?'

'Flying Officer Noble and I have made a list of those,' Richard responded. 'The first risk is weather; that's at Tangmere, en route, and in the target area. Preliminary forecasts for the operation don't raise any concerns. Our take-off minima at Tangmere are not high, given the generally low terrain there. In any event, we head straight out to the coast after take-off. We also decided that a low cloud base in the target area wouldn't be fatal to our plans, provided it's no less than four hundred feet. Our attack is planned lower, so the actual strafing runs would be largely unaffected. The bigger risk is visibility. If there is any precipitation, then en route navigation over France becomes difficult, particularly as we must dead-reckon our way to position to our respective run-in fixes. At present, the forecast doesn't indicate any issues.

'The second risk is interception. Because we are three aircraft, flying at low level, well south of normal routes between Britain and France, it's low risk we will be seen crossing the Channel. Once over France, we follow the Somme river valley so we will be relatively unobtrusive, flying low, with reduced engine power. Rising terrain on each side of the river will, to a degree, screen us from anyone viewing from a distance, but there is no doubt we will be seen by people close to the river, so someone is likely to report our presence if we are recognised as British aircraft. However, we will be only a few minutes from our target once we are over France. I doubt any warning could reach a Luftwaffe fighter base and result in an interception before we have the opportunity to attack Glisy aerodrome. Our problems are going to be post-attack. Everyone will know we are there. We head for home as fast as possible, but I expect we will be intercepted at some point, probably crossing the Channel as we head to Lympne. That's a risk to us, not the mission, of course.'

Sidey nodded.

'The next risk is ground defences. We know there are two gun-pits at the northern end of Glisy aerodrome. They are light ack-ack. The Germans might recover from the surprise of our attack in time to start shooting at us, but there's not much we can do about that. Also, we decided it would be unlikely any parked display aircraft would have time to get airborne and confront us. I think that covers everything?' Richard said, looking at John.

'Yes, that's it at present,' John replied. 'We did consider serviceability issues, but decided it was low risk, and at worst any en route issue is likely to affect only one of our three aircraft. The mission could proceed with two if necessary.'

Before Sidey could respond, there was a sharp knock on his office door, and Bland came in.

'Good evening, Squadron Leader. I wanted to see how planning was going for the operation over France.'

'Thank you, sir,' Sidey replied. 'The planning for Operation Sneaker is proceeding well.'

'Excellent. Take me through the mission, please.'

'We haven't completed all we intended to discuss yet, sir. I was going to seek your sign-off when complete,' Sidey responded.

'Maybe so, Squadron Leader, but you can explain the bones of the op now, I'm sure?'

John could see from Sidey's face that he was not happy, but there was little the squadron leader could do. Short of point-blank refusal, he would have to spend time going through everything again.

'Certainly, sir, a quick summary,' Sidey said.

Sidey spent the next five minutes outlining Operation Sneaker to Bland, who sat listening intently while he talked.

'You plan to use three aircraft, Squadron Leader?' Bland asked when Sidey had finished. 'Why not four? That won't make any difference to our resources and might ensure a good outcome.'

'That may be so, sir, but the intelligence chaps are happy with a three-aircraft strike, and all our planning is around that number. We think it's the right number.'

'There will be four, Squadron Leader. I have decided to join you in a fourth aircraft and participate in the mission.'

John caught Richard's eye. They both knew the CO was not up to the demands of this operation.

This is going to be awkward, John thought. *How do we tell our Commanding Officer he is not sufficiently competent for the mission?*

'Gentlemen, that's all for today. Please return at thirteen hundred hours tomorrow to finalise matters and plan transit to

Tangmere,' Sidey said, looking at John and Richard. The look on his face told John that Sidey was not happy with developments.

John and Richard saluted the senior officers before leaving.

'Wouldn't want to be Dave Sidey right now,' said John, once they were out of earshot. 'How's he going to tell the CO that he won't be taking part in the attack?'

'God knows,' Richard replied, sighing heavily.

John knew it was a situation Sidey had to get right. The stakes were too high not to.

CHAPTER THIRTEEN

'There's been a change of plan,' Sidey told John and Richard when they sat down with him the next day. They looked at him expectantly. 'Wing Commander Bland is going to be involved in Operation Sneaker.'

Damn, thought John. *Sneaker is a precision operation involving high risks. We cannot afford to have anyone with us who may not perform.*

'When the CO and I discussed the plans last evening, I took him through the mission's risk profile,' Sidey continued. 'Interception as we make our way back across the Channel is one of those risks, as we talked about yesterday.'

Neither John nor Richard said anything. John wondered where this was leading.

'I have persuaded the CO he could best contribute to the mission by providing exit cover,' Sidey continued. 'He has agreed. Wing Commander Bland will lead a section of six Spitfires to rendezvous with us as we leave France, after we have completed our attack at Glisy.'

That's a good result, thought John. Bland will be involved, but not as a member of the mission over France. Fresh aircraft joining them as they left France would be useful, as the three Spitfires would be low on ammunition after the strafing. They would also be marginal on their fuel, so would have a limited ability to dogfight if they were intercepted.

'Very good, sir. That will be useful,' John said.

'I thought you would both appreciate the new arrangement made with the CO,' Sidey said, with a knowing look at John and Richard.

A crisis had been averted, and there was no doubt in John's mind that the presence of six Spitfires, to provide cover on their return, would be valuable.

'Now, let's go over everything once more to confirm we are still happy,' Sidey said.

'Hello, chaps, what are you doing in our neck of the woods?' asked a young, but prematurely grey pilot from one of the squadrons based at RAF Tangmere, as John and Richard walked to the officers' mess. They had just been attending to the parking and refuelling of their aircraft. Sidey had gone ahead to speak to the station's adjutant, ensuring arrangements were in place for the overnight stay of three pilots from 415 Squadron.

John shrugged. 'We're using Tangmere for an operation we have tomorrow,' he replied nonchalantly. There was no way he was going to talk about a special mission, and the need to use Tangmere to reduce the chance of being observed.

'Three of you coming down from Hornchurch for an op? Must be special,' the local pilot continued.

'Not really. Just an exercise using a different base,' John lied.

That did the trick. The questions ended. Instead, the local began talking about how good the food was at the officers' mess, and how visiting pilots were always welcome.

'Hope you enjoy your time with us,' he said cheerily, as he walked away.

'You're becoming a fluent liar, John,' Richard said with a grin. 'It's worrying.'

They both laughed, but at the same time they recognised the importance of confidentiality around a mission that depended on the element of surprise.

Later that evening, after dinner, which had been as good as promised by the new friend they had encountered earlier, John and Richard chatted with Sidey. The three pilots were sitting in a quiet corner of the lounge in the officers' mess, well away from others in the room.

'Here is tomorrow's forecast,' Sidey said, putting a foolscap page down on the table between them. 'Light and variable winds. The only cloud is some high cirrus over northern France.'

'That's good,' John said. 'Virtually no wind means little effect on our ground speed or track, so we will have no excuse for getting our timing wrong or getting lost.'

'Intelligence expects to receive the report from the French Resistance on aircraft parked at Glisy by o-nine-hundred hours tomorrow, our time. The latest weather at the target area will also be confirmed then,' Sidey said. 'Once I have that information, we will meet to confirm the attack scenario to be used — A, B, or C — and go over the procedures and timings.

'I want to make our attack at twelve-thirty hours, their time; they are an hour ahead of us. I would be delighted to upset the lunch the officers might be having around then, both pilots and the visiting senior brass. That dictates we should be airborne at ten-forty-five hours. Happy with that, gentlemen?'

Both John and Richard were satisfied and had no questions.

'All right, we will meet in the ops room tomorrow morning at ten-hundred hours, ready to go.'

The next morning, John and Richard made their way to the ops room to meet Sidey. John appeared relaxed, but that belied a growing apprehension, which was normal in the circumstances. *Any pilot who does not experience some degree of anxiety before a mission would not be human*, he thought. But there was also an advantage: the adrenalin would help him fly and operate with an increased precision as he focused on his tasks.

'I've had the call from intelligence,' Sidey said once they were all seated in the ops room. 'The Resistance has reported that the Luftwaffe aircraft have all been parked in a line alongside the eastern side of the runway vector orientated northeast-southwest. That's the stalk of the T we sketched for our planning.'

'Scenario A then, sir,' John said.

'Yes, with a slight twist.'

John raised an eyebrow in question.

'Let me explain,' Sidey continued. 'The Resistance observer reported that the parked aircraft were lined up on the eastern side of the runway. She counted forty-five aircraft, mostly single-engine but some twin-engine as well. She also said there was a large marquee on the western side of the vector, at the southern end. Probably the social hub for attendees. One aircraft is parked on that side, by itself, about three hundred yards from the marquee. It's described as single-engine. A low picket fence has been erected around it, so it's clearly a special display. I think it's the new fighter, the Focke-Wulf. We should target that particular machine. When you strafe the aircraft lined up on the eastern side of the runway, I want you to adjust your line at an appropriate point, and shoot at the Focke-Wulf on the western side.'

'It will only involve a minor heading adjustment, so that should be no problem, sir. I agree, if it's Germany's new fighter, hitting it would send a strong message to Göring.'

'All right, that's agreed. You two do it. Adjust your strafing line as required so that the new aircraft is also attacked. By the way, given the accuracy and tight timing involved, I have decided that we should add one more layer to ensure any conflict between number two finishing his strafing and me starting is minimised. As you complete, Flight Lieutenant Cowles, I want you to call that. It will give me a last assurance that you are not in the way.'

'Yes, sir. I will call "complete" as I enter my turn out,' Richard replied.

Sidey nodded. 'The Resistance has also reported that the weather at Glisy is fine and sunny, with no wind, as we expected.'

Great, thought John. *What a disaster it would have been if bad weather had prevented the op.*

'They also reported that the two anti-aircraft gun-pits on the northern side of the northwest-southeast runway vector are operational. We already knew this; however, interestingly, they say neither battery was manned.

'I don't think we should assume that the anti-aircraft guns at the aerodrome are not crewed at all. It's possible no-one there feels the need to have them manned early in the morning, but whatever the reason, I'm sure there will be crews close to the pits, ready to move to action stations if required.'

'It's surprising, sir, that the AA is not manned and ready at all times, given there's a war on and this is an operational aerodrome,' Richard commented.

'I agree, Flight Lieutenant, but Herr Göring may be inadvertently helping us here. As you know, the main driver for the day at Glisy aerodrome is Göring's desire to reinforce Luftwaffe capability and power with the senior Wehrmacht officers present. So, he puts on an impressive line-up of aircraft to be inspected, introduces the new Focke-Wulf, has his fighter pilots present to brief and answer questions, and, importantly for us, does it in north-western France to show he has confidence the skies are his. The RAF hasn't been seen in the Amiens area since the Expeditionary Force was there before Dunkirk, so he believes his own rhetoric; the RAF is mortally wounded and not a threat in the air over France. If the gun-pits are unmanned as a consequence of the same arrogance regarding the abilities of the RAF, then that's their problem and our advantage.'

John and Richard both smiled their agreement.

'I think that's about as far as we can take it now,' Sidey concluded, 'although I have a couple of housekeeping matters. Call signs will be Sneaker one, two, and three. Any position report we make should not name the actual town we are referring to. I don't want any call picked up by the Germans revealing where we are or where we are going. When we split our tracks at Hangest-sur-Somme, we will refer to Hangest as "Initials". Our respective fixes at Cardonnette and Sains-en-Amiénois are simply to be referred to as "Finals". On our way back, any report as to position should be your bearing and distance from the Somme River mouth, which we shall code as "Rendezvous". Incidentally, that is where Wing Commander Bland and his flight will be waiting for us. Is there anything else we need to cover?'

'Nothing from me, sir,' Richard responded.

'Nor me,' said John.

'Very well, let's go down to dispersal and check over our machines. I want us wheels-up at ten-forty-five hours.'

'Tangmere, this is Spitfire Echo Bravo Delta. Taxiing for take-off as a flight of three,' Sidey called as he led the Spitfires towards the end of the runway.

'Roger, Spitfire Echo Bravo Delta, conditions are calm and you are cleared to use runway zero seven when ready. Do you have a call-sign allocated, and what's your destination?'

'Roger, cleared to take off from zero seven when ready. We will be taking vectors airborne and have no call-sign allocated as yet.'

Sidey could have said the call-sign was Sneaker, but they had agreed to say as little as possible about the mission to anyone. That included not confirming a call-sign, or naming a destination, in response to a controller's query. John appreciated that such an approach may raise suspicion, but that could not be avoided.

Five minutes later the three Spitfires were airborne from Tangmere. They had taken off to the east, and were soon over the sea, flying low towards the French coast, which was presently invisible to them at their height of fifty feet. At that level, they would have to be a lot closer to France before they would see its coastline, John knew. He was leading, as sneaker one. Fifty yards behind him, and two to three wingspans out to his right, Richard was sneaker two. Sidey's aircraft was following, as sneaker three.

'Land in sight,' John called, as they closed on the French coast. It was about ten miles ahead, he estimated, as he scanned anxiously. *Where is the Somme estuary? Ah, there it is, a couple of miles north. I wasn't far out.* He was about to call a heading change to the left, when he saw numerous buildings on the southern shore. *That's not right. There's nothing like that on the south side of the Somme estuary shown on the map.* John felt a rising panic.

Stop, think, analyse, he told himself. *We can't be far off track over such a relatively short distance, holding a steady compass heading in low wind conditions.* He had seen from the sea's surface that there was little wind, as the forecast had predicted when they had flown across from Tangmere. *Yes, that estuary to the left, north of track, is definitely too small. It's not the mouth of the Somme.* John scanned around and saw a larger estuary to the south. *That's it — must be*. He glanced quickly at the small map on his knee. *Yes, of course, the first area I saw will be the Bay of Authie, and the town to its south, Fort-Mahon-Plage. That's the Somme to the right, about four miles. Great.*

A slight adjustment of track soon had the three Spitfires heading directly towards the Somme river estuary. A few minutes later they were over the estuary, cruising at two hundred miles per hour indicated, the relatively low airspeed resulting from the reduced power setting they had adopted for this stage of the mission. It would be power up and high speed as they initiated their low-level attack on Glisy aerodrome. John was happy that after all the planning and preparation, the operation was now about to begin.

Moments later, they were over the river itself, following its shallow valley towards Amiens, approximately forty miles ahead. They were no more than fifty or sixty feet above the terrain. As they passed the town of Abbeville, the elevation on each side of the river started to increase. John remained as low as he safely could. He was pleased they had closely studied the map and aerial photographs of the area as part of their preparation. *You wouldn't see a wire stretched low across the valley, and it would be catastrophic if one of us hit something like that,* he thought. Soon the small town of Hangest-sur-Somme loomed up.

'Initials,' John called as they flew over the town. Sidey took his cue and turned to the right, heading southeast towards his run-in fix, the town of Sains-en-Amiénois. John and Richard eased their aircraft up out of the river valley, tracking towards the town of Cardonnette. Four minutes later, they were over the town. They were so low that John could see upturned faces looking up to see what was flying so close overhead. John rolled his Spitfire into a turn to the south. He was now heading directly towards the target. 'Finals inbound,' he called, at the same time increasing engine power so that his indicated airspeed moved up to three hundred miles per hour.

CHAPTER FOURTEEN

John's Merlin engine sang as his Spitfire hurtled towards the aerodrome and the Luftwaffe aircraft parked there. Richard, who had dropped back to a position six hundred yards behind John, followed. *We will join Herr Göring's display in seconds, and Jerry is going to be surprised when we suddenly appear overhead,* John thought. His earlier pre-mission nerves had gone, replaced by cold and focused concentration.

Looking ahead, John could see the Luftwaffe aircraft parked on the eastern side of the aerodrome's main runway vector. There was a single aircraft parked on the opposite side — the new fighter, the Focke-Wulf 190, he decided. He glanced at his air speed indicator. Three hundred miles per hour. The aircraft's altimeter was showing five hundred feet above sea level. That was three hundred feet above the airfield's elevation. *On speed, at commencement height — now, slight pitch down and ... shoot!* The Spitfire screamed in low, a stream of fire from the eight machine guns tracking along the ground towards the line of aircraft.

John could see the rounds impacting the targets from his opening salvo. One of the Luftwaffe aircraft exploded. He banked slightly to the right, so his Spitfire was now pointing towards the other side of the runway, where the Focke-Wulf was proudly parked. He carefully positioned his gunsight just short of it, and fired a long burst. His fire initially threw up the ground in front of the Focke-Wulf, but then moved on to hit the aircraft itself as John "walked" his salvo towards it, as he had been taught to do when strafing. The German aircraft bucked and jumped on its wheels as it was hit, such was the force of the stream of fire from John's guns.

Then John was past the Focke-Wulf, and he turned his attention to the remaining aircraft lined up on the eastern side of the runway. He saw numerous figures running from the marquee at the far end of the aerodrome. *Run, you blighters, run*, he thought, but he did not direct his fire at them. While he was happy to shoot at enemy aircraft, he would not target the people on the open ground below.

His strafing had hit numerous aircraft, with several bursting into flames. He pulled his aircraft into a steep right-hand turn and headed west, staying low as he raced in the direction of the French coast. *That worked well*, he thought to himself, at the same time wondering how Richard, who would be six hundred yards behind him, was doing. Just then he heard Richard's call, a call he knew Sidey would be keen to hear.

'Sneaker two is complete.'

So far, so good, thought John. Sidey should now be beginning his strafing from the opposite direction. They had a margin of about ten seconds between Richard finishing and Sidey starting. Then he heard Sidey's radio call, confirming his strafing run was also complete. *Mission accomplished*, thought John. *Time to head for home.*

John and Richard were low over the French countryside, heading for the mouth of the Somme. They knew they would be about two miles ahead of Sidey. They were watchful. The Germans would be very unhappy about the attack. Avenging the damage done to aircraft and Luftwaffe pride would be their priority. As they passed south of Pont-Remy, easily identifiable by its historic stone bridge across the river, John saw a group of eight aircraft approaching from the northwest. They were Me 109s.

'Bandits, eight of them, three o'clock,' he called.

'Roger. Got them,' said Richard.

'You hear that, sneaker three?' John called.

'Affirmative,' was the short response from Sidey.

'They've spotted us,' John called to Richard when he saw the one-o-nines begin to peel off, one after the other, and dive towards them. 'Let's hope we can reach the Channel before they catch us.' He was conscious of the fact Bland was leading a flight that was waiting for them just off the French coast. *They will relieve three low-fuel and virtually out-of-ammo Spitfires*, he thought, as he crouched low in his cockpit seat and leant forward, willing his aircraft to go faster to escape the imminent danger.

It was not to be. While the one-o-nines had not yet got close enough to shoot, as John and Richard passed abeam of Abbeville, six more Luftwaffe fighters appeared. They came from the south, and neither John nor Richard, who had both been busy watching the fighters approaching from their north, had seen them coming. Sidey, several miles behind, called a warning.

'Six more one-o-nines, coming down on you from your seven o'clock!' he shouted.

John quickly looked back over his left shoulder. He saw them immediately. They were only about two thousand yards away and would soon be close enough to begin shooting.

Moments later, John felt his aircraft shudder as fire from the lead Me 109 riddled his rear fuselage. He pulled up steeply, banking left in the direction of the Luftwaffe aircraft shooting at him. Richard followed. Their turn had the effect of rapidly closing the distance between them and the attacking aircraft, which flew right past them at high speed. Now the Germans had to turn before they could take another shot at the Spitfires making for the Channel and relative safety.

As John watched, the attacking fighters split into two groups. Four turned left, pulling hard into a steep turn so they could launch another attack. The other two turned right, but did not come around far enough to get behind the two fleeing Spitfires. Instead, they rolled out of their turn halfway through it and headed east. *Going after Dave*, John decided. He saw also that the original fighters he had sighted, eight of them, had now closed up with them and were about to join the fray. Fourteen versus three. *Not great odds*, John thought, at the same time wondering how much ammunition he had left. Perhaps a third?

A line of tracer flashed over his cockpit, missing by no more than a few feet. John rolled his aircraft steeply to the left, but did not stop the roll when his wings were vertical. Instead, he continued the roll through an inverted position, until his wings were again vertical. Then he pulled hard into a right-hand turn. To a following aircraft, what appeared to be an escape manoeuvre to the left suddenly became a steep turn to the right. Unfortunately for John, the Luftwaffe pilot, still on his tail, was not fooled. Another extended burst of fire from the Me 109 hit John's aircraft, this time raking the nose area. *Damn*, John thought, *I need to shake him*. He pulled his Spitfire up into a steep climb, planning to go into a loop, with a roll off the top into a tight spiralling dive. That had worked well before in several of John's previous encounters with the enemy.

As he became vertical, there was a loud bang. Parts of the cowling flew off, and the engine stopped in an instant. '*Christ!*' John shouted in shock. He pushed the nose of his aircraft down, to avoid a stall. Jerry must have hit something vital, he decided. Initially at fourteen hundred feet when shot, he was now too low to bale out safely. John scanned the ground in front of him as he fought to stabilise his damaged machine. He spotted a field to the left where some sheep were grazing. He did not like the look of the surface condition, but there was no time to get the landing gear down anyway. The field was coming up fast. *It's a bit short, but I'm not going to travel far along it on my belly.*

Coming in low over the field's perimeter hedge, John started to flare the aircraft, hoping to hold off surface contact for as long as he could. With no engine noise, he had become a silent glider. *The sheep haven't heard me coming — I'll hit them.* As his Spitfire sank onto the ground, it hit an undulating area which had been obscured by the lush grass covering the field. The aircraft skipped and bounced across the uneven surface. The thumping noise of the aircraft bouncing along alerted the grazing sheep, which scattered at the strange and sudden sound. John worked his control stick, trying to limit the height of each bounce and skip, and to soften the ground impacts that followed each one. He pushed his rudder pedals hard, to keep the aircraft as straight as he could. There was a loud bang from the right wing. John looked across, just in time to see the sheep the aircraft had hit flying through the air. Then, suddenly, the Spitfire came to a stop.

John pulled back the cockpit canopy and was out within seconds. There was some smoke from the engine area, and while there was no flame that John could see, he was aware you could never be sure what was happening under the cowls. He had seen Spitfires crash-land back at the station. Aircraft showing nothing more than a few wisps of smoke had suddenly exploded into a conflagration with little warning, so he did not waste any time getting out. As he stood next to his crashed Spitfire, his attention was drawn by the sound of nearby aircraft. About a mile west, he saw Me 109s dogfighting at relatively low altitude, no more than two thousand feet. *Bland and the team are there*, he realised. He could see six Spitfires engaging with the Germans, and he was pleased they had not waited to rendezvous at the Somme mouth. Instead, they had come into France by some miles. Jerry had come after, and caught, the Spitfires that had attacked Glisy, sooner than expected. Perhaps they'd been airborne nearby when they had been alerted about Spitfires attacking Glisy, he thought.

John knew he should find somewhere to hide. The fact that one of the attacking Spitfires had been shot down and had crash-landed would have been reported. Soldiers would soon be out looking for him. Then he had an idea. *They will only search for someone who has escaped the landing and is thought to be hiding in the area. Jerry needs to think I did not escape.*

John ran back along the field, to where the sheep he had struck during his landing lay. He dragged it back to the wreckage. Grunting with the exertion, he wrestled the dead animal up onto the Spitfire's wing, then hefted it into the cockpit. Reaching in, he adjusted the sheep's body so that it was lying back on the cockpit seat. John put the safety harness around it, pulled his leather flying helmet onto its head, and strapped on his goggles. *Not perfect, but it might fool someone taking a cursory look at burnt remains*, he decided.

A thick black column of smoke rose from the Spitfire John had set alight. The smoke had climbed up into the sky, clearly signalling the aircraft's whereabouts to any searchers. Just over a mile away, peering from behind a screen of trees at the edge of a forest, John watched as a German patrol arrived at the crash site. Six soldiers were carefully approaching his burning aircraft, fanning out in a line, rifles at the ready. John understood their caution. For all they knew he could be lying in wait, service pistol in hand, ready to shoot at them when they got close. The line of soldiers crept forward, watchful. Thirty yards short of the burning wreckage, the patrol stopped. Then one of the soldiers ran quickly towards the nose of the aircraft, bent low as he moved forward. The flames were subsiding now, and there was less smoke. The soldier peered around the nose of the aircraft, then stood up, no longer bending and scurrying. *He knows I'm not there, waiting for him with my gun*, John thought. *Now, let's hope my scheme works.*

After a few minutes the man in charge of the patrol moved up towards the cockpit. John knew he would not be able to get too close, because of the heat. *With any luck he will decide I died in the crash and subsequent fire*, thought John.

Moments later, John saw that his subterfuge had worked. The soldiers were leaving. If someone came and looked more closely, they might see what he had done, but that may not be for some days, if ever. He was pleased, but knew he now had to move deeper into the woods. He walked slowly and carefully to keep noise to a minimum, and to avoid tripping. A sprained ankle, or worse, would not do. His mind raced. He had to find somewhere to shelter before it got dark. He could not wander through the forest at night — that would be asking for trouble. And food — where would he find something to eat? But the bigger issue, John knew, was how the hell would he get out of France?

After walking for nearly thirty minutes, John sensed he was nearing the edge of the forest. The trees were beginning to thin, with more light getting in through the canopy. Sure enough, he soon reached the edge of the treeline. He found himself on a low hill, looking down into a wide green valley. There was a farmhouse below, with washing hanging on a line.

As he watched from the cover of the trees, John saw a young woman emerge from the front door. She was carrying a bucket as she strode purposefully around the end of the building and out of sight. A moment later she reappeared. This time she was walking backwards, reaching into her bucket and scattering seed on the ground for the chickens following her. John thought he might be able to get some eggs. He would slip in after dark to see if he could find any.

It had been dark for over an hour when John left his hiding place on the edge of the forest and cautiously made his way across the open pasture towards the farmhouse. Sure enough, as he crept around the side of the house, there was a large chicken coop. He glanced towards the house. A light was on in one room, but the rest of the building was in darkness. He headed towards the coop, hoping his arrival would not cause the hens to start squawking. Unlatching the door, he edged in, feeling under the shelf where the birds perched. Yes, two eggs there. He picked them up, but must have moved too quickly, as one of the hens jumped and flapped its wings vigorously. It sounded loud, but, John reasoned, not so loud it would be heard inside. He moved slowly back towards the coop's door, careful not to knock into something and make a noise. He reached the door without incident. Moving the latch to its open position, he quietly pushed the door and stepped through.

The metallic click was unmistakable. It was a pistol being cocked. Its cold muzzle was pressed into the nape of his neck.

'On your knees, hands on your head, or you die now,' a voice said quietly.

CHAPTER FIFTEEN

John sank to his knees, hands on top of his head. He realised the person holding the gun, while not sounding German, certainly knew what they were doing.

'Who are you?' he was asked.

'RAF pilot. Forced down in a field on the other side of the woods. My aircraft burnt, but I got out. I was hungry and came here looking for food.'

The pistol was removed from John's neck and he turned around slowly.

'You are French?' he asked. It was the woman he had seen feeding the hens earlier.

'Yes. I am Celine.'

'Hello, Celine, I'm John. I thought you might be German when I felt your gun, and thought I was at risk of being shot.'

'*Monsieur*, you *were* at risk of being shot. I would have pulled the trigger if you had not complied or if I had not believed you were who you said you were.'

'Well, I am very pleased you didn't shoot me. Thank you. But how did you decide I was telling the truth, that I am RAF?'

'I had heard about a crashed Spitfire. And you are wearing flying kit and sound English, so I decided you are who you say you are. Come inside, I will give you something to eat.'

John was hungry. He wolfed down the bread and honey Celine gave him. He had not eaten since breakfast, just before he and his fellow pilots had departed Tangmere on Operation Sneaker.

'Thank you,' he said with a grateful smile. 'Where did you get the Luger? Not the usual weapon found in a French farmhouse, I think.'

'I took it from the body of a German officer some weeks ago.'

'Oh?'

'A trap was arranged by the underground movement. The officer had thought he was going to have a night of love with a young French woman, but I am a member of the Resistance.'

John stared at Celine. She was obviously capable of looking after herself.

'We must hide you while we plan how to get you out of here. The Germans will be searching for you. Your aeroplane crashed nearby, so they will scour this area.'

'They think I died in the crash and the fire which destroyed my aircraft,' John replied.

'Why do they think that?' Celine asked, looking surprised.

'I put a dead sheep into the cockpit. They will see that and think it's me, I hope.'

'Ah, a trick. You may well have deceived them. We shall see in the morning. If there is a lot of activity around here tomorrow, with trucks and troops out on the roads, we will know you have not fooled them, *monsieur*. You must go to my hayloft in the meantime. I will talk to my friends in the movement about how you might escape from France. Come with me.'

Celine led John back outside. About eighty yards beyond the chicken coop, he could just make out a small building in the moonlight.

'That is my barn,' Celine said. 'Climb up to the loft and sleep at the far end. You should be safe there. I will bring you some food in the morning, before I go to the village to see those who may be able to help.'

'Thank you,' John replied.

After Celine had left, John broke down a small bale of hay to spread on the timber flooring. *That will be slightly more comfortable*, he thought, grateful the night was not cold.

John dozed fitfully most of the night, but was fully awakened by Celine clambering noisily up the ladder. He glanced at his watch. Eight o'clock. It was later than he had expected.

'Quick, the Germans are coming.'

John followed her back down the ladder, and stood next to her as she cautiously peered out the door.

'My friend Jacques saw a German patrol at your crashed aircraft very early this morning. They must have come back to check the wreckage again. I think they have found that you did not die yesterday, and now they search for you,' Celine said with a grimace. 'The Germans will know you cannot have got too far from the crash site. There are soldiers everywhere. They must really want you. What did you do?'

'I was one of three Spitfires that attacked Glisy aerodrome,' John answered.

'Ah, that was you? I heard about it. They are very angry and will be pleased to find you, so now I understand the effort they make. I will take you to the village. There are people there who can help you. It's not too far from here, but we will have to walk, and not on the roads. The Germans will be patrolling, and if we meet them, you will be caught. You have no papers, and I presume you also have no French?'

'Only some basic schoolboy French, but not enough to fool anyone if we meet a German squad looking for a British pilot.'

'Then we will travel cross-country, but it will take time. Being in the middle of a field is no good. It will be necessary to use hedgerows, woods, and treelines. It will be slow, and we must be very careful.'

'Should we wait for nightfall, so we are less likely to be seen as we move?'

'No. I think they will be here soon, searching for you. If we find there is no cover available at some point on our journey, we can wait until it gets dark, but for now, we must leave here. We will be safer hiding in the countryside.'

John nodded. Celine was more familiar with the area and with the way in which the Germans would conduct their search.

'Lead on,' he whispered.

Celine took him back towards the forest through which he had first approached her small farm.

'We get into the trees,' she said, 'and then we move south, just inside the treeline so we are not easily seen.'

They moved quickly and quietly through the forest. After twenty minutes, they reached its southern extremity. Celine knelt down next to a large tree and looked across the open fields that stretched in front of them.

'See that small hill there?' she said, pointing to a low peak some five miles away.

John nodded. 'Yes.'

'The village we must reach is in the valley on the other side.'

'Not much cover,' John said, looking across the open fields.

'We will follow the river down there,' Celine said, pointing towards what looked to John to be a small stream rather than a river. 'The willow trees that grow along its banks will give us some protection. Come.'

They ran down to the river, which was probably no more than ten yards wide. As they reached it, John could see it was not very deep either. He doubted the water would come much above his knees.

'We will stay on this side,' Celine instructed, 'and move from tree to tree. We will pause beside each tree and look to ensure the adjacent fields remain empty before moving again. The trees on the riverbank will help us, but they are not as good as the forest, so we must be more cautious.'

She bent low, squeezed through some bushes, and ran to the near bank of the river. John followed. Within moments they were both beside an old willow tree that leant precariously out over the water.

'Keep your eyes open,' Celine said as they began moving along the bank. The trees were not close together, as they had been in the forest, nor was there much undergrowth to help protect them from anyone watching. John was scanning in all directions as he moved.

'Celine,' John called urgently after they had been moving along the riverbank for about fifteen minutes. She was ten yards ahead of him. 'Germans, over there.' He pointed to an adjacent field, on the other side of the river. A line of soldiers was walking across the grass towards them. Ten men, he counted, each carrying what looked like a submachine gun.

'Get down,' Celine ordered. They both dropped to the ground.

'I don't think they have seen us,' Celine said. 'The trees on the far bank interrupt their view. Anyway, they would show more urgency if they knew we were here. We will stay low and quiet, behind the trees here. I don't expect they will cross the river. The Germans don't like to get their feet wet, unless absolutely necessary.'

John pressed his body hard against the muddy ground on which he lay. As the soldiers got closer, John could hear them calling to each other as they walked. He had no idea what was being said, but it sounded like casual chatter between colleagues. There was even occasional laughter as someone said something amusing. Then the voices began to fade as the soldiers moved past, continuing across the large field adjacent to the river, but heading in the opposite direction to the way Celine and John were going. It looked as if the Germans were heading to the forest. *Lucky timing*, John thought. *We could have met them as we emerged from the trees.*

'Time to go,' Celine said, ten minutes after the soldiers had passed. John had been impressed by her patience. She seemed happy to lie low and give the Germans plenty of time to move on, before attempting to continue. He looked back towards the forest. The patrol they had managed to avoid was approaching the edge of it and was now spread out in a line. Then, the soldiers all stepped forward at the same time and disappeared into the trees. John got up and once again began following Celine slowly along the riverbank.

An hour and a half later, the small hill Celine had pointed out earlier was just ahead. The river curved off to the left of the hill and entered a valley. They continued to follow the river's course. As they made their way through the valley, John could see a low stone bridge ahead. Two trucks, both carrying soldiers in the open-backed vehicles, crossed the bridge as he watched.

'They are everywhere today,' Celine muttered. 'They want you. It will make it harder for us.'

They continued carefully, and soon they were under the bridge itself. It was low, so they had to crouch.

'Wait here,' said Celine. 'It is too dangerous for you to go up onto the road now. Tonight will be safer. Get comfortable. I will go into the town and come back when it is dark.'

With that she scrambled up the bank to the road and left. John sat down on the hard ground beneath the bridge. He knew it would be an uncomfortable wait, but he had no choice. German soldiers knew he was somewhere in the area, and they were looking for him. John could hear people walking over the bridge, talking as they moved, just above his head. He recognised the language: French. *Just locals, thank goodness, not Germans.* John passed the time watching the local wildlife. There were ducks on the water, paddling around in circles. Looking for food, he guessed. There were some large birds nearby, too, crows by the look of them, busily scavenging through the undergrowth. Heavy vehicles rumbled across the bridge. Probably trucks — farmers or military lorries, he wondered? John recognised that he was nervous.

Not long after dusk, John heard movement as someone came down from the roadway. It was Celine.

'Come now, John. It is dark enough and no-one is about, because of the curfew. We must not be seen, otherwise we will be stopped and probably arrested for breaking curfew, even if they do not know who you are.'

John stood up, his legs stiff after sitting in his cramped position for so long. Celine climbed slowly back up the bank to the road, and peered left and right, before softly calling to John to follow. They moved quickly along the wide grass verge next to the roadway, constantly looking around. The main street of the town was directly in front of them, and John could see right along its length. It was deserted, and the shop windows were unlit. The only light came from the windows above some of the shops. Probably accommodation for the shopkeepers, John decided. A set of headlights suddenly appeared at the far end of the main street. It was a truck, coming towards them.

'Germans,' Celine hissed. 'Quick, in there.' She gesticulated towards an alleyway. John saw there was a stack of what looked like forty-four-gallon drums, with their tops cut off, in the alley. They ducked in behind them, just in time. The truck was carrying a squad of soldiers, and a light was being shone from the driving cab. Its beam roamed over all the doors and recesses of the buildings in the street as the vehicle travelled slowly along the road. A beam of light pierced the blanket of darkness covering the alley in which they were hiding. Celine and John pressed themselves closer to the wall behind the drums. The light moved on, and darkness fell once more as the truck continued past.

'Quickly,' Celine said as she stood up. She paused at the end of the alley and looked around the corner.

'It is clear,' she called back to John.

'Where are we going?' John asked as he came up alongside her.

'To my friend, Albert, not much further down the street. He has arrangements for you. An aeroplane is coming tonight to pick you up.'

'Oh? That's wonderful, but a surprise. How was he able to do that, and so quickly?'

'Albert is head of the Resistance in northwest France. Your superiors in England are very keen to get you out. Extracting you from France, before the Germans find you, seems especially important to them, so it is being done tonight. Now come.'

Celine ran along the main street before turning into a narrow lane. John was close behind her. At the end of the lane was a small cottage. This was Albert's home, Celine told him, and he would wait there until one o'clock in the morning. Then they would make their way to a secret landing area for tonight's operation, and meet the aircraft sent for John.

When John entered the cottage, he was introduced to Albert by Celine. John was surprised. He had expected Albert, the local Resistance leader, to be a young man, fit and agile. But he was an old man, about seventy, John thought, and he certainly did not look fit, nor agile. But John quickly learnt he should not make judgements about capability based on looks. Albert was sharp-minded and completely in control of arrangements, as their discussion soon showed.

'Welcome to my home, *monsieur*. Tonight, we have a Lysander coming for you. He will be here at two o'clock. There is a partial moon, which will help the pilot make his landing. The wind is southwest, ten to fifteen miles per hour, which is good, because the length of the strip we are going to use is short, and a headwind will help. Also, a south-westerly blows away from the town, making it less likely the aircraft will be heard by anyone there.'

'Thank you, Albert. I appreciate you arranging this for me.'

'It is not a problem to help a pilot of the Royal Air Force, especially one who helped destroy German aircraft at Glisy. Your success is their agony. It is very good. Now, we will leave for the landing area at one-twenty, travelling by bicycle. It is easier to be discreet on a bicycle. A vehicle would attract attention. When we get to the landing site, my men will use torches to guide the Lysander to a landing. You must wait with me. The aircraft will quickly come to a stop when it touches down, then it will turn around and come back towards us. Because the landing area is not long, it needs to start its take-off run from where we will be waiting, at the beginning of the strip.'

John nodded his understanding.

'The pilot wants to be on the ground for seconds only,' Albert continued. 'You will approach the aircraft from the rear, not its front. There is a ladder attached to the left-hand side of the fuselage. That is there so people can quickly get up and into the rear cockpit area, even if the plane is moving. Do you have any questions?'

'No, that's all clear, thank you.'

'*Très bien*. Until later then, my friend. There is some bread in the kitchen, and maybe some jam. Have what you want.'

As John chewed the jam sandwich he had made himself, and sipped the cup of tea Celine had put in front of him, he thought about what was to come. He found himself thinking about the skill and daring of the pilots who flew into Occupied France under cover of darkness, and landed on improvised landing areas guided only by a few people on the ground with handheld torches. John knew that Lysanders had advanced systems to enable a pilot to slow it for landing. It had leading-edge slats on its wings to enhance low-speed lift, and large slotted flaps. Even so, bringing an aircraft in at night to an unknown and unlit field was impressive flying. John had a lot of respect for anyone who could do that. He knew also that there had been some talk of a full Special Duties Lysander squadron being formed if the current covert operation trials being undertaken with the aircraft showed promise. A dedicated service to assist the intelligence services and their operatives. *Well, if I'm the beneficiary tonight of one of their trial flights, I'm happy about that*, he thought.

'It's nearly one-twenty. We will go. It will take us thirty minutes if we have no problems,' said Albert as he led Celine and John outside. Three bikes were there for them to use. Albert saw John looking around and must have guessed what he was thinking.

'The others will make their own way to the landing site,' he said. 'We will ride on the bike path. Follow me.'

John took a bicycle. It was slightly small for him, but sufficient. Albert was already twenty yards down the track, pedalling fast. Celine and John followed.

CHAPTER SIXTEEN

As they rode together, out of the village and then through the moonlit countryside, John saw no-one else. All was quiet. After about twenty-five minutes, Albert turned down a path that disappeared into a stand of oak trees. After making their way through the trees they emerged into a large, open area.

'This is where he will land,' Albert said to John, as he dismounted from his bike. 'It's a hay field, just cut, so perfect for us tonight.'

'Set up,' Albert called into the night and John saw movement — men he had not noticed before disappeared back into the darkness to prepare for the arrival of a British aircraft coming into Occupied France.

'Come with me,' Albert instructed. John leant his bicycle against a tree and fell into step behind Albert and Celine, as they walked towards the end of the field.

Ten minutes later, John detected the faint sound of an approaching aircraft. It was still some distance away, and he could tell that its engine must have been throttled right back to near idle. Albert's assistants had heard it too, as they now flicked on their torches. Albert had described to John how they prepared for one of these night-time arrivals. Three of his men would be at the touchdown area, showing the pilot where the landing threshold was situated in the darkness. Another two would be at the far end of the strip, marking its end point, and also helping the pilot with his height perception as he looked along the length of the strip when landing. John found himself wondering about the touchdown technique. Probably not the usual landing flare, he decided, more a harsh round-out input made at the last moment and at low speed. No doubt there would be a burst of power added at the same time, to ensure the aircraft's arrival was not too solid. There would be nothing delicate about the landing technique in these circumstances, he thought.

John could hear the engine much more clearly now, but it was still a relatively unobtrusive sound, just a dull grumble, with some variations in volume as the pilot adjusted his power from time to time. Necessary, John understood, for a pilot descending towards a newly mown hayfield on a dark night, assisted only by a partial moon and some torches. There was a sudden, short roar from the aircraft's engine. John knew that would be the pilot giving the Lysander a burst of power to arrest his rate of descent before making a heavy, but safe, touchdown on the field as he saw the ground at the last moment. Moments later he heard the Lysander engine briefly roar again. He could just make out the shadowy outline of the aircraft as it turned around, to taxi back to the beginning of the landing area. He appreciated that the strip was not long enough for the aircraft to take off from where its landing roll had ended. It needed to backtrack to the threshold before departing. *That requires quite a lot of extra noise and time on the ground. Hope there are no bloody German soldiers out near here tonight*, he thought.

As the Lysander reached the end of the strip, close to where it had initially touched down, the engine roared again as the pilot turned around, so that the plane was facing back down the strip, ready for take-off. It sat, unmoving, with its engine ticking over.

'Go, go, go, my friend. And good luck!' called Albert.

John dashed towards the waiting aircraft. He was ten yards from it when he heard shooting and saw muzzle flashes ahead of him, on the far side of the field. John ducked and ran harder. He realised the Lysander pilot probably could not hear anything inside his cockpit above the noise from his engine, although he would no doubt see the flashes from the shots being fired and know there was an ambush. John sprinted towards the aircraft, running as hard as he could. He heard machine-gun fire start up, and saw a salvo of bullets hit the Lysander's rear fuselage, now just a few yards in front of him. The aircraft shuddered like some mortally wounded beast. Then the engine roared, and the plane started to move down the strip. John realised that the pilot was not going to risk staying on the ground any longer. He was taking off.

Damn, where's the ladder? John thought to himself. He had just reached the aircraft, which was now moving at running speed. He could not see the ladder. *Where is it? Another few seconds and it will be too late. The plane will have accelerated out of my reach.* The engine's noise was loud. He knew the pilot would have slammed his throttle forward for full power to escape, and the Lysander was continuing to accelerate. *There it is! Grab it, quick, before he's gone.* John reached out and managed to get hold of the rail at head-height, then he swung his feet up onto the lowest rung. He clung there for a moment as the aircraft continued to race along in the darkness. He was conscious of the increasing wind-flow as the Lysander accelerated, but was determined not to let go. Gasping with effort, he hauled himself up the ladder and threw himself into the rear cockpit area.

'Shut the canopy!' a voice shouted from the front.

John reached up and grabbed the frame of the canopy, pulling it closed. He banged the locking pins into position, then wrestled with the various straps of the safety harness as the aircraft bumped along. And then the plane was airborne, climbing smoothly into the night sky.

'Thanks,' John called to the pilot hunched over the controls at the front of the cockpit.

There was a grunt of acknowledgement. John could see he was busy trying to maintain control of his damaged aircraft, which had been raked with machine-gun fire. There had obviously been some Germans in place, hidden on the side of the field, waiting for the Lysander to land. *How did they know it was coming tonight?* John wondered. Somebody must have informed. It was clearly a planned ambush.

'Quite a to-do,' John said to the Lysander pilot once they were established in the cruise, heading across the Channel for England.

'It was. We nearly didn't make it out,' the pilot replied. 'We were lucky they didn't start firing at us as soon as we landed. If they had started shooting earlier, I don't think either of us would be here now.'

'Maybe they thought you would shut down and be on the ground for longer.'

'Perhaps,' replied the pilot, 'but we plan to be on the ground for a minimum time, so there is never an engine shutdown. We have even tried pick-ups on the move, but we are still experimenting at this stage, to see what works best. That's why we have put the special grab-ladder back there, which saved you tonight.'

'I suppose we'll never know why they didn't start shooting earlier,' John said. 'A guardian angel must have been watching over us tonight. Whatever the reason, I'm happy to be going home.'

'Me too,' came the reply from the front cockpit.

They landed at RAF Tangmere, the base from which Lysander covert operations were being trialled.

'Debriefing in the morning,' the duty officer had said on their arrival. 'The sergeant here will show you to your room.'

John was asleep the moment his head hit the pillow.

'We have a Spitfire here which is available for repositioning,' said the wing commander in charge of special operations trials at Tangmere, who was about to conduct John's debrief. 'My CO has spoken to yours at Hornchurch, and it has been agreed you should take it back. It will replace the aircraft lost when you were shot down over France.'

'Yes, sir,' John replied in acknowledgement.

'The full mission debrief will be conducted by your people and intelligence when you get back to Hornchurch, but I want to discuss with you what you observed and get your thoughts on the Resistance people you met. I would also like your view on any operational aspects you noted during your uplift conducted by our Lysander. Let's begin at the beginning; what happened immediately after you crash-landed?'

John took the wing commander through the events, including how he had tried to cover up the fact he had escaped from the crash by dragging a sheep into the cockpit, hoping its remains, once he had set fire to his aircraft, would be mistaken for his.

'Must have been hard work manoeuvring an animal that size into the cockpit?'

'I was a farmer in New Zealand, so I'm used to handling stock, and it was dead, so it wasn't struggling against me. I hit it with my wing when I was skidding along the field during my forced landing. Anyway, it's amazing the strength you can summon in a situation like that. I knew I would be the subject of an intensive search if I wasn't found in the crashed wreck, so I had to do something.'

'What did you do after you had set fire to your aircraft?'

'I was in the open — in the middle of a large field. There were no houses nearby. I had seen that as I came down, so I didn't expect anyone to appear. But I had been shot down by an Me one-o-nine, and I knew he would have called that into his base. I had to hide, and quickly, hoping my sheep ruse would prevent a search for me being organised. There was a forest a short distance away, so I started towards that, moving as quickly as I could.'

John described how he had come across the small farmhouse, and how he had waited for nightfall to set about finding some food.

'I planned to help myself to some eggs in the adjacent henhouse,' he said. 'Raw eggs would have been better than nothing — I was damn hungry. As it turned out, I didn't get them. The owner must have seen me, and the next thing I knew there was a gun barrel pushed against the back of my neck.'

'Good lord! How did you get out of that?'

'It was a woman called Celine, and luckily, she was on our side. She worked with the local Resistance. She fed me, sheltered me, and led me safely to a nearby village the next day. There, I was introduced to Albert, a leader in the underground movement. He must have had contacts with someone here, because my extraction was arranged very quickly, that same night.'

'Yes, our liaison officer was contacted, and the decision was made to get you out straightaway. We had heard the Germans had made your capture top priority. They were pouring personnel into the area. Also, there was a full moon a few days ago, so we knew there would still be some partial moonlight for our pilot if we went in last night.'

'And I very much appreciate your people getting me out, sir. The Germans must have looked more closely at the wreckage of my aircraft, so it would probably just have been a matter of time before I was found.'

'Yes, I expect so. We know the person managing the operation on the ground in that part of France, Albert. He has been involved in several operations for us recently.'

'Yes, he was in charge and he had six others with him. Five men, who marked out the landing area with torches, and Celine.'

'Do you think he managed the operation well on the ground? I only ask so that we can give any advice that may help the success of any future operations.'

'I understand. From all that I saw, it seemed fine. The landing area was sensibly marked, both in terms of when they did that, and how they did it. Albert had me in a good position for a quick turnaround, once the Lysander had landed, stopped, and backtracked to the beginning of the strip. If I had one comment, it would be to use a longer landing strip so the aircraft can come to a halt, load, or unload, as required, and then immediately take off without having to backtrack. Returning to the beginning of the strip creates quite a lot of additional exposure for a covert op — more time on the ground, and more engine noise as the aircraft is turned and taxied.'

'Yes, noted thanks, Flying Officer. I agree, but longer landing areas are not always easy to find. Despite the slots and flaps on our Lysanders that reduce the strip length needed to something much less than conventional aircraft require, we usually need to backtrack after landing. There are few night-time covert operation areas long enough, even for our Lysanders, with their short landing and take-off capabilities.'

John nodded his understanding of that explanation.

'The pilot of our aircraft reported German intervention?'

'Yes, once the Lysander had taxied back to where I was waiting next to the touchdown area, it turned around to face back down the strip, ready for its take-off. I ran towards the rear cockpit to climb aboard. Albert had told me to look out for a small ladder attached to the fuselage. I was just a few yards from the aircraft when there was shooting from the other side of the field. I managed to grab the ladder and clamber into the rear cockpit as the aircraft was beginning to accelerate away. A machine gun had opened up just as I reached the Lysander. If I had been a couple of paces more from the aircraft when the shooting started, I wouldn't have been able to get to the ladder. The aircraft immediately began moving in response to the shots being fired — it was a close thing.'

'Our policy is that if there is any shooting, the pilot is to get out of there as fast as he can, whether his load is on or not.'

'I understand that, sir, and I didn't mean to suggest that I was put at undue risk. I understand your pilot must observe your procedures to accommodate the events of the night. Better to leave me than risk losing everyone and the aircraft. Do you know what happened to Albert and his team?'

'We understand three of his men died. The others, including Albert and Celine, all escaped.'

John nodded grimly. He was delighted some had got away from the German ambush, but saddened his recovery had cost the lives of others.

'It could have been worse if the Germans had opened fire earlier. We might not have got anyone back and lost our Lysander,' the wing commander commented.

'Yes, I thought that was an operational mistake by the Germans,' John agreed. 'They should have started shooting sooner.'

'We think they got the information about our operation from a member of the Resistance who had been arrested and interrogated on the afternoon of your exfiltration. The SS appears to have learnt about your uplift from a landing-field sketch being carried by that prisoner when they were detained, which is likely how the ambush came about. But we think some deception might have been undertaken by the prisoner, and that helped us succeed in getting you out of France.'

'Oh, what was that?'

'Well, we can't be sure, of course, but you said it yourself. Why didn't the Germans take their prime opportunity? They could have taken out the Lysander as it manoeuvred on the ground instead of waiting until it had repositioned and was ready to take off. That would have brought our mission to an end and presented them with something they really wanted: one of the Spitfire pilots who had ruined their day at Glisy, as well as getting our aircraft and pilot.'

'So, what were they doing?'

'We think they thought more was to happen, perhaps that the Lysander would shut down on the ground for you to board. Then they could move in quickly and cleanly, capturing the aircraft and all those there. If the Germans thought that was what was planned, their mistake saved the night for us. You never shut down on these ops. Quickly in and quickly out. That is our procedure, and engines are kept running at all times.'

'You mentioned a deception by the Resistance member held prisoner by the SS?' John queried.

'Yes. We think the Germans might have been deliberately misled during the interrogation. They knew an uplift was planned as a result of finding the sketch being carried, so they would have focused on the detail of that uplift during their interrogation process. It would have been very difficult for the prisoner being questioned to say nothing at all. The Nazis use some very unpleasant methods to get people to talk. Those in the French underground are by and large brave and resourceful, and they have developed some techniques to help themselves when being questioned in difficult circumstances. If under duress, they may include false matters when speaking about things that they know the enemy is already aware of, in this case the planned landing. Appearing to provide some detail about such matters can take some of the pressure off, yet not provide anything valuable to the enemy. Certainly, the SS appears to have got it wrong in the ambush of our aircraft.'

'I have the greatest respect for the Resistance and what they do in occupied France,' John replied. 'If the prisoner took the opportunity to mislead the SS about the detail of the Lysander pick-up, and that made the difference for us last night, he is heroic.'

'*She* actually, Flying Officer, and yes, if that's what she did, she was heroic. Unfortunately, we have been advised this morning that she died during interrogation.'

'But not before she may have helped me,' John said quietly.

The wing commander just nodded.

CHAPTER SEVENTEEN

John's flight back to Hornchurch from Tangmere was uneventful, a pleasant afternoon at the controls of his replacement Spitfire. He was pleased there were no issues of any sort, with the aircraft or with the weather. It was so quiet, it might have been peacetime, he thought, as he cruised northwards.

That evening, John found some of the chaps in the bar, enjoying a pre-dinner ale. Richard greeted him warmly.

'Hello, John. How are you settling back in after your French holiday?'

Charlie, Craig, and Greg all roared with laughter. It was such a loud and sudden outburst, people around the room paused mid-conversation to look around.

John grinned. 'Thank you, Richard. I am very pleased to be back, and in one piece. I had a close call getting out of France in a Lysander.'

'Tell us about it, John,' Craig said.

John took them through everything that had happened, from his shoot-down and subsequent forced landing in a field, to clinging onto the ladder of the Lysander as it came under machine-gun fire during the ambush by German soldiers. The others listened in silence, bar the occasional exclamation.

'You won't know this, John, because you've been busy running around the French countryside, but the Luftwaffe have started to bomb infrastructure in our cities now, particularly London, as well as continuing to attack us where they can. It started a few days ago, and the view is that more bombing of cities should be expected. They can't knock us out, so now they are having a go at targets that will impact civilians as well.'

'Bastards,' John exclaimed. 'I had wondered if the Luftwaffe might adopt a new strategy if they didn't gain the air superiority against the RAF they wanted.'

'Göring has to show Hitler he can achieve something. Having a crack at specific targets that will also mean civilians are hit, affecting the morale of the populace, is an easy enough task for him,' Richard responded.

'I'm confident that we can upset their plans,' John said, surprised at the depth of his own patriotic feeling as he said that.

'Gentlemen, dinner is served,' the mess orderly announced.

The next morning, John and Richard met with Sidey to debrief on the Glisy mission.

'Operation Sneaker was a complete success,' Sidey said once they were all seated comfortably in his office, with cups of tea provided by his assistant. 'In saying that, I don't overlook that you were shot down, Flying Officer Noble, but that ended well for you.' John knew he had been lucky. He was alive, and the attack on the aerodrome had achieved what it was designed to do, so overall it was a good outcome, as Sidey was saying.

'Going over the mission,' Sidey continued, 'we made landfall in France at our planned entry point. Our split at Hangest-sur-Somme saw us positioning to our respective run-in fixes, and your "inbound" call, Flight Lieutenant Cowles, enabled me to ensure I wasn't on scene early. I came in about eight seconds after your call, so our planning worked well in that regard. The spacing between numbers two and three was always critical.'

'Did you encounter any flak?' John asked. 'Neither I nor Flight Lieutenant Cowles saw any. We caught them unawares, as we had hoped, but were they ready when you came through?'

Sidey nodded. 'Some AA rounds did explode near me, so they had got themselves organised by the time I came in. I only saw two air bursts, and that was when I was at least halfway along the runway, so coming in from the opposite direction may have helped slow the response. Got a few shrapnel holes in my starboard wing. The strafing runs themselves achieved their purpose, so I am happy with that part of our mission, but our exit back to Britain was not as tidy as I would have liked, with multiple Luftwaffe fighters onto us very quickly. It was always going to be difficult with just three of us, low on fuel, facing determined Luftwaffe fighters, but those blighters appeared much sooner than I had expected. The intervention of Wing Commander Bland's section was timely, and we owe him some gratitude for his decision to come inland and not wait out over the Channel. Now, do either of you have anything you want to say about the operation?'

'Not really, sir,' John responded, 'but I must say that spending time on our strategy for the attack, and the in-depth planning of the mission proved valuable. Our focus on the basics — speed, height, timing, approach tracks, and attack direction — all contributed to a successful outcome.'

'I agree, Flying Officer. It was a difficult operation, but we were able to achieve what was sought. I thank you both and congratulate you. I can tell you that the Prime Minister, who was very keen on the operation, is delighted with the result.'

The new Luftwaffe bombing strategy, targeting industrial targets, as well as communication and public utilities, put enormous demands on the squadron pilots as the weeks passed. The German attacks came regularly, and large numbers of enemy aircraft were involved in each attack.

'God, I'm tired,' John complained to Richard one evening as they ate dinner. Others at the table, hearing John's comment, murmured their agreement. They were all feeling exhausted. That day the squadron had scrambled on four occasions to meet inbound attackers.

'We are all feeling it, John,' Richard responded, 'but at least we can be satisfied we are getting a return on our commitment. Chain Home is putting us in the right place at the right time, and the lads are flying and fighting well. Jerry's bombers are copping it. We had three Heinkels destroyed today, with four more being classified as probables. Our squadron lost no-one.'

'I wonder how long this will go on,' John said. 'The Luftwaffe first started coming over England in significant numbers in mid-July. Surely they must be feeling the pinch of the significant losses they have experienced? How long can they keep up so many offensive operations?'

'There will be a lot of people who would like to know the answer to that question, John,' Greg replied. 'The Germans changed their tactics regarding our airfields, so that says to me they were not satisfied they were achieving enough to justify their effort and losses. Maybe they will eventually reach the same conclusion about their general bombing of targets in population centres. Certainly, if they suffer too many losses of men and machines they are likely to review their strategy, I would have thought.'

So, we just keep at it,' John said.

'Of course, John, we have no other choice. If we continue the success we have been achieving, I think Jerry will decide to change tack,' Greg replied.

John agreed with that. RAF Fighter Command's steadfast defence had been successful to date, and he thought that must mean a change would be coming sometime soon. The Luftwaffe would not continue their costly bombing offensive indefinitely, unless it saw that it was bringing Britain to its knees, and right now that was certainly not the case.

John and his fellow squadron pilots had some relief from German attacks because of poor weather at the end of the second week of September. That forced the Luftwaffe to curtail operations for a few days, but on Sunday, 15th of September, it dawned fine and clear again. John was in the officers' mess, having breakfast. Richard Cowles and Greg Somerville were with him. So was Craig Thomson. It was six in the morning, and they were due to be in the ready room in thirty minutes, to await the day's events.

'The buggers will come today,' John said. 'They will be keen to get on with it after being held back by the weather conditions over recent days.'

'Yes, they will,' Richard replied, 'but at least you've had those days to catch up on your sleep, John, so that's good.'

'We have had a quiet time recently, but there's no doubt that's about to end,' Greg added, as he munched some toast he had just smothered in marmalade.

'I hear London was bombed in the early hours of this morning, so today's attacks have already started,' Craig commented. Then the telephone rang.

'It's a scramble,' the person answering the call announced to the room.

John, along with other pilots, was on his feet in seconds, running to dispersal.

'Jaunty Squadron, follow me, climbing angels eighteen, heading one zero zero,' Sidey called. The Spitfires of 415 Squadron were soon at eighteen thousand feet, flying a course that roughly followed the southern shoreline of the Thames Estuary far below.

'Dorniers sighted, one hundred plus,' Sidey called a few minutes later.

John saw them, and saw also that other fighter squadrons were already there engaging with them, and with the Me 109s that had been flying as cover for the German bombers.

As John joined the engagement, he loosed off a long burst at one of the Dorniers. He saw his fire impacting its rear fuselage and tail section. It dipped down out of the Luftwaffe formation, slowly turning back towards France. *Damaged and going home,* John decided. He turned towards another of the bombers.

'John, on your six!' someone shouted. *That sounded like Craig,* John thought, as he rolled violently to the left and accelerated into a dive. He looked back over his shoulder. Two Me 109s were behind him. *Damn.*

John rolled to the right and pulled his Spitfire into a tight turn, back towards where he expected the pursuing German fighters to be. As the nose of his aircraft carved around the horizon, he waited for the Me 109s to come into his view. But they were nowhere to be seen. *Where did they go?* he wondered. As he asked himself that, multiple rounds impacted the rear of his aircraft, shaking the fuselage with their force. John did not hesitate. The Luftwaffe pilots were clearly closer to him than he had realised when he had started his turn towards where he had thought they were. Now, instead of being head-to-head, they were tight on his tail. John rolled inverted, then put his aircraft into a vertical dive. Looking back, he saw the Germans follow. He transitioned from his steep dive into a spiralling turn to the left, but after one tight descending orbit, and still being followed, he abruptly changed his spiral to the left to a spiral to the right, then stopped his descent after a few seconds, and entered a maximum rate turn. That worked. He got inside the chasing Messerschmitts' turn radius and was able to begin to close up behind them. Seeing what John had done, the German pilots rolled away, disengaging from the chase.

John climbed back towards the Dornier formation. Coming up from beneath, he was not obvious to either the Dorniers or their escorting fighters that seemed to be mainly above the bombers. John got in a quick burst that went into the belly of one of the bombers. It showed flames almost immediately and started to go down. Now at the same altitude as most of the Dorniers, John turned towards the nearest of those aircraft and fired. He hit the cockpit area, and the bomber fell out of control. He realised he must have incapacitated the pilot.

Tracer flashing past his nose alerted him to another German aircraft attacking him. It was an Me 109, out to his port side and about three hundred yards away, but getting closer by the second. John turned steeply towards the approaching enemy fighter and dived underneath it, to get himself clear of that threat. There were no other Luftwaffe aircraft near him, and John realised that, in any event, he did not have sufficient fuel to continue dogfighting. He turned for Hornchurch, descending power-on at high speed. He wanted to put some distance between himself and the Germans as soon as he could.

Back on the ground at Hornchurch, John saw that some of the squadron had already returned. Sidey landed a few minutes later. While the ground crews re-armed and refuelled the Spitfires, the pilots gathered in the ready room.

'Everyone got back from that one, I see,' Sidey announced. 'Well done, chaps. Talk to the intelligence officer with your reports as soon as possible. Jerry seems to have decided this is going to be a big day, so we need to be ready to go again in short order.'

Sidey was right. An hour later there was another call to scramble. All the squadron pilots were back in the air a few minutes after that, climbing towards Dungeness, where the next wave of attackers was expected to cross the British shoreline. Control reported one hundred plus, which they had identified as bombers, with another one hundred plus fighters coming in above and behind the bombers.

Level at twenty thousand feet, and on a course to intercept the approaching bombers, John's squadron received an unexpected call from control.

'Jaunty Squadron, change of instructions. Abandon your track to intercept the inbound bombers. Other squadrons will deal with them. You are to hold at angels twenty over Biggin Hill.'

'Roger, control,' John heard Sidey respond. 'Jaunty squadron, you will have heard that. Follow me in current formation to overhead Biggin.'

'And Jaunty,' the controller continued, 'you should expect multiple one-o-nines. We see some of the fighters leaving their bomber escort duties and now following a track directly towards London, presumably on a target of opportunity mission.'

John realised there were so many German fighters available to escort the bombers, that some could be spared for alternative operations, the so called "free hunting" that the Luftwaffe occasionally allowed its fighter aircraft to undertake. But none of the free hunters looking for targets of opportunity, nor any bombers, arrived over Biggin Hill, and after loitering in the area for thirty minutes it was time for the squadron to head back to Hornchurch.

'Wonder where the threat to Biggin got to?' John commented to Richard as they walked in from their aircraft after landing.

'God knows,' was Richard's reply, 'but I can tell you this. There must have been over five hundred German fighters and bombers over England for that last raid. That is huge.'

'I bet my friends at control were busy,' John said with a grin, as he thought of those he had met in the Uxbridge control room during his recent familiarisation visit.

'Gentlemen, if you had not already picked up on it, today is big. Two large waves have come in, and the number of enemy aircraft involved has been substantially larger than we have experienced in the past,' Sidey said to the pilots gathered in the ready room. 'We are to be ready to go again as soon as we are called, although I'm not sure if that will happen. Jerry has sent so much over today, I doubt they will have more to come. I have never seen so much activity.'

'Scramble.' The call came from the airman managing control's direct telephone line into the ready room.

'Well, shows what I know,' Sidey said with a short laugh at his misjudgement as he led the way, running to the squadron's parked Spitfires.

'Jaunty Squadron, proceed direct to West Ham. The Bromley-by-Bow gas works are under attack,' John heard when they were airborne.

'Wilco, Jaunty is setting heading this time for intercept,' Sidey responded, confirming that his squadron would undertake what was required — stopping the bombers from destroying the gas utility.

Minutes later the Spitfires of 415 Squadron were attacking the bombers they had located over West Ham. Cloud nearby was giving adjacent areas some protection from the Luftwaffe. If the bomb aimers could not see they could not effectively bomb, John knew, so the cloud was a partial saviour for some potential targets, he guessed. Swooping in on the bombers, a mix of Dorniers and Heinkels, the squadron had good success, with three bombers taken down in the first moments of the encounter. John shot down a Heinkel, and as the Germans broke off their raid and set off for the safety of France, he, along with the other pilots, harried them all the way to the Channel. John did not shoot any more down, but saw several Luftwaffe aircraft plunging earthwards as they unsuccessfully tried to get away.

John was concerned at the level of enemy activity he had seen during the day's battles. He thought it must be the largest number of aircraft ever sent over by the Luftwaffe in one period, and he found himself wondering how the Germans had managed to mount such a large attack, and if Britain would have enough aircraft itself to keep intercepting and defending against them.

'Christ, what a day,' John exclaimed that evening as the pilots of 415 Squadron were having dinner. 'I have never encountered so many aircraft in one day. I thought Jerry was running out of steam, but clearly not. Large numbers sent today, and in three principal waves. Do we know how it went overall?'

'Air Ministry is saying about one hundred and eighty German aircraft were shot down, with us losing forty,' Craig said.

'That can't be sustainable for Jerry,' Richard noted.

'You wouldn't think so, but it's a wait and see game now, I think,' John replied.

CHAPTER EIGHTEEN

John read the Fighter Command memorandum to all squadrons the day after the enormous Luftwaffe raids of the 15th of September, thanking all pilots for their dedication in defence. It also confirmed that while the RAF had been stretched, it had been able to meet every inbound enemy formation. It must have been a close-run thing, John decided, pleased the RAF had been able to successfully respond to what had clearly been a maximum effort by the Luftwaffe.

Over the following weeks, 415 Squadron continued to be scrambled most days, getting some relief only when the weather was so bad the Luftwaffe remained grounded.

In mid-October, John and his fellow pilots began to see a new tactic being employed by the Germans. They started using fighter-bombers that would sweep in at high altitude, and then dive to a low level to drop their bombs. Because these aircraft came in at about 25,000 feet and could reach their targets within twenty minutes of being identified by British radar, the Spitfires and Hurricanes of the RAF were finding that they could not get up to intercept them in time.

'I wonder if we should mount high altitude standing patrols?' John had said at a squadron briefing when these attacks had been raised by Sidey.

'I think that is what may be being planned,' Sidey had replied.

Sure enough, in following days John had found himself patrolling at 25,000 feet, awaiting an alert from control that high-flying Luftwaffe fighter-bombers had been identified inbound.

As October drew to a close, John and the other squadron pilots noticed that the level of Luftwaffe activity over Britain was subsiding. Certainly, it was much less than in earlier months. 415 Squadron was not being scrambled as often, and when an intercept was made, there appeared to be fewer enemy aircraft involved.

'Jerry seems to have reduced his forays in recent times,' John said to Richard as they sat in the officers' mess one evening. 'Dave Sidey says Fighter Command has confirmed enemy aircraft attacks are substantially down.'

'I think the problem for Göring is that he has not got the return he wants, given the scale of the Luftwaffe's operations against us. It's bad enough that he wasn't able to subdue the RAF, as he announced he would, but he has lost a large number of aircraft and crews on his offensive ops generally,' Richard responded.

'I understand that, but he started with a lot more than us, and we have taken losses too.'

'True, but the difference is that we have had successful defence of the air over Britain to show for the losses we've suffered. I don't think the Luftwaffe has much to show for its losses at all.'

415 Squadron had been at readiness since dawn on the 1st of December. That was three hours ago, and no call to scramble had been received. *Where are the buggers?* John wondered.

The telephone in the dispersal hut rang. The waiting pilots looked up expectantly.

'Take a break. Four-one-five Squadron has been released from standby until twelve- hundred hours,' said the young man whose turn it was to answer the telephone in the hut.

Unheard of, thought John. *What are the Germans up to?*

He got up from his chair and began walking towards the mess. *Bit early for lunch, but a cuppa would be good*, John decided. Richard was in the lounge when John arrived. They sat down together.

'We are seeing less and less of the Luftwaffe. Night bombing, in particular, seems to be the new way for Jerry.'

'Yes,' Richard responded, 'the intensity of their daytime activity has reduced significantly. Their prime focus does seem to be night-bombing now.'

Just then they were approached by a mess orderly. 'Excuse me, the CO would like to see you both in his office,' he said.

Richard and John got up and made their way out of the mess, heading for Bland's office.

'I think our CO may have turned a corner,' Richard commented as they walked. 'Certainly he's flying and planning better now, compared to his earlier days. I was very thankful he decided to come inland, past the French coast, on Operation Sneaker. He and the others were able to divert the attention of the one-o-nines sufficiently to allow us to get back. Well, all of us except you, of course, but it was a good move. The outcome could have been a lot worse without his intervention.'

John nodded. 'I'd written him off, but I'm prepared to be nice, if you are right and he has turned a corner. Anyway, let's see why he wants to see us.'

'Gentlemen, I have asked you here to advise that you have both been awarded the DFC. Congratulations.'

John and Richard were momentarily stunned. Neither of them had expected it, as was clear from their stammered replies.

'Ah, thank you, sir.'

'A surprise, sir, but appreciated.'

'You are going to Buckingham Palace next week, where King George will personally present your honours. Squadron Leader Sidey will be with you. He has also been awarded a DFC.'

The king, John thought. *I wish my parents weren't on the other side of the world. They would have loved to see this.*

'And Flying Officer Noble,' Christopher Bland continued, 'you have also been promoted to Flight Lieutenant. Well done. Thank you, gentlemen.'

John and Richard took their cue and left.

'The Distinguished Flying Cross, presented to you at Buckingham Palace by the king! Oh John, that's wonderful,' Mary said, when John telephoned to tell her the news.

'Is there any chance you could come to London for the investiture ceremony? It's on Wednesday next week, at two o'clock.'

'I'm not sure, but I will ask. I would think for something like this I could get away for a day or two. I will see what I can do.'

John thought the dinner he and Mary had just savoured, in a well-known restaurant in Mayfair, was one of the best meals he had ever had. His investiture at Buckingham Palace had occurred that afternoon, and Mary had been able to take leave from the hospital to attend. John had expected a relatively formal occasion, but the king had chatted in a friendly and relaxed way with those he was decorating for their service, and John had enjoyed the surprisingly informal atmosphere.

'That meal was wonderful, Mary. Your father's suggestion was first-rate,' John said.

'Father loves this place and thought we would enjoy it. Pre-war, it was very expensive. Not so bad now, with fewer offerings because of the war.'

John laughed. 'Ah, he understands fighter pilots and nurses don't get paid much.'

'Father knew we wanted a special night, so he thought it would be all right.'

'Good for him,' John replied. 'The Mirabelle with its reduced wartime pricing is just what we wanted.'

'Let's go back to the hotel, John.'

John was surprised. It was only nine o'clock. 'Bit early, isn't it, Mary? I thought we would visit some clubs.'

'I don't want to go partying around the city. I want to go to bed.'

'Of course. If you're tired, that's no problem. I'll pay the bill and we will go now.'

Mary smiled at John. She leant forward and whispered across the small table. 'I have no intention of sleeping, not for quite some time.'

John blinked and then called for the bill. After a moment looking at it, he signalled for the maître d' to come over.

'Is there a problem, sir?' the maître d' asked.

'Yes, the bottle of champagne we had has not been included on the bill.'

'That's very honest of you, sir. Thank you for pointing it out. However, I understand from the waiter who served you that you are a pilot in the RAF, and you fly a Spitfire.'

'Yes, we did have a bit of a chat about flying while he took our orders.'

'The Prime Minister recently spoke in the House of Commons about our fighter pilots, and their battle against the Luftwaffe. He said we owe you a lot, noting that just a few of you have done so much for us all.'

'Yes, it was kind of him,' John responded.

'Well, sir, so far as the Mirabelle is concerned, one of Mr Churchill's few does not have to pay for his champagne. Please accept it as a small expression of our gratitude for what you and your fellow pilots are doing.'

John was on standby at Hornchurch, but any call to fly looked unlikely. The weather that December day was foul across the whole of south-eastern England, the Channel, and also over France. *Unlikely we will see anything of Jerry*, John thought.

He looked out through the window of the dispersal hut. The windsock on the airfield whipped vigorously in the wind. It was probably forty miles per hour, with occasional gusts substantially higher, and it was continually veering and backing through at least forty-five degrees. The cloud base might have been five hundred feet above the ground, but heavy rain affected visibility, which was down to four hundred yards at most. The morning was effectively unflyable, John thought.

'Flight Lieutenant Noble.'

John looked around. The CO was standing at the door of the dispersal hut.

'Yes, sir?'

'I want you to engine test a Spitfire,' Bland said. 'Flight thinks it's not achieving sufficient boost.'

'Certainly, sir, as soon as the weather improves.'

'I know it's marginal out there, Flight Lieutenant, but sufficient to test fly, I think. So get on and do it now, please, while Jerry continues to be quiet.'

John was dumbfounded. How could the CO think undertaking an engine test in these conditions was appropriate? No flying would be safe at the moment.

'With all due respect, sir, in my judgement the weather is not safely flyable at present. I will take it up as soon as it improves.'

Bland said nothing as he abruptly turned and walked out of the hut.

'What the hell was that about?' John asked Richard, who had been standing nearby and would have heard the exchange.

'I agree with you, John. It would be madness to undertake a test flight in these conditions.'

'Why would he ask for it then?' John queried.

'God knows. Trying to show he's in charge?'

Three hours later, the weather had improved slightly but remained poor for flying. The squadron pilots had been released from any level of readiness. No-one expected enemy operations today. Richard and John were in the lounge having a cup of tea when Bland strode over to them.

'Right, weather has improved enough to get on with it. Let's get that test flight done.'

'I don't think it has sufficiently improved yet, sir,' John responded.

'Rubbish. Get on with it, Flight Lieutenant.'

It was too much for Richard. 'Sir, I agree with Flight Lieutenant Noble. No flight, and certainly not just a test flight, should be conducted at present. Conditions have improved in recent hours, but remain, in my opinion, too marginal.'

Bland looked stung. He had the highest regard for Richard. 'Oh, for Christ's sake, I'll do it myself,' he blustered.

The CO marched out before either John or Richard could say any more.

'I think that Wing Commander Christopher Bland,' said Richard, 'is struggling to prove himself, and is feeling the pressure. We kept him out of war ops leadership at Dunkirk. Then we developed some alternative oversight arrangements to ensure he didn't actively lead us in the air during the air battles of recent months. When he wanted to participate in Operation

Sneaker, Dave Sidey blocked that, although he did arrange for Bland to help with providing cover on our exit from France. As a consequence, he will be well aware of the views held in the squadron regarding his competency. He's not that daft. I think what we are now seeing is Bland trying to retake control and reassert himself. That's why he demanded you conduct the flight test today, in my view.'

'Maybe.' John was uncertain about Richard's theory.

'Look, John, he wants it done, and we've told him it's not a good idea because the present weather conditions make it too dangerous. Any rational pilot would come to the same conclusion. It's just a test flight, so there's no urgency, but Bland says it has to be done now. He is effectively saying our judgement is faulty. Successfully doing it himself is a way to demonstrate that he is right, and we are wrong.'

'You may be right, Richard, and if you are, it's an unfortunate state of affairs.'

A few minutes later they heard an aircraft starting up. They moved to the window that overlooked the operational area. A Spitfire was taxiing into position for take-off.

John shook his head as he watched. 'How's he going to check the boost properly if he can't get above five hundred feet because of the cloud base?'

John's question was answered as they saw Bland accelerate and lift off, the aircraft's wings jerking and ducking in the turbulence, the tail swinging wildly. Bland's aircraft climbed straight ahead, and into the cloud.

'Oh, the silly bugger is going to try to get on top, to run his tests at altitude,' John said.

'Yep, he will have his hands full. Difficult flying conditions, and there's bound to be some icing as he gets higher,' Richard agreed.

An hour later, John heard the sound of a Spitfire. He looked out of the window. It was Bland. *Just as well the weather conditions have improved since your departure*, John thought, as he watched Bland taxiing back to dispersal. *Otherwise you would have struggled to land.*

A few minutes later, Bland walked into the lounge and approached John and Richard.

'In my office in five, please,' he said before walking away.

Richard and John exchanged looks, then stood to follow Bland towards the block where his office was situated.

'Gentlemen, come in and sit down,' Bland said, when they knocked at his door. 'I have completed the test flight I asked you to do, Flight Lieutenant Noble. All is well with the aircraft. You declined to fly the test. And you,' he added, looking at Richard, 'supported that decision.'

What's coming? John wondered. *Charges for failing to follow orders?*

'I have decided you were both right,' Bland said, leaning forward, as if to reinforce what he had to say. 'I accept that it was not appropriate to initiate a test flight in the conditions we had earlier. I made an error of judgement in flying today, and the consequences were nearly fatal.'

John was surprised. *Why is Bland being so frank, and what on earth has happened that almost killed him?*

'In the air, I had to work hard to maintain control of the aircraft,' Bland continued. 'I climbed through dense cloud and there was severe turbulence for the first five thousand feet. It was unrelenting and kept me very focused on the blind flying panel. It would have been easy to become disorientated in those conditions. When I got on top, above the cloud at ten thousand feet, it only took me twenty minutes to complete all the tests I wanted to do. Satisfied with the engine's performance and responses, I began thinking about my return to Hornchurch, but I had made a mistake. I had not paid any attention to the direction in which I had been flying while undertaking the testing. My failure to maintain any positional awareness meant I was uncertain where I was.

'I couldn't see the ground because of the continuous cloud cover below me. I knew descending through the cloud would be dangerous, as there might well be high ground in my path. I decided that risk would be minimised if I flew east. As my general heading while above the cloud had been easterly, I thought descending in that direction would most likely bring me down somewhere over the English Channel, well clear of any hills. So, I flew a heading of one hundred degrees, reduced power, and trimmed the aircraft for a slow descent through the cloud. I knew it would be rough, and, sure enough, I encountered severe turbulence. The aeroplane was shaken to a degree I have never previously experienced. There were substantial updrafts and downdrafts, and that made maintaining aircraft attitude and speed control difficult.'

Bland paused. John could see he was upset.

'After a few minutes, I noticed my rate of descent was increasing, and my airspeed was building too. To counter that, I raised the aircraft's nose. Despite doing that, my speed continued to increase, along with my rate of descent. I couldn't understand why that was happening. I pulled back on the control stick some more, in an attempt to reduce my speed and descent rate, but that didn't work. They both continued to build. I also started to feel an increasing gravitational loading, building quite quickly, pressing me into my seat. The air speed was moving through the Spitfire's limit in the turbulent conditions, and the altimeter was continuing to unwind. I admit I was becoming confused, unsure of why the aircraft was doing that.'

John and Richard exchanged glances as Bland shared his near-death experience.

'I was worried things were rapidly moving beyond my capabilities,' Bland continued. 'I was in a bad state; I think I was becoming disorientated. I couldn't understand what was going on, and why the aircraft wouldn't respond to my control inputs. I had raised the aircraft's nose, but I was still going down and my speed was continuing to increase. The g-forces I felt were continuing to build. I thought it was over for me. Then I remembered a comment made to me once by Squadron Leader Smallbone. He had noticed the difficulty some pilots had when flying blind in cloud. Their lack of experience flying on instruments had some of them unknowingly entering a spiral dive.

'The trouble is, it sneaks up on them, Tony told me at the time. They don't notice their wings aren't level when they are flying on instruments, with no outside visual reference to assist them. A wide, spiralling descent slowly develops, eventually showing up on their instruments as both an increasing rate of descent and increasing airspeed. When the pilot sees speed building and height being lost, he immediately takes the usual step to stop those things. He pulls back on the stick to raise the nose, but in a spiral dive that makes it worse. That doesn't raise the nose relative to the horizon. Because the wings aren't level, it just acts to tighten the spiral dive the aircraft is in. The result is more speed and a rate of descent that goes exponential as they wind their machine into an ever-tightening spiralling dive.

'Remembering that conversation, I realised what was happening. When I gathered myself and looked carefully at my instruments, I saw my heading was continually changing, and the artificial horizon showed I was in a steep bank to the left.

Then I knew I was in one of the spirals Squadron Leader Smallbone had talked about. I rolled my wings level, reduced power, and slowly eased out of my dive. When I did that, I soon had everything back under control.'

'A near thing, sir,' John said.

'It *was* a near thing. And it made me realise that I'd got it badly wrong, insisting that the test be conducted in marginal conditions. You were right to tell me that it was inappropriate. I accept I have exhibited poor judgement. The result is that I nearly died today. I survived, but my self-confidence has gone.'

John was keen to reassure the CO. 'We are all learning and growing from our experiences, sir,' he said. 'You can take some comfort from the fact you coped in extreme circumstances and now understand why things went as they did.'

'Yes, I understand that, Flight Lieutenant, but my near fatal loss of control wasn't the only lesson today. Once out of the cloud, I was confident I would be able to see where I was and get myself home. At five hundred feet I emerged from the cloud base, but it wasn't the waters of the English Channel below me. Instead, there were large open fields. I still had to ascertain my position and set a heading for Hornchurch.'

'You were obviously able to do that without too much difficulty, sir,' Richard said.

'Not really, Flight Lieutenant. Conditions were clear under the cloud base, with good visibility. I scanned all around, looking for some identifying landmark. I could not see anything familiar. Then I saw an aerodrome about two miles away, directly ahead of me. A mown landing strip, with a bright orange windsock at one end. I decided to land there and find out where I was. I lowered my undercarriage, put down my flaps, and reduced power. On my landing approach, passing through two hundred feet, I realised there was a line of aircraft parked next to some low trees on the southern side of the aerodrome. I could only look quickly, because I was concentrating on my landing, but I saw enough. They were Me 109s. I was over France.'

'Oh, goodness,' John exclaimed, before he could stop himself.

'Flak began exploding around me as the German aerodrome defences started shooting. Looking back, I think I tried to land at the former French Air Force aerodrome near Crochte, ten miles east of Dunkirk. I am very angry with myself for my stupidity. I know France is only about thirty minutes' flying time from base. I also know the squadron pilots have been warned many times about that proximity, and how easy it is to inadvertently end up over France. But that's what I allowed to happen.

'So, gentlemen, there it is. My stupidity and lack of awareness exposed me to situations that could have been disastrous. I had time for reflection as I made my way back, and I find myself questioning my capability as the commander of a Spitfire squadron. I can also acknowledge my in-air leadership has been lacking, initially through lack of experience in war ops, but also in more recent times because my strategic judgement is simply not the best. The reason I have asked you here is to let you know that I am determined to change. I will address the issues we have had in the squadron to date as a result of some of my decisions, and I will have an appropriate conversation with Squadron Leaders Sidey and Smallbone to embed what I propose. I am letting you know because you have been, shall I say, on the frontline trying to deal with the issues I have created.'

The room fell silent. Neither Richard nor John knew how to respond. It was a bit awkward. This was a very unusual conversation for a senior officer to have with two of his juniors, but John appreciated Bland's honesty and determination to change. He realised just how badly the CO had been affected by the day's events.

'Thank you, sir,' said John. 'We appreciate you talking to us about what you now plan to do, and I think we will all benefit.'

Richard mumbled his concurrence.

'One last thing, gentlemen. I will do my part from now on, and you will see a change in me. That said, this conversation never took place. I want to avoid any speculation and gossip in the squadron about how the change the squadron pilots will see has come about. Agreed?'

'Yes, sir,' they both replied.

CHAPTER NINETEEN

By the end of 1940, it had become clear to John and the other pilots of 415 Squadron just how critical the ability of the RAF to successfully resist the Luftwaffe during the Battle of Britain had been. Hitler had postponed, indefinitely, Operation Sea Lion, Germany's planned invasion of Britain, and the Luftwaffe had been obliged to change its tactics. Because Göring had been unable to neutralise the RAF, as he had promised Hitler, German aircraft had begun bombing British cities, particularly London, but the Luftwaffe had suffered significant losses during daytime raids. The Germans had then varied their tactics again, and there was increased nighttime bombing. The British press called the Luftwaffe's bombing campaign *The Blitz*.

Happy to have survived four months of intensive aerial warfare during the Battle of Britain, and several demanding encounters since that time, John knew that he and his fellow pilots still had a lot ahead of them. The German forces were just across the Channel, and he did not think that they would simply cease hostilities at this point in the conflict. Nevertheless, John was pleased to see that, by the end of 1940, Luftwaffe activity over England had substantially reduced. The Germans were not coming as often as they had been previously, and when they did come, the numbers of aircraft involved were considerably less than had been the case during the difficult days of July through to October. Not having to stand by every day in the ready room, waiting anxiously for the next raid, was a huge release.

John also saw that as a result of fewer attacks now being mounted by the Luftwaffe, Fighter Command had moved from organising responsive defence, to planning offensive operations. By mid-January, some eleven weeks after the end of the Battle of Britain, he found he was being sent out on numerous patrols over Occupied France, flying sweeps along the French coast, and sometimes penetrating further inland, looking for any targets of opportunity. Occasionally German fighters were encountered, but not in significant numbers, and when John and his squadron did meet them, the Luftwaffe did not appear keen to engage. John recognised that the dynamics of the air war were now quite different. *The result of us being able to defy the odds, successfully defending Britain against the massive attacks launched against it by a much bigger air force,* he confirmed to himself.

During a quiet period between missions, John knocked on the door of Richard's room, having received a message from Bland. 'The CO wants to see us at midday,' he said as he stuck his head in through the doorway.

'What about?' asked Richard.

'No idea, old chap.'

Sidey was waiting outside Bland's office when they arrived. 'Gentlemen,' he said by way of greeting.

'We were asked to see the CO at midday, sir,' John told him.

'Yes, I know. All three of us are to meet with him,' Sidey responded.

As he said that, Bland emerged from his office and invited them in. Once they were seated, he got straight to the purpose of the meeting. 'I have had a special request from Fighter Command. You gentlemen are to provide air cover for a special ground movement within England,' he said.

John was surprised. Air cover for local ground movements? That was new, and what ground movements needed protection?

Bland continued, 'You may be aware that the PM is not using his official country retreat, Chequers, at present. The security services consider the property insufficiently secure for him to use during wartime.'

'I wasn't aware of that, sir,' said Sidey.

'Yes, they think it's too easily identified from the air, and, consequently, could be targeted by German aircraft. Apparently, one of the problems is that on all but the darkest nights, the property's entrance road is discernible to anyone flying above, enabling identification of the site. The alignment of the road virtually "points" at the home itself, so until some camouflage is installed to hide the road surface, it's a no-go for Mr Churchill. I hear there is some suggestion of covering the surface with sods of turf. Seems extraordinary, but that's what I'm told.

'There is a concern that German Intelligence is planning an attack on Mr Churchill,' Bland went on. 'Some indicators of that have been picked up recently. Consequently, security around him is being stepped up, especially when he is travelling outside London.

'The PM wants to use a property known as Ditchley, in Oxfordshire, as his country retreat whenever he feels the need for a brief escape from London, given that Chequers is not available. Apparently, he has decided that he will have a weekend at Ditchley next month. So, in mid-February, date to be confirmed, he is going there for a few days' rest and relaxation.

'You will be wondering what this is all about. Well, while using Ditchley is less of a risk for the PM than Chequers, the security services still consider that a visit to Ditchley is not without risk. To protect against that, whenever he goes to Ditchley there will of course be the usual military presence provided on the ground there, and the PM will also be accompanied on his road journey from London to Oxfordshire by appropriate security personnel. The issue for us is that the security services are concerned about an aerial attack on the Prime Minister's convoy while he is en route. They think he is exposed as he travels through the countryside. Because of the German threat to the PM that they have identified, security did not want him to take a trip to Ditchley, but he wouldn't have it. The PM has told the security services he is going, and they have now reluctantly agreed, but subject to one further precaution — air cover.' Bland paused, smiling at them. 'It has clearly been difficult for some at Whitehall, but there seems to have been an outcome achieved that all can live with. You three are to be the PM's air cover, at his special request.'

John was surprised, and he could see the others were too.

'A special request, sir?' asked Sidey.

'Yes, Squadron Leader. He wants the three pilots who flew the Glisy mission. As you will recall, that mission was something he pushed for personally, and he was delighted when it was successfully completed. He has said that if he must have air cover on his journey, he would like you to provide it.'

'This is the route the PM will be taking tomorrow,' Sidey said to John and Richard as they examined the map of England he had spread out on his desk. It was mid-February and they were all in Sidey's office for a briefing regarding the Prime Minister's upcoming road trip to Ditchley House. 'I plan that we pick his convoy up at Northolt, and escort him from there.'

John looked closely at the map. Roads proposed to be used by the Prime Minister's convoy had been marked with a dark pencil. The pencil line began in Whitehall, making its way through various built-up areas to Northolt, then past Beaconsfield, to Wheatley, through Woodstock, and then, after what looked to be about another five miles, it took a sharp left to follow the road leading to Ditchley House itself. The journey from the point where the PM would clear greater London was approximately fifty-five miles, John calculated, after making some quick measurements against the scale at the foot of map.

'We will start the cover at Northolt, because he will be travelling through urban areas prior to that, and I doubt an attack is likely there. In any event, it would be too difficult for us to be effective in those areas. We will have to leave that part of his trip to his accompanying ground security.'

'I agree, sir,' John replied to Sidey. 'And I see that from Northolt to Ditchley is about fifty-five miles. Hour and a quarter for the PM's convoy?'

'Yes, I think that would be the maximum. They will not be stopping, and they will keep up a reasonable speed. So, certainly no more than seventy-five to eighty minutes, I would think,' Sidey replied.

'There will be a radio operator in one of the accompanying vehicles, and a discrete air/ground frequency has been established for use in communications between us and the convoy,' he continued.

John and Richard both acknowledged that comment with a brief nod.

'Given the speed disparity between us and the convoy, what do you have in mind, sir, regarding how we operate?' Richard asked.

'I have been thinking about that. One of us will fly at a reduced airspeed of one twenty-five, one thousand feet above ground level, orbiting the convoy. The other two should be, say, four thousand feet, flying at standard low-cruise speed, to ensure some height if Jerry does turn up. Once we have sighted the convoy, number one aircraft will position to undertake continuous wide low speed orbits around it at one thousand feet. Numbers two and three will patrol at their higher altitude, flying observation patterns, but staying within ten to fifteen miles of the convoy.'

'Yes, sir, agree with all that,' John said, as Richard murmured his concurrence. 'How do you propose that comms be managed?'

'All three of us will be on frequency, but I will communicate with the convoy. Our call-sign is *Cover*. The convoy is *Ground*, and they will also be monitoring sector control. Either of you can come in on the radio, of course, if something occurs that you want to point out. I will be cover one. You are two,' he said to John, 'and Flight Lieutenant Cowles, you are cover three.

'Chain Home should spot any enemy aircraft that might pose a threat to the PM's convoy as they approach our coast, and other defensive capability will be scrambled to meet them in that case. I don't see Jerry having any real chance of successfully getting far enough inland, beyond London, to be a problem for us on this operation, even if there was to be such an attack attempted.'

'Do we know what tomorrow's weather forecast is looking like?' John asked.

'Preliminary forecast has a high overcast with little wind, so that should be okay,' Sidey replied. 'We will check it again in the morning. I am aiming to pick up the convoy at about fifteen hundred hours, as they pass Northolt. If there is nothing else, gentlemen, be back here at thirteen hundred tomorrow please, planning to be airborne at fourteen forty-five hours. We don't need to take off until fifteen minutes after the convoy departs Whitehall. It will take them about thirty minutes to get to Northolt.'

The next day, the three Spitfires tasked with protecting the Prime Minister's road convoy took off from Hornchurch at fourteen forty-five hours, as planned. The Prime Minister's convoy had departed Whitehall on time. At their briefing immediately before taking off, Sidey had confirmed that the meteorological reports for the area in which they would be operating were as expected. He also described the convoy to them, so they would be able to identify it from the air. The convey would be led by a grey staff car, carrying armed security service operatives. The PM's car would be next — his well-known armoured dark green Humber Pullman — and after that a light truck with a squad of eight from the London Infantry Brigade.

John, Richard and Sidey were soon airborne and following their planned route. On their second orbit of the Northolt area, Sidey called that he had sighted the Prime Minister's convoy. Sidey, as number one, set up a low-speed orbit in the general area of the convoy, at one thousand feet, while John and Richard climbed to four thousand feet to begin their wider observation patterns overhead. As they climbed, John heard Sidey call the convoy radio operator, who was probably operating his equipment from the truck at the tail of the convoy, John decided.

'Ground, your air cover is in place,' Sidey said. Two key clicks from the operator on the ground acknowledged Sidey's call.

John was watchful as he flew. After twenty minutes, and as he was commencing his fourth wide orbit above the convoy's route, he saw three low-flying aircraft approaching from the northeast. He was lucky to have seen them. They were very low, and their black fuselages made them difficult to pick out in the approaching dusk against the backdrop of the terrain they were over. They seemed to be travelling very quickly. *What are they?* John asked himself, as he peered down towards them.

As he strained to see them, John realised they were twin-engined aircraft, and there were two vertical fins on their rear empennages. *Oh, Christ*, he thought.

'All stations, three Messerschmitt one-tens inbound from the northeast, low level and fast. Passing west of Chesham this time. Cover two and three are heading to engage,' John transmitted.

As he said that, John rolled his Spitfire towards the Bf 110s. He saw Richard was positioning slightly behind him and to his right. They both dived towards the approaching low-level Messerschmitts.

'With you in one minute,' Sidey called.

John knew that it would be just Richard and him as this started. The engagement would be underway before Sidey joined them.

The radio operator in the truck at the rear of the convoy heard the transmissions and called, 'Roger, Ground convoy is stopping on the roadway at a position where we have some tree coverage. Keep me advised.'

John had the lead Luftwaffe aircraft in his sights. They were effectively head-to-head. He fired an extended burst and saw the long, glassed cockpit on the German aircraft explode into fragments. The aircraft fell out of control from a height he estimated to be about thirty feet. It impacted the ground in a huge fireball within no more than two or three seconds. He turned his attention to the next German attacker.

This aircraft banked steeply to the left as John pulled his Spitfire around behind it to enable him to shoot. The rear gunner in the Bf 110 fired a long burst at John. The tracer told John it was close, but nothing hit him. Another burst of tracer was closer, and John banked hard right. As he did that, he saw the Messerschmitt's starboard engine hit, and it started smoking, clearly badly damaged. He realised Richard had got the German.

The third Bf 110 was now getting close to where the convoy had stopped, although it was likely that the tree-cover meant that those on the road would not be seen easily enough to allow an accurate attack. John saw that the Luftwaffe aircraft was continuing to follow the road towards a treed area where he thought the convoy was parked. John knew the firepower of an Me 110 was substantial, and even if it shot into the trees blind, there was a risk it could hit the convoy vehicles sheltering in there and do some real damage. He was wondering if he would be able to reach the German in time to prevent him shooting, when the Me 110 exploded as multiple rounds struck it. Sidey's Spitfire appeared. He had taken out the third would-be attacker.

As protection missions went, the three Spitfires of 415 Squadron had excelled. All three German aircraft were down, and no shots had been fired at the Prime Minister's convoy.

Sidey was very pleased, as he showed when back on the ground with them at Hornchurch.

'Well done, chaps. That was a surprise attack, but we responded well and put up a good show, taking them all down. I have been advised that the PM was unaffected, apart from having to park under some trees for half an hour until the all-clear was given.'

'I am surprised we had no warning, sir. I thought control would have got them on Chain Home and alerted us,' John said.

'I wondered about that myself. It seems they crossed the Channel at extremely low height, and entered England by coming in over the sea, down the centre line of The Wash. Chain Home didn't pick them up, they were so low. First thing known about them was a report of three low-flying and fast twin-engined aircraft crossing above an Observer Corps post near Sutton Bridge. They called it in to control, but we were already engaging by the time the convoy was contacted. Good thing we saw them and were able to stop them. The one-tens have huge firepower, and would have done some serious damage if they had managed to unleash on the Prime Minister's convoy.'

CHAPTER TWENTY

'Gentlemen,' Bland said, 'your air cover operation yesterday went well. The Prime Minister is very pleased, as you would expect, given that the German plans to assassinate him failed when you took out the three attackers.'

I have been thinking about the operation, sir,' John said, 'and I find myself wondering how the Germans knew about the Prime Minister's travel plans, and where they would be able to intercept his convoy. For them to come down The Wash at just the right time, they would have needed to know both timing and route, certainly a lot more than simply the day of travel.'

'They did,' Bland replied. 'I have been advised that a person on the PM's staff, who worked in the Cabinet War Rooms, was arrested last evening and charged with spying. It appears that person had passed on the Prime Minister's route, day of travel, and proposed departure time, to German intelligence a few days ago. Knowing when Mr Churchill would be on the road, and where he was going from his rooms at Whitehall, was enough to allow an operation to be planned by the enemy. The person arrested has confessed all this, and told the security services that the Luftwaffe had aircraft coming in from an airfield in Holland. Those aircraft were low, so they were not spotted there by Chain Home. Literally wave-top height, we think, seeing they weren't seen by radar. If you chaps hadn't been there, we may well have had a different outcome yesterday.'

'Quite an exercise by the Luftwaffe planners,' John noted.

'Yes, it was, and now the Prime Minister wants to thank you

personally. He has invited you to Ditchley House this afternoon to have tea with him.'

Sidey, John and Richard all smiled at that. *Tea with the PM*, John thought. *That's different. Wonder what he's like in person.*

'His private secretary advises you should be there at sixteen hundred, so you need get away from here by fourteen thirty, to be on the safe side. Can't have you being late for Mr Churchill, can we?' Bland continued with a smile.

'I will need to check the availability of the squadron car, sir,' Sidey said, 'otherwise we will have to persuade one of the other squadrons to lend us some transport.'

'No, you won't. Take my vehicle,' Bland responded.

To John, this was another example of Bland's new approach to squadron life. There was no question that the CO was now a changed person. Always friendly and welcoming, he was becoming known amongst the squadron pilots and ground staff as an empathetic, helpful commanding officer. John had noted on several occasions in recent times that Bland always ensured his pilots were getting the support they needed in their operations, and in their lives. It was a good position for them to be in as they readied themselves for the next phase of the war, whatever that was going to be.

The Prime Minister looked up from his desk as Sidey, John and Richard were shown into his study. It was a large room, with an area at its far end where there were comfortable chairs and a long couch. In front of the couch there was a long, low wooden table, with plates of sandwiches and teacakes already spread out over it, awaiting his guests.

'Welcome to Ditchley House, gentlemen. Come in. We shall sit over there,' Churchill said, gesturing towards the afternoon tea set on the table at the end of the room.

After introductions, and the PM expressing his thanks and admiration for what they had done the day before, they settled into the comfortable chairs and began enjoying their food.

'You know, I went to the control centre at Uxbridge a few months ago and sat in with the clever chaps there who run fighter control,' said Churchill. 'I saw wave after wave of the German aggressors come in while I was there, and group after group of our fighters being sent up to intercept them. We were alerted by our radar, and we responded using what appeared to me to be very good control systems.'

'Yes, sir. Chain Home has been very good for Britain, and the procedures established to use the information it provides have been first class,' Sidey said.

'My thoughts too, Squadron Leader, although I did worry when the officer in charge at the control room told me he was at risk of running out of reserve squadrons. Fortunately, he didn't, but it highlighted to me the narrow margins involved in the great air battle we were facing at the time. It was knife-edge, and the skill and devotion of people like you, gentlemen, was key to its outcome. Indeed, I believe it may have adversely affected the outcome of the entire war if we had lost the Battle of Britain. So good for you, and all your fellow fighter pilots.'

'Thank you, sir. We do recognise how important it was that we were able to successfully resist the Luftwaffe attacks.'

'Indeed, Squadron Leader. After Dunkirk, I warned that the Battle of France had been lost, and that the Battle of Britain was about to begin. I understand the critical role all our valiant airmen have played in standing up to the Luftwaffe. It was vital that the Germans failed in their attempt to gain air supremacy over the Royal Air Force.'

'Of course, sir, no doubt about that,' Sidey replied.

'As you will be aware, I spoke in the House last August about the debt of gratitude this country owed to our fighter pilots for the superb effort they were making. You all had to fly and fight constantly, and with great skill and fortitude, undaunted by the odds you faced. There was no succumbing to the fatigue and weariness the constant alerts must have brought to you all. I saluted the valour and devotion of all of you involved. Not to put too fine a point on it, I think the RAF's fighter pilots really are marvellous, and you showed me that again yesterday. Thank you.'

While appreciating what Churchill was saying to them, John was feeling slightly self-conscious at the depth of feeling the PM was expressing. He dipped his head in acknowledgment as Churchill looked directly at him.

'Enough from me now,' he continued, 'except to record that what I said in the House fairly sums up everything I think about the fighter pilots of the RAF. At the time, I wanted everyone to understand the effort being made every day, and to join me in acknowledging the debt all of us consequently owed to just a few.'

As 1941 went on, while there were continuing engagements with the Luftwaffe , John noted that the enemy's daylight operations over England continued to diminish. Less frequent raids were occurring, and when they did, the numbers of enemy aircraft involved were usually much lower than John had known previously. Still a long way to go, he realised, but in his view the air war, certainly over Britain and the Channel, had reached a point where the RAF seemed to be on top of the Luftwaffe. Opening a second front in the east probably hadn't helped the Germans, he thought. Like most others, John had been surprised when they had launched Operation Barbarossa against Russia, in late June.

Relaxing in his favourite deep leather armchair in the lounge of the officers' mess at Catterick, and sipping a cup of dark-looking tea, John was chatting with some of his fellow 415 Squadron pilots. It was a pleasant day in August, and they had been back from 11 Group duties at Hornchurch for some time now, given there was little Luftwaffe activity in the south-east of England requiring their presence. The station adjutant came in and stood looking around the room for a moment, before seeing John. He walked briskly across the lounge towards him. *He's in a hurry*, John decided, noting the adjutant's quick steps as he approached. *What's up, I wonder?*

'Flight Lieutenant Noble, the CO would like to see you in his office as soon as possible, please,' the adjutant told him.

'Certainly. I'll be there in a moment,' John replied.

'Very good.' With that, the adjutant spun round and left the room as quickly as he had come in.

'Our usually relaxed adjutant seemed a bit *agitato* this morning, John. Why has the boss summoned you so urgently? You haven't been doing unauthorised beat-ups again, have you, showing off to Mary in your Spit?' Greg Somerville asked with a broad grin after the adjutant had left.

There were some chuckles from others in the group. They could all recall the incident Greg was referring to. John had incurred the ire of the squadron's Commanding Officer for some extreme low-level flying over his girlfriend's house. Mary lived with her parents. He hadn't known at the time, but her father was a senior officer on 13 Group staff and had been at home on leave. Unimpressed by John's performance, Mary's father had made an official complaint.

'I have no idea what it's about,' John replied, ignoring Greg's suggestion, 'but I'll find out soon enough.'

'Good morning, Flight Lieutenant,' Bland said with a smile as John entered his office. 'Sorry about the short notice, but Command wants my urgent confirmation on an issue this morning. Have a seat.'

Once John was seated, Bland went on, 'There is growing concern regarding what may be brewing in Southeast Asia with the Japanese,' Bland said. 'You may have heard that they have now moved into French Indochina. Intelligence says they forced their way in but managed to do it without any major military action. The thinking is, their objective is to close supply routes to China. That will help them in their rather nasty war with the Chinese.'

John nodded his acknowledgment. He was aware of the Japanese movements and had heard stories about the atrocities they were committing in China. He had also seen in the newspapers that Germany had signed an agreement with both Italy and Japan, to cooperate in developing the revised world order they envisaged. Germany would lead a new Europe, which it had said it was currently reshaping, and Japan would lead a new Southeast Asian order. It was all a bit scary, John had thought at the time.

'Whitehall wants to beef up our defensive capabilities to protect our interests in that part of the world. There is concern the Japanese might have plans to plunder our natural resources down there, and those of the Dutch. The thinking is that Borneo, Malaya, Hong Kong, and the Dutch East Indies could be at risk.'

'What is proposed, sir?'

'The Royal Navy is moving some of its major capital assets to Singapore, in case the Japanese try to expand their influence into Malaya or the Dutch East Indies. The *Prince of Wales* and the *Repulse* will be sent out there. The RAF is going to position some Hurricanes to Singapore as well, to improve air defence capability. Because those aircraft will not be there for some months, the current RAF presence is going to be reinforced in the meantime with a couple of squadrons from the Australians and New Zealanders. I understand those squadrons will be equipped with an American aircraft, the Brewster Buffalo, pending the arrival of the Hurricanes.'

John wondered why he was in the CO's office being told all this, but it soon became clear.

'The squadrons being sent to Singapore by the Aussies and New Zealanders don't have any pilots experienced in air warfare. Consequently, the RAF has agreed to send some of our chaps down to Singapore to work with these new outfits for a few months, to help them set up. You are to be one of those pilots, and you will lead the New Zealand squadron based at Kallang airfield.'

John was surprised, but did not show it.

'As well as being a New Zealander, you have been through the entire air war here so far: Dunkirk, the Battle of Britain, the Blitz, as well as our current operations. You're a resolute fellow when you put your mind to something, and that's just what will be needed in Singapore to get its improved air defence set up and operating well. I'm not aware of anything we have planned here that would preclude you from going — is that as you see it?'

'No, there isn't anything specific, sir.'

'Good. That's settled then. The world of Raffles and Singapore Slings it is for you,' Bland said with a grin. 'I don't think you will find it too demanding down there. The Japanese are unlikely to take us on directly at Singapore — it's a fortress. Sending in major naval assets and beefing up air defences will telegraph to the Empire of Japan that we won't tolerate any nonsense. And, of course, they are unlikely try anything, given the American fleet in Hawaii. If the Japanese launch against us and look to start plundering the oil reserves in the area, the US will probably engage them with all that they have in Pearl Harbour. So, in those circumstances, I think you will be back in a couple of months, once things are in place in Singapore.'

Hope you are right about all that, John thought, but he did agree his experience would be useful in establishing the new air defence capability Singapore needed. Nevertheless, he was disappointed about being sent there. He enjoyed his role in 415 Squadron, and he wasn't keen to fly the Buffalo in any war operations against the Japanese, should that ever become necessary. He was aware their Army Air Force had some capable aircraft, and the Buffalo was considered inadequate in both performance and reliability. *The sooner the Hurricanes get there, the better,* he thought.

'When do I go?'

'Arrangements will be put in place as soon as I confirm your availability with Command, which I will do straight after this meeting. Preliminary planning has you flying to Cairo, via Lisbon and Gibraltar, the day after tomorrow, before you continue on to Singapore from there, but that's not yet confirmed. I expect more detail about your transit soon. I'll advise you when I have that. In the meantime, get packed up and make any personal arrangements you consider necessary, given you are off to foreign parts for some time. Also, Flight Lieutenant, you have been promoted to Squadron Leader on this secondment. Congratulations.'

The next day, John was told his flights to Cairo were no longer happening. Instead, he was to report to Liverpool, and from there he would sail to the west African port of Takoradi for onward transit to Southeast Asia. His travel arrangements from Takoradi would be advised on arrival in Africa. John, who always liked to be precise and well-prepared in the things he did, would have preferred more clarity about his travel arrangements from Africa, but, as he told himself, there is a war on. He couldn't be a pedant about detail.

'I'm sorry, Mary. It's an overseas posting to Singapore, and it will take me out of Britain for several months. Not sure when I will be back.'

John had telephoned Mary to tell her of his departure overseas, and he could sense her unhappiness as they spoke. He would have liked to have said his farewells in person, rather than over the telephone, but he had no choice. She was being kept very busy at the hospital, so calling her was all he could do in the time available before he left.

'Write to me, John. We've had lovely times together during the last year and a half. I'll be a very sad girl if it all just peters out now, because you have to go away.'

'Of course I'll write. Chin up now, Mary. Worse things could have happened to us, and they didn't, so keep the faith, darling, and I'll see you when I'm back from my secondment.'

'Whenever that might be,' Mary responded, still unhappy.

'Bye. I love you,' John whispered, as he hung up.

Back in his room, John thought about what he needed to do to organise himself for his Singapore secondment. He also started to think about what could happen while he was there. *Hopefully the Japanese won't have a crack at us*, he thought. *Surely the presence of the American Pacific fleet in Hawaii will stop them trying anything like that, and if I get the promised Hurricanes in Singapore soon, that will be useful in setting up a robust air defence strategy. Yes, it should all be fine,* he decided, but he did feel a bit down. He was not keen to go to Singapore, and he worried about the future of Britain. The Americans had not entered the war in Europe, so Britain was effectively the last man standing, facing the Germans. He appreciated that the Eastern front they had opened with Russia would take some pressure off, but he was also aware that the Russians seemed to be struggling. German forces were advancing deep into Russia, and he wondered whether that meant Germany would soon have the ability to once again mount a major offensive against Britain.

Then will we be able to survive in the longer term, against the might of Germany? he asked himself. *Will they eventually overwhelm us? We have defied the odds so far, but what happens next? Time will tell,* he thought, as he started to prepare for his temporary secondment to Singapore.

A NOTE TO THE READER

Dear Reader,

I hope you enjoyed *Defying the Odds*, the second novel in the *John Noble Fighter Ace Thriller* series. In writing the series, the abundance of publicly available historical material has been very useful. It has enabled me to weave my fictional stories through actual events and activities of the past. I researched RAF Fighter Command's World War Two practices and procedures, and reviewed notes and records from the time. I also had access to a Spitfire pilot's logbook. What I read in that logbook helped me develop the stories in a way that I hope will give readers some understanding of the trials and tribulations a fighter pilot would have faced in the air, at the time.

While this book is a work of fiction, the stories told are inspired by real people and actual events. In some cases, the missions reflect wartime operations flown and aerodromes used, but I have invented the squadron numbers. They were not allocated to a fighter squadron at the relevant time.

While the *John Noble Fighter Ace Thiller* series is a fictional series, the stories told can serve as a reminder of the debt owed by many of us, to the fighter pilots of the RAF during World War Two.

Thank you for taking the time to read *Defying the Odds*. If you would like to rate this book on **Amazon** or **Goodreads**, or leave a review, that would be appreciated. Readers are welcome to get in touch with me via my **Facebook Author Profile** at **"David Mackenzie NZ writer"**.

Kind regards

David Mackenzie

Sapere Books is an exciting new publisher of brilliant fiction and popular history.

To find out more about our latest releases and our monthly bargain books visit our website:
saperebooks.com